THE
DRAWING GAME

THE
DRAWING GAME

A Sketch in Crime Mystery

Volume 3

Deirdre Verne

gatekeeper press

Published by Gatekeeper Press
3971 Hoover Rd. Suite 77
Columbus, OH 43123-2839
www.GatekeeperPress.com

ISBN Paperback: 9781619845725
eISBN: 9781619845732

Printed in the United States of America

For Gail Patricia

ONE

I HAD A NEW man in my life. Wispy threads of hair, a full belly, and hopelessly incontinent. Baby Roon nuzzled his tiny face toward my breast and parted his lips. My mother leaned over my shoulder and cooed softly while my sixteen-year-old daughter, Gayle, tickled Roon's feet.

"Feeding time," I said as I handed the bundle of pink swaddling back to my best friend Katrina, who, without complaint, hadn't fully buttoned her shirt in months. "Trina, about the pink," I hedged. "When are we switching him to blue?"

"Don't label," my goth-inspired daughter said.

I shook a lavender bunny in front of Roon's face. He reached out and snatched it from me. "Maybe he'll be color blind," I offered. I wondered how the stuffed rabbit felt about his own purple pelt.

"You get what you get and you don't get upset," Katrina said, repeating an oft-used Freegan motto. "I don't care what it is as long as it's free," she added.

"Can I hold you to that?" my mother, Elizabeth Prentice, asked.

"Because I've got a box of Teddy's baby clothes in the basement, and it would make me happy to see them again."

Katrina rolled her finger into Roon's fist. "Ce, are you good with this?"

Unlike Katrina, I needed a second to digest my mother's offer. "So the choice," I asked, "is between pink onesies or out-of-date, yet gender-appropriate clothes once worn by my now deceased brother?"

Katrina and my mother nodded. Teddy, my brother, had been dead nearly two years, but dragging out his moth-balled baby clothes was new territory for all of us. I looked at my mother, a beauty still, despite the recent tragedies in our life. Even her battle with alcohol hadn't compromised her good genes. I had joked during her recovery that the alcohol seemed to have worked as a preservative as opposed to a poison.

"It's a good memory for me," my mother said, and I believed her.

I reached over and plucked the strawberry polka dot cap off Roon's head. "It's time, little buddy. I can't let you wear pastels to your parents' wedding. To the basement," I announced.

I'm not going to mince words. I grew up in a mansion. A good old-fashioned, Long Island Gold Coast mansion. I high-tailed it out of Tara after high school and now reside a few miles away in a historic building called Harbor House. Like its name, my current residence belonged to the first harbor master in Cold Spring, who (not surprisingly) was also a Prentice.

My family goes back, way back, as does Harbor House. As it turns out, both my house and family have been in recent need of an overhaul. Since my brother and father's deaths, my life, and that of my mother, had been on a slow but upward trend. My mother, a recent graduate of rehab, was relearning everything she had lost to alcohol, like cooking, driving, and most importantly painting, an activity we now enjoyed together.

Harbor House, with its sagging porch and chipped paint, was another story, one that involved an inheritance. The home was given to me, free and clear. And since Freegan's adore anything with zeros, the DIY repairs have been more than worth the effort. It helps that the harbor master's former residence overlooks majestic Long Island Sound. The grounds' fertile and sun-drenched soil make it a perfect setting for the self-sustaining farm I maintain along with my roommates, Katrina, Jonathan, and Charlie. We're a down-to-earth group of Freegans who practice our anti-consumerist ideals by living on society's left-overs. What with growing our own food and the occasional Dumpster dive, we have everything we need. It's cheap living, but as Katrina had pointed out earlier, Freegans can't be choosy. However, Katrina was more than pleased when my mother offered her palatial spread as the site for her and Jonathan's upcoming nuptials. We were there today, at my mother's, to help plan the big event. The sooner the better, since we couldn't possibly let Baby Roon spend the rest of his life as the town's bastard. The poor kid was already being raised a Freegan; legitimizing his birth seemed to be the responsible thing to do.

And then there was Gayle, the daughter I hadn't met until a few months ago. We'd been separated, mother and daughter, by science. A test-tube kidnapping of sorts. Like a Sea Monkey in a bowl of water, my daughter grew without me, via a surrogate. She was subsequently raised by a lovely family who thankfully allowed me into her life during the last few months. We had decided—my roommates, my mother, and Gayle's father—to use Katrina's wedding as the venue for announcing both Roon and Gayle to our extended family. My mother's home, with its period opulence and excess, seemed just over-the-top enough to complement our modern-day clan.

I opened the basement door and Gayle gave me the thumbs up. "This is going to be cool," she said, and she was right. The thing about mansions is that, structurally, they require a substantial foundation, making the basement of my childhood home big enough to host a polo match. The Prentice family had lived in Cold Spring Harbor for two centuries and pretty much anything they had owned in that time ended up in the basement.

"Control yourself," I whispered to Katrina. As a good Freegan, I knew she'd be hard-pressed to pass up an opportunity like this.

She eyed Roon. "This won't be any fun without two free hands."

The burden of motherhood, I thought.

I flicked on the light and we descended the solid oak stairs, which, despite their age, were surprisingly stable. They don't make mansions like they used to.

"This rocks," Gayle said as she made her way through the maze of Prentice castoffs. A men's black cashmere dress coat caught her eye and within seconds, her slim shoulders disappeared beneath a swath of Prentice history. I hadn't raised Gayle, but she definitely had Freeganism in her blood.

"Can I have it?" she asked.

My mother smiled. "Of course. What else would a girl wear with combat boots?"

I pulled down a box with my name on it, popped the top, and discovered a stack of clothes I had worn in high school. I held up a pair of lowslung jeans and a cropped t-shirt.

"Drop the clothing and walk away," Katrina teased. "I'm cheap, but there's no way I'd let you repeat that fashion mistake."

I turned to Gayle and offered my hand-me-downs.

"Not cool," she replied. "Give it ten years. Vintage takes time."

I closed the box and headed over to a stack of games. Half of them, including the Trivial Pursuit game I held, were still in the wrapper.

"I hated board games," my mother said.

"No kidding," I added. "You never played games with us, but this," I said as I spotted a tangle of wires, "these old gaming consoles and cartridges might fetch a pretty price on eBay. Teddy had a huge collection."

"All yours," my mother said.

I made my way across the basement to a dust-caked window. Now here was a memory worth revisiting. Just a little push on the frame and the window gave an inch. Cold wintry air rushed in, and I smelled freedom, as intoxicating as it was in my teens. This window, familiar after all these years, was my secret exit and entry point, my escape route from the dysfunctional, non-game playing Prentices. I looked down and sure enough the stool I had used to heave myself through the opening was still in place. I stepped up for better leverage and the window gave a creaky yawn as I loosened it from its hinge. I peered across the Prentice grounds with the grass just below eye level. The sun had dropped, but I could make out the changes in the landscape.

"What a shame," I sighed. "I can almost see the new development from here."

"There's no stopping progress," my mother lamented. "When you were a child, the next house was almost a half mile away." She was right, but now a new development had wedged its way into the neighborhood. I'd have a hard time slipping out unnoticed these days, what with ten new houses hovering along my escape route. Too bad, but in a shrinking economy, even the wealthy were hard-pressed to support a five-acre spread a stone's throw from Manhattan. The taxes on estates like my mother's home could fund a Third-World country. The neighboring lot, which had previously held a home just as majestic as hers, had recently been torn down and subdivided into half-acre plots.

On the upside, the new homes were entirely eco-friendly—solar powered, Leeds certified, and fabulously overpriced. From what I'd read in the local paper, these mini-mansions were targeted at eco-techies, the modern-day equivalent of the Yuppie. These buyers craved the gadgets a fully wired house provides. For this crowd, it was less about the green message than the ancillary stuff required to make the green go. Want to reset your home's temperature after you've left for work, press here. Wondering if your cat triggered the kitty door? There's an app for that too.

The Prentice home, with its three-foot-thick stone foundation, hadn't been rewired in a hundred years. I stepped down from the stool and wondered how long we'd be able to keep it in the family or at least prevent it from going up in flames.

My mother picked up an ancient, coal black pistol and aimed for an old wash basin. "Don't get me started on the new development. And the name! Green Acres? Who are they kidding? Ever since those houses were built, my electricity has been temperamental."

As if on cue, the only working bulb in the basement flickered.

"See?" my mother said, gesturing toward the bulb with her pistol. And just like that, without my mother even firing her ancient gun, our sole source of electricity expired. Darkness descended on the basement, and I struggled to make out familiar shapes. Luckily the sound of my mother's cursing coupled with Roon's cries helped me to establish our locations. I blinked a few times in search of light, and my eyes moved reflexively to the faint glow offered by my escape window.

As I waited for my vision to adjust to what little light shone in, I felt for the stool with my feet. I stepped up again and then looked back over my shoulder into the darkness.

"Can you guys see me?" I yelled.

"Barely," Katrina replied. "You look like a floating hologram."

I turned back toward the window and squinted. I caught a faint glimpse of a moving object though the window. Could it be? Did I just see someone on my family's property?

TWO

"DON'T MOVE," I SAID as I shifted in Katrina's general direction. "I don't want you to walk with the baby in your arms. There's too much crap on the ground. And Mom," I called into the darkness, "no broken hips."

Roon let out a ferocious wail. "I guess the keg is empty," Gayle giggled.

"I curse you with twins," Katrina replied over her son's protests.

I turned back to my clouded window and scrubbed at the dirt with my elbow. It was late February, just a month shy of our clocks' annual leap forward. At six in the evening, there was still a glow, but not nearly enough daylight to make out anything definite. That being said, I was almost sure I had seen something. Male, jeans, medium height, and very large hands. That last part seemed ridiculous, but I held onto the image. Even if I'd had my drawing pad with me, that wasn't much to go on. And the oversized hands? It was winter. Maybe the person I saw was wearing heavy gloves.

"Gayle, don't you have a flashlight app on your phone?"

"I left my phone in the kitchen."

"How long before the lights usually go back on?" I asked my mother.

"About a half hour, maybe forty minutes" my mother said.

"We can wait it out," Katrina offered. Roon's cries started to subside.

"Fine," I said as I lowered myself onto my stool. We remained in our positions for what felt like an eternity before I cracked. "I'm crawling. Don't laugh," I instructed as I moved slowly across the dusty cement floor.

"This is silly," my mother said as my hand met her foot.

"Nice shoes." I wasn't kidding. My mother had expensive taste. I tickled her ankle.

"Stop that."

I inched my way to the staircase on all fours. It was so dark now, I might as well have had my eyes closed. To prevent bumping my head, I crawled a bit then stretched forward with my hand, which got old and tiring pretty quickly. Every few feet, I swapped arms to give my shoulder a break. When I got to the stairs, I sat down and took a breather.

"How long do you think we've been down here?" I asked.

My mother's voice called to me from across the room. "Close to an hour? Get yourself up those stairs and find a flashlight."

I climbed north in search of a battery-operated solution. I pushed back the basement door and was welcomed with a smidgen of natural light. Even so, I walked along the hall with my hands trailing the chair rail toward the kitchen. About halfway down the hall, I heard Gayle's phone trill and then stop. My mother's land line immediately followed, and I walked toward the sound. I picked up the wall phone on the third ring.

"Prentice residence."

"It's Frank."

"Hey. Wait, you're not calling to cancel our date, are you?" I was confused. Detective Frank DeRosa, my boyfriend, had never called my mother's house. I didn't even know he knew the number.

"You're not carrying your phone." This was true. I wasn't a fan of constant communication, plus I was too cheap to bother figuring out how phone minutes worked. Turning off the phone did the trick. "I tried Gayle's number first," Frank added.

"Wow, you're really going the extra mile to get out of dinner."

Frank used his best cop voice. "Can you stay put for a few hours?"

I wasn't sure if my uneasiness was the result of possibly being stood up or if I sensed something else wasn't right. I moved to the nearest window in search of the stranger I had spotted earlier. The entire landscape was now dark. Green Acres, with all of its modern amenities, was also experiencing a blackout. "What the hell is going on Frank? We lost the electricity here almost an hour ago and then I spotted a guy on our lawn. And now you're telling me to stay put?"

Frank blew into the phone with such force I could have sworn it ruffled my hair.

"What gives?" I asked.

"You know the new development behind your mother's house?"

"I'm staring at their useless solar-powered rooftops right now."

"A break-in was reported in the last hour," he said and then paused. "It's the third one in the past month."

"That information would have been helpful a few weeks ago. It's not like my mother has a security system."

"New home break-ins are common." Frank down played my

concern. "Thugs see a new home and think new stuff. Top-of-the-line technology, flat-screen televisions. You get the picture."

I considered the collectibles goldmine in my mother's basement and let out a sigh of relief. It would take one high-class thief to brave the bellows of the Prentice cellar.

"Whoever the person outside was, he's gone. No one is in our house."

"Did you get a face?" Frank, as always, was eager for the clues my sketches might reveal.

I twirled the phone cord around my finger. "Unfortunately, no. He was wearing a jacket and his face was obscured. He was moving quickly." I left out the silly part about his hands.

Frank covered the phone and yelled out the nearest cross street for my mom's house. The background din at the Cold Spring Harbor police station ticked up a notch, but I could barely make out a sentence with the phone pressed against Frank's rib cage. I pressed my ear to the receiver and listened as the activity level rose to a near fury. For a minor tip involving an empty-handed man near, but not *at* the crime scene, the corresponding police reaction seemed excessive.

"Give me a minute," Frank said. "Something's come up." Then the sound muffled as he re-covered the phone.

I used the time to ponder the thief's movements. Had he broken into a Green Acres home and then headed toward my mother's house? Or were we his original target? I stared down hard on the dim outlines of the Green Acres homes. From my mother's kitchen, they looked like scattered Lego pieces in a darkened playroom. I wondered whether the person I saw was even the culprit. He didn't seem to be carrying anything, although I guessed that jewelry or cash could easily be shoved in a pocked. As I considered the possibilities, my mother's kitchen lit up like Times Square. You never realize how many lights you've left on until they all ignite at once. What a waste of electricity. I needed to get my mother some electrical timers before she blew a fuse.

"Frank," I yelled into the phone, hoping he would realize I was still on the line. No such luck. It had been almost two years, but I still hadn't gotten used to dating a cop. My love life was now at the mercy of my fellow citizens' actions. In this case, I was about to come in second to a power outage and a possible break-in. My needs, it seemed, were met only when the entire town was on its best behavior. Frank's sweet spot was Sunday at ten in the morning, when most of the town was either at church or reflecting on why that hadn't gone to church. In my experience, Frank's attention was easily sidelined by a range of local crises. Be it a bar fight or a stranded kitten, Frank DeRosa took pride in being on the scene. He cared about our little town, and I liked that about him, but I also looked forward to a night out in my little town. I yelled for Frank again. My voice echoed right back at me and, given no other choice, I hung up. It wasn't like he didn't know where to reach me.

I passed my mother, Katrina, and Gayle coming up from the basement. Gayle was perspiring under a dozen layers of vintage garb. "You look like homeless person in August," I noted. My mother handed me a box labeled baby clothes, and I shoved it along the floor to the kitchen. When I finished with the first box, I went down to the basement for more—ten boxes in all. Given the total count, it appeared that my brother and I had never been naked in our lives. We would have had had to be clothed twenty-four hours a day, twelve months a year to successfully wear all of these outfits. I stared at the wall of cardboard. What had seemed like a good idea earlier—sifting through my dead brother's baby clothes—now turned my stomach. I carefully lifted a lid and sure enough, a stack of Teddy's neatly folded pajamas peered back at me. I recognized another outfit from a matching set we'd worn for one of our numerous photo sessions. I let the flap fall back into place.

"You guys start with the baby clothes," I said. "I want to see if the street out front is lit."

That was a lie. I was more interested in the heavy-handed thief lurking in our snow-covered azaleas. I opened the front door and walked to the middle of the circular driveway. The circumference was so large that Teddy and I used to pretend we had a private jogging track carved into our front lawn. We even hosted a mock Olympics in grade school. Extending out from our Olympic village like the handle of a pinwheel was the main drive that led for a quarter mile to the road. I jogged forward a few yards and then wrapped my arms across my now shivering chest. I was about to head back to the baby fashion show when a black-and-white came barreling toward me.

I stepped aside as it slowed to a stop and Officer Cheski rolled down his window.

"I thought Frank told you to stay put," he said.

I smiled. Cheski knew me better than to assume I'd follow directions, but for the first time in our friendship, he didn't smile back. "Get in," he said, and I did as I was told.

"I knew something was wrong" I said.

"The guy that built Green Acres," Cheski started.

"Simon Fletcher," I added. Everyone in town knew the fabulous Simon Fletcher, a TED-worthy environmentalist who had designed and built Green Acres. I knew Simon personally because he had hired me a few years back to do a portrait of his wife. I believed that

13

painting was currently hanging in the master bedroom in the old-money mansion the Fletchers had purchased two lots away from my mother's house. Simon Fletcher hadn't just bought the plot next door to my mother but the adjacent one as well, and our homes essentially bookended the new development he had built. Over the past five years, Simon had renovated his home and used it as his main residence. Then he developed Green Acres as his personal experiment in low-carbon living.

"He's dead," Cheski interjected before I could even begin to reel off a list of Fletcher's green accomplishments. "Worse," Cheski continued, "Charlie was at Fletcher's house when the murder occurred. Frank has him at the station now."

I had one foot out of the car door when I turned back to Cheski. "Let me get my drawing pad and a coat."

When I returned to the kitchen, the table was covered in miniature outfits with expensive labels. Teddy, I remembered, had spent his first few years posing as Little Lord Fauntleroy. I winced at the clothes as much as the memory of my dear brother dressed like an English prince.

I patiently explained the burglaries to my mother, Katrina, and Gayle. I strategically left out the part about the possible intruder on our property as well as Simon Fletcher's murder. And of course, I neglected to add the kicker: Charlie, my closest childhood friend and Harbor House roommate, had been found at the Fletcher home, apparently with a dead body. Instead, I conjured up something plausible.

"One of the residents at Green Acres may have seen someone, and Frank wants me to get something on paper as quickly as possible. I think it would be best if you could all stay here for a few hours. Just until the police check the area." In truth, I didn't want

Katrina to return to Harbor House and wonder why Charlie wasn't home. As Harbor House's den mother, she felt it was her job to keep tabs on its residents, and it wasn't beyond her reach to track Charlie down.

"You're being dramatic," my mother said. "I'm fine by myself."

"How about if we order a pizza and hang?" Gayle asked as she removed a few items of clothing. It was clear to me she wanted a second go at the basement, and staying for dinner would be a good excuse.

"I'm game," Katrina offered and with that I grabbed my backpack, a coat, and a scarf that Gayle had pinched from the basement. I headed outside, where I found Cheski waiting.

I jumped in the cruiser and turned to him. "Did Charlie see anyone?"

Cheski stuck a stalk of celery in his mouth and drove with his free hand. Since we had met two years ago, during my brother's murder investigation, Cheski had become a regular at the food co-op, dropping twenty pounds off his senior frame.

He handed me a fresh stick, which I gladly took. Freegans are like that. We never turn down free food.

"I don't know who saw what. All I know is that someone with a bit of muscle cracked Fletcher's head open," Cheski paused. "Charlie was at Fletcher's. What the hell was Charlie doing at Fletcher's?"

I bit down hard and a spray of celery water shot across the dashboard. "They're buds, Fletcher and Charlie," I said. "Charlie was developing an app for the Green Acres homes."

"Let me guess. An app that flushes your toilet from another room?"

I took another stalk out of the bag. "Perfect for the multitasker, but I'm with you. I don't understand the appeal of half these phone

15

applications, but people gobble them up and Charlie is a whiz at programming."

"Do you really think there's a toilet-flushing app?" Cheski asked.

"There's an app for everything. The problems with toilets is people don't realize their commode uses thousands of gallons a water a year. And forget a shower or a bath, you're literally throwing out the water. You could end up butt dialing your phone flushing app and suddenly your water bill has doubled."

Cheski shook his head. "I'll bet that gets under your skin," he said.

"I don't worry about these things at Harbor House," I replied. "Charlie installed a system that fills the back of the toilet with the used bathroom sink water. He also intercepted the shower and tub water before it flows to the public sewage system. Now it gets redirected to the fields."

"I'm not even sure that's legal," Cheski said as he looked at a bag of carrots, "and I'm not so sure I want to eat your produce anymore."

"With Roon's daily baths, you might have a point," I said. "Who knows what's going down that drain."

Cheski winced, and I decided it was time to ask Charlie if sterilization was part of our water system. Knowing Charlie, he had already solved the problem and applied for a patent.

"Don't worry about it," I said. "If a need exists, Charlie has figured out a way to turn it into cash. He's the richest Freegan I know." This was true. Charlie had lived with me at Harbor House for seven years and although his heart was into the Freegan movement, he loved a challenge with a payoff. Especially the financial kind. I had no idea what he did with his money, since he lived as simply as the rest of us, but I assumed his bank account was bursting. Over the years, he had sold his coding solutions to start-ups as well as major corporations.

Cheski took a hard turn that forced the celery to the back of my throat. I looked at the older man's face. He wasn't happy, and it had nothing to do with the cleanliness of my vegetable garden.

"Is Charlie okay?" I asked, although I found it hard to believe my friend was in any danger. I had spent the better part of my childhood watching Charlie weasel his way out of tight corners. He had an escape artist's reputation for extricating himself from even the toughest binds. In high school he had been nabbed red-handed surfing the principal's computer, and somehow he walked out scot-free. "The principle's got a fetish," he had whispered to me in study hall.

"Cheski?" I said waiting for an answer.

Cheski spit a wad of half-chewed vegetables out the window like it was a ball of tobacco.

"At it stands, Charlie is Frank's only suspect."

THREE

The station house, located in a sleepy residential neighborhood, was not built for high-profile murder investigations. The parking lot boasted ten guest spots, and by the time Cheski and I arrived, cars were parked up on curbs and curious neighbors were lingering in their driveways. An aggressive local television reporter had camped out by the front door. Unfortunately my father's and brother's deaths had made me a recognizable figure in town, and the savvy reporter was quick to pick up on my presence.

"Not you again?" she said through red-stained lips.

I looked carelessly over my shoulder as if she had spoken to someone behind me.

Cheski man-handled my elbow and drew me to a side entrance. "Nosy bitch," he mumbled as we entered the station house.

We had no problem finding Charlie. He was standing by himself, back against the wall, dressed in his standard uniform of a t-shirt and jeans. I turned toward Frank's office and watched as my boyfriend strode purposefully toward me. My eyes shifted back to Charlie, who pouted like a lost puppy, and I realized I had no idea who I was here for—Frank or Charlie. I felt for my drawing pad, my security blanket and the source of my stability. If a suspect had been seen at Fletcher's mansion, I was confident I could make sense out of this madness. For certain, my drawing skills would allow me to translate a witness's memories quite accurately onto paper. The faster I drew, the faster I could put a stop to whatever was unfolding at the Cold Spring Harbor police station.

Easy enough, but what if the face in question was Charlie's? A face I had known my whole life. A face I had kissed, literally, a thousand times as a teenager. I looked at Charlie. His unkempt blond curls obscured his eyes, but I knew something had a taken a bite out of his swagger.

I nodded at Frank and then walked in Charlie's direction. It was awkward. Frank was on duty, his game face on. Charlie, on the other hand, couldn't seem to settle on a facial expression. He seemed to be waffling between crying and laughing, and I was concerned the combination of the two would trigger a breakdown. I had to make a choice between the two men and, at least for the moment, Charlie won.

"Let's get out of here," I said to Charlie.

Cheski handed me the keys to his Subaru. "You'll need these. Charlie's car is at the scene."

Frank stood by the door. "It would be easier if I could ask you a few more questions," he said to Charlie.

"Not for me," Charlie replied as he bolted toward the exit.

Frank reached for my hand. His touch, surprisingly soft, reminded me that this was my boyfriend. I loved Frank. We were *in* love. I watched Charlie walk through the parking lot, his long stride hitting a jogging pace. He definitely wanted out of here. I turned back toward Frank.

"This is a mistake," Frank said. "It's important Charlie stays and answers questions." Point well taken. Charlie and Frank were, to the best of their abilities, friends. It had been rough at first, what with me dating Charlie and then dating Frank.

"I'll call you later," was all I could think to say to my boyfriend.

———

Outside, Charlie and I circumvented the aggressive reporter, who was now busy questioning unwitting neighbors.

"I need to drive," he said.

I gave Charlie the keys, we climbed in, and he headed north on West Neck Road until we entered a small public beach. We cruised past the empty ticket booth and Charlie drove the car so far forward, the front tires sunk into the beach sand. He got out and slammed the door.

I pointed to an outcropping of rocks. "Let's sit," I suggested, and we walked across the moonlit beach. The frosty air gathered in tiny clouds around my mouth, but it wasn't nearly cold enough to drive us back to the confines of the car. Charlie's anxiety was palpable, his gasps so loud, I could barely hear the water lapping against the shore. I made myself as comfortable as humanly possible on a damp rock and waited until Charlie was ready to speak.

"I had a meeting with Fletcher," he began. "It went well. We finished up, and he said he had to take a call." Charlie's voice was tight, and I rubbed his back to slow him down. He nodded and continued. "I hung around for a bit with Fletcher's wife, Jamie. Then I left."

"What time was that?"

"Maybe five thirty."

"Then what?"

"I stopped for gas, got home," he said and then paused, "and went to the bathroom."

I nodded. Hard to challenge a bathroom break. "Go on."

"Then I saw Jamie's text inviting me to dinner, so I got back into the car."

"Okay."

"As I was driving back, I noticed the lights in the neighborhood were out. I parked in Fletcher's driveway, went back into the house, and made my way into the great room, where I basically tripped over Fletcher's body." Charlie threw his shoulders forward and then tossed his lunch across the rocks. He sat back and wiped his mouth. "Crap, Ce. Fletcher's head was bashed in."

Charlie's description of Fletcher's condition was consistent with Cheski's info. I covered my mouth, thankful that Charlie couldn't see my horrified reaction in the dark.

"By what?" I asked, and I realized I had no idea what had caused Fletcher's death.

Charlie spit into the waves. "I don't know. Something hard. Really hard."

I cringed. I didn't know what level of force was required to crack a skull, but I remembered the time Teddy fell off the jungle gym at school and got a concussion. There was very little blood and although Teddy's skin had split, his head was intact. If Fletcher's skull was injured, then Charlie and Cheski were right—something hard and powerful had made contact with his head. This wasn't a tumble off playground equipment.

"So then it was just you and Jamie?" I asked.

"Jamie came up behind me." Charlie shook his head. "Then I

heard the front door open and Nicky or Ricky, whatever Fletcher's assistant's name is, walked in and dialed 911."

"It's Ricky. He worked for them when I painted Jamie's portrait," I said, remembering a college-age assistant bringing Jamie a sparkling water. I thought about the people in Fletcher's house. Jamie, Charlie, and now Ricky. "But you weren't there when it happened?"

"No."

"So why are Cheski and Frank so upset about you being in the house after the murder?"

"I don't know. I guess because I was the one found by the body." Charlie rubbed his face hard. "Let's face it. The cops arrive at the scene of murder and I'm standing over the body with blood on my shoes. I'd suspect me too."

"This is different. You're not a stranger to Frank."

"That's what I thought. In fact, I was so relieved to see Frank, I almost started to cry. Then the whole thing went south. Jamie was hysterical and Frank took Ricky aside That was weird." Charlie paused as he remembered the events. "No one took me aside," he said. "It freaked me out."

"Frank tried to speak with you at the station," I reminded him, and then I tried to establish a mental picture of Fletcher's assistant. If my memory served me, and it always did, Ricky was a slight, young male, confident and very attentive to the couple's needs. He had called me a few times to reschedule Jamie's portrait sitting, and I remembered him as highly efficient without being pushy.

So," I continued as I tried to piece the events of the evening together, "you, Ricky, and Jamie were all in the great room when the police arrived?"

"Yes."

"Was anyone else in the house during your meeting with Fletcher?"

Charlie shrugged. "I don't know. It's not like I asked for an attendance roster."

Of course not, I thought. Who expects to be invited to dinner only to stumble over the host's body? Yet the facts remained: Four people, one dead, no murder weapon, and as far as I could tell, no motive on Charlie's part. There had to be an explanation.

I grabbed Charlie by the shoulder. "Come on," I urged. "We're not making any progress sitting here."

FOUR

THE FRONT DOOR OF the tidy Cape Cod opened on the first knock.

"Hey, where's Gayle?" Kelly Goff, Gayle's father, asked as he stepped back from the door. He shook Charlie's hand and pecked me on the cheek.

"She's eating pizza at my mother's," I said. "Katrina will bring her home."

Kelly, a recent widower, had raised Gayle from birth with his husband, Michael. Their cozy home had a storybook feel, and I couldn't have been happier that my biological daughter had grown up in such a loving environment. Who would have thought the little house with amazing curbside appeal was only a stone's throw from Harbor House and that for the last sixteen years, my surprise daughter had been living right under my nose?

I hadn't asked Gayle, the child of two men, if she ever thought she'd be reconnected with her genetic mother. I do know that the loss of one of her dads had been traumatic. Managing a bad hair day is tough enough for a teenage girl, much less the death of parent. I had hoped to fill that void, or at least act as distraction to her pain. Luckily Gayle had no preset conceptions on the role of a female in her life, since she had been raised by two dads. In that respect, it was easy for both of us to start with a blank slate. And, by the grace of God, Kelly was more than happy to include me in their life. That's why I was here. Kelly was a good guy. Solid.

Charlie walked aimlessly into the den and sunk down into an overstuffed leather chair.

"Charlie's in trouble," I said to Kelly.

He blinked. "Are you here because I'm a lawyer?"

"Yes," I admitted. I didn't know many lawyers, but I trusted Kelly implicitly. He seemed to have done a damn good job with Gayle and since Charlie was like family to me, the first person I thought of was Kelly.

"I'm an immigration lawyer," Kelly replied. "Unless Charlie is from Canada, I don't think I'm going to be much help." He chuckled at his own joke, but Charlie remained stoic. Sensing the severity of the situation, Kelly pulled up a chair and placed a hand on Charlie's shoulder.

I nodded my head as if to say "go on."

Kelly took my cue and addressed Charlie. "Whatever this is, I'll tell you right now that I'm probably not the right lawyer, but I'll listen and I'll advise where I can."

Charlie's computer-oriented brain launched into a logically paced and relatively calm description of the events that occurred at Simon Fletcher's house. Kelly was as flabbergasted as I had been upon hearing the news. About halfway through Charlie's story, he glanced at me in utter disbelief. I shrugged.

"You found Fletcher's body?" Kelly asked.

Charlie nodded. "Fletcher was facedown on the floor. Jamie

walked in behind me and started to scream and then Ricky walked in."

"Did Jamie have blood on her?"

"I don't know." He paused. "It was dark. The only thing I remember is that she had changed clothes. When I came back, she had on a robe."

Kelly reached for Charlie's hands and pulled his arms towards him as he examined Charlie. "No blood?" he asked.

"I had a long-sleeve shirt on and sneakers. The shirt was clean. I gave it to Frank, and I let him take pictures of my hands and arms."

I looked at down at Charlie's flip-flops and my heart kicked up a notch. He too looked down. "It was dark and I stepped into a pool of blood. I gave the sneakers to the cops." He pointed to his feet. "These are from the station's lost and found."

"Okay," Kelly said as he recounted the same details I had at the beach. "So you and Jamie were discovered at the scene by Fletcher's assistant, Ricky."

Charlie nodded again. His retelling of the events was consistent with the version he had told me earlier. A few additional details had surfaced, like the blood-stained shoes, but otherwise Charlie told the same basic story. As I had learned from Frank, people who lie never vary from a precise story line, because it's the only one they've memorized, like a script. Any other version and the contradictions would surface and reveal the deceit. People who tell the truth are comfortable with the facts. As a result, they'll tell the same story, but never the same way twice. As far as I was concerned, Charlie fell into the latter group.

Kelly stood up and walked over to a built-in liquor cabinet. He was a big guy with a big heart, but Charlie's ship seemed to be taking on water mighty fast. Kelly reached for three cocktail tumblers and poured a shot of something dark into each. He handed me a glass and in keeping with my Freegan philosophy on free food and drink, I accepted his offering, as did Charlie.

We titled our heads back in unison. I wasn't prepared for the burn, but the shock got me thinking.

"What about the burglaries?" I asked. "Someone tried to break into the Green Acres homes during the power outage tonight. Who's to say that this wasn't a break-in gone bad?"

Charlie sat bolt upright. "What burglaries?" he said.

My news had also caught Kelly off-guard. "I hadn't heard about any burglaries in the neighborhood," he said.

I recounted what Frank had told me about the break-ins, and I described what I had seen through the basement window. "It's not isolated. There were a few burglaries last month at Green Acres."

"And Frank can't put two and two together?" Charlie said.

Low blow, I thought, but I had to admit I wondered the same thing myself. "Frank's a professional," I said. "He knows about the break-ins, and he's aware I saw someone. I think he was being truthful about wanting to talk to you. If there's a murderer out there, his job is to keep the public safe. What if your information can help?"

Charlie shook his head. He wasn't buying my logic, but Kelly wasn't ready to give up so easily. "Go back to the part where Jamie texted you."

"Right," I urged. "She texted you and asked *you* to come back. Had she not invited you, you'd have been safe and sound at Harbor House."

Charlie handed his phone to Kelly, who scrolled through Charlie's recent calls.

"You got a text at six twenty-eight p.m."

Charlie's expression lightened. "That sounds about right. I left Fletcher's when the lights were on, but I guess when I returned the lights had gone out."

"The lights at my mother's went off at about six. If you left around five thirty, as you said, the lights would have been on at Fletcher's as you were leaving."

Charlie nodded. "That's right. I didn't notice the lights were off in Fletcher's neighborhood until I drove back."

"The lights went back on shortly after seven," I noted. "But it was dark in the house when you were standing over the body."

He nodded again. "All of a sudden the lights went on." He shivered at the memory of seeing Fletcher's body.

Kelly's smile turned south as he placed the phone on the tumbler tray. "The text was from Fletcher's phone."

Charlie blinked rapidly.

"*Let's keep this going, come back for dinner*," Kelly read. "Why did you think this text was from Jamie?" he asked.

Without taking his eyes off the phone, Charlie reached for the liquor bottle and took a swig. I tried to structure a timeline in my head. Charlie left Fletcher's a half hour before the lights went out, he received a text at six thirty and returned to find Fletcher dead before seven.

"I don't know," he stammered. "I just assumed that wives make the dinner and do the invites."

My eyebrows shot up at Charlie's sexist comment. "Jamie Fletcher is the type of woman who sits to have her portrait painted. She's not interested in serving people dinner."

Charlie passed the bottle back to me. "This is insane," he yelled at me. "I didn't kill anyone. I just wanted a free meal. Isn't that our goal?" Charlie's last comment was nasty and directed at me.

"Sure, so now it's my fault we're Freegans," I shot back.

Kelly placed his arms between us as if refereeing a boxing match. "Hey," he interrupted. "Charlie's innocence is not in question here, so let's put the history between the two of you aside. I'm concerned Charlie left the station, and this text makes it look like he had a reason to see Fletcher again."

"No," Charlie said, his anger peaking. "That's not what happened."

"You were doing a business deal," Kelly said. "Were the two of you in agreement on the terms?"

"That's why I thought Jamie invited me back," Charlie said, "to celebrate the deal."

It seemed so logical, yet Charlie's earlier actions, before he had even considered escaping from the station, had bothered me. He had given Frank a statement, handed over his clothing, and left his car at the scene. Barring any new evidence, there wasn't any reason for him to stay and I was comfortable with that decision. It was the events leading up to the murder that I questioned. Why have dinner with Fletcher and his wife? I spent a month painting a portrait of Jamie, and I never felt the need to linger and chat. She wasn't unfriendly or rude or even critical of my work. She held the poses I asked and never complained when I needed a few extra minutes. I don't think people understand how boring it can be to sit for a portrait, but Jamie was a trooper and she was pleased with the finished product.

Interestingly, I wasn't. I hated the portrait I had painted for the Fletchers. It was lacking an emotional dimension, which I consider crucial in my work. It can happen when the artist and the patron don't connect, and that was exactly the issue with Jamie. We never clicked. I didn't lose sleep over it; the cause of her distraction was

29

obvious. The whole of her being was wrapped up in her husband, Simon. Her attraction, laser-like, left little room for others. I was simply the help.

As I remembered it, Jamie requested a short break every twenty minutes and used the time to communicate with her husband. And that was in addition to the pop-ins Simon regularly made during our sessions. I guessed, at the time, that Simon Fletcher had a good twenty years on his wife, and I had assumed this had been a second marriage for him. A daddy complex, I thought, but it had bothered me only to the extent that it compromised my work. For me, the painting fell flat. It was clear that Jamie was devoted to, almost obsessed with, her husband, but my painting would never make the cover of a Valentine's Day card. Of all couples to be a third wheel to, why would Charlie accept an invitation from the Fletchers? A free meal? Even I had limits on free, because what I'd found over the years is that sometimes free things have hidden costs—as Charlie had just come to discover.

Kelly repeated his statement. "But you still left the station when Frank asked for more time. That doesn't look good."

"I know," Charlie said, rising from his chair. "I have to make this right. Maybe we should go back and talk to Frank?" As he put his phone in his pocket, it bleeped. Charlie looked at the message, and his face relaxed. "It's Katrina. She wants me to help her draft plans for a wedding huppah after she puts Roon to bed." I stared out the window and saw Gayle coming up the driveway with a bag full of clothing. I wanted to be there with Gayle while she tried on her stash of clothes from my mother's basement, and more than anything I wanted to help Katrina plan her wedding. So did Charlie. He was a wizard with a circular saw, and if a homemade huppah was in the wedding couple's future, then Charlie was the man to build it. Roon's birth and Gayle's arrival had upended our lives in the most wonderful way, and all of us wanted nothing more than to celebrate these events. We'd been looking forward to raising the roof, not raising bail.

I handed Kelly my empty glass. "Charlie, I'll drive you home and then I'll return Cheski's car. If Frank is still at the station when I get there, I'll talk to him." Then I turned Kelly. "Does Charlie need a lawyer?"

"Not necessarily, but should this escalate, I have someone in mind. Let me hear what you get out of Frank and we'll go from there," he said as he prepared to welcome his daughter. "I think you're right: Charlie should go home. He's done nothing wrong. If Frank wants to talk to him again, we'll get him a lawyer."

Gayle stepped into the foyer, her radar on high alert. Three adults talking in hushed tones was enough to make my already hyper-aware daughter suspicious. "Why are you all here?" she asked.

"Because Frank thinks I killed someone, and I was asking your dad for advice," Charlie blurted out.

"What?" I exclaimed. "Were you raised by *wolves*? Who says that to a teenager?"

"He's kidding," Kelly chided as he wrestled his daughter into a bear hug.

That lie will last about five minutes, I thought as Gayle eyed me from under her father's hefty bicep.

FIVE

BY THE TIME I returned to the police station, Cheski was long gone, but Frank's office light was still on. I handed Cheski's keys to the desk cop and pointed in Frank's direction. The cop signaled an approval, but as I headed to Frank's office my legs tightened. I replayed the evening's events one more time in my head. I focused only on the facts.

Frank finds Charlie at the scene of a murder. The victim's wife is present, although she arrives after Charlie. An employee of the family is also on the scene but shows up after the wife. Concurrent with the murder, a blackout occurs and a burglary is reported in the same neighborhood as the murder. An unidentified man is seen on a neighboring property. Charlie, a suspect, has blood on him, but his arms and hands are unscathed. Charlie's phone received a text from the victim, who was dead minutes after communicating with Charlie. I repeated the events to myself again, and I still didn't like the ending. I had three strides before I entered Frank's office and at this point, he could probably hear my footsteps. I slowed down and continued with my train of thought.

Fletcher—or possibly Jamie, as Charlie had insisted—texted Charlie before the murder. The entire distance from Fletcher's home to Harbor House was no more than fifteen minutes. If Charlie returned immediately upon receiving the text, it would have taken him no more than fifteen minutes to get back to Fletcher's. That would put him on site at about six forty-five, but according to Charlie, he was standing over the body when the lights went on. It must have been close to seven at that point. That left maybe fifteen minutes unaccounted for. I stopped walking.

I'd taken one step backward when I heard the desk cop behind me. "Frank," the cop called out. "Your girlfriend is here."

So much for a quick exit. Short on options, I walked into Frank's office and sat down. Frank handed me half of a ham sandwich on rye.

"Date night," he said through a mouthful of mayonnaise. He wiped his mouth and added, "Charlie didn't kill anyone, but he needs to come in again or I'm going to have a hard time explaining his presence at a murder scene to the powers that be."

I studied the ham sandwich and realized I hadn't eaten anything since Cheski's celery and Kelly's shot of liquor. The growl in my stomach rivaled Roon's cries for milk.

"Eat," Frank said, "and then we'll talk."

We ate in silence, but my head was rotating faster than a salad spinner. What did Charlie do with the extra time? A horrible thought crossed my mind. One that I could barely imagine but needed to be considered. Would the extra time have been enough to crush a man's head in and wash the blood off? Maybe Charlie never left the house in the first place. And what about Jamie? She was there too. What had she told Frank?

"What did Jamie say?" I asked.

"She said Fletcher called Charlie and asked him to join them for dinner."

"She's a liar," I yelled.

Frank put his hand out like a stop sign. "Try to remember that I've already spoken to everyone on the scene. You've only spoken to Charlie."

He had me there. "So what did Jamie say?"

"Not a whole lot. She was disoriented, in shock I suppose. I asked her a few questions, but it was unproductive at best."

Frank had picked the tomatoes out of his sandwich. I reached across the desk for his discarded veggies and layered them between my bread. Eating off of others' plates was a Freegan habit that Frank had grown used to. "How about Ricky? He was there. What's his story?'

Frank swallowed his last bite of sandwich like it was sandpaper, and I wasn't sure I wanted to hear what he was about to say, given Charlie's earlier suspicion about Frank and Ricky talking in private at the scene. He took a swig of coffee and cleared his throat. "Ricky thinks it was a lover's quarrel."

"Thank God," I said as I leaned over the desk to high-five Frank.

He caught my hand and pulled me closer. "Between Charlie and Jamie. Not Jamie and Fletcher."

"Excuse me?" I said.

"Ricky insinuated that there was something going on between Jamie and Charlie. He thinks Charlie had a thing for Jamie."

I released Frank's hand and threw the remainder of my sandwich on his desk. I then proceeded to spit out a string of expletives so offensive that a jumbo size bar of soap would have dissolved upon contact with my tongue.

I heard the desk cop come charging down the hall. I spun my chair around and pointed directly at the unsuspecting officer. "Just a lover's quarrel," I said calmly and turned back to Frank.

"You know how to deliver a punch line," he said as he relaxed back into his chair. Then he waved the desk cop away.

I frowned. "So now what?"

Frank wiped his hands and threw out the remains of our deli dinner. "Fletcher's skull was severely damaged on the right side. I don't know what the murder weapon was, but someone with a solid swing put a fatal dent in his head."

I thought about Jamie and I considered Frank's description of the murder. "You think a man killed Fletcher."

"Most likely," he responded.

A tomato slice seemed to be lodged in my throat. Two men were on the scene, Charlie and Ricky, and Charlie had a few pounds and inches on Fletcher's assistant. "What else you got for me?" I said, clearing the remnants of my meal with a cough.

"One of the residents at Green Acres did see someone during the blackout. I'd like to take you to their house tomorrow and see what you can put on paper."

"Happy to do it."

"There's a condition."

I didn't like conditions.

"If we engage your services, you work for us and not Charlie. The whole . . ." Frank moved his hands around in a tangled circle. "The whole friendship thing with Charlie and then Charlie being at the scene of a crime . . ."

"And you and me dating," I added. I wondered if Frank's jealousy was really the issue.

Frank nodded. "It's too close for comfort. So I'm asking you to work solely for me."

"I reject your offer," I said without pause, and I meant it. There was no way I could turn my back on Charlie, and Frank wasn't giving me any options. I could, of course, agree to his arrangement, and then back out if the evidence worked against Charlie. Switching teams in the middle of an investigation would strain my relationship with Frank, but opting out of his offer now would likely have the same effect. If I chose not to help Frank and sided with my ex-boyfriend, this deli sandwich on greasy paper might be our last date. The only win-win situation would be if I lent my skills to Frank *and* we proved Charlie's innocence.

Frank waited for me to run through the scenarios his offer implied. Two choices involved a potential break up and the third had merit but also contained an element of risk. What if we couldn't exonerate Charlie? And what if I sketched the proof that ultimately put Charlie in jail?

"Do the math, Ce. We'll get further working together than separately."

He had a point.

I looked at my watch. It was almost midnight. "I've got a huppah to help build," I said as I leaned across the desk to kiss Detective Frank DeRosa. "You still owe me a date."

"Sleep on it. If you want to work on this case, call me in the morning."

Translation: I'd be sleeping by myself until I made a decision, and as far as Frank was concerned, there was only one option.

Despite the late hour, Charlie and Katrina were in full huppah swing when I returned home. Katrina had sketched out her vision for an open wedding canopy draped with colorful fabrics. Charlie had made a list of items for the lumber yard. "Most of the wood we'll get from the scrap pile," he said. "If we want the four supporting posts to match, we may have to purchase those, but I have some old barn boards that we can use for barter." Katrina's project was good therapy for Charlie.

I pointed to the drapery covering the canopy. "What's the theme?"

Katrina smiled brightly at me. She had no clue what had happened at the Fletcher mansion today or that her huppah draftsman was avoiding the police. For all we knew, this incident would resolve itself within days, leaving no reason to upset her. We didn't have television and Katrina only read week-old newspapers, if she read any at all. Less than a year earlier, we had ditched poor Katrina on the day of Roon's birth in search of another criminal. Good sport that she was, she chose to name her son in honor of the victim, Bob Rooney, a fellow Freegan and the manager of the town's recycling center. As generous and forgiving as Katrina had been at the time, I didn't want to repeat the pattern. Her wedding was our redemption, a chance to get our families back on track. I sat down and gave her my full attention.

"I researched a traditional Jewish wedding huppah," she said eagerly, "and I discovered that couples sometimes ask wedding guests to donate a piece of material that represents something important in their lives. The huppah is then decorated with the donations as a symbol of the couple's new home."

I neglected to mention that her new home was technically still Harbor House.

"That's nice," I said and then paused. "Trina, is Jonathan Jewish?"

Jonathan, Katrina's beau and a former Harbor House roommate, was currently in medical school at Yale. Katrina had scheduled the wedding to coincide with the end of his school year and although she was happy to marry a future doctor, their separation had been difficult.

"No. Neither of us are Jewish, but ideas are free and I really like this one."

I gave Katrina a big hug. Roon must have sensed someone had moved in on his territory because his cries wafted down the stairs. "He needs me," Katrina said and headed upstairs.

Charlie and I sat quietly at the table for a few minutes before he broke the silence. "What did Frank say?"

"He wants me to do some sketches."

"If you could pitch in that would be great," Charlie said. "Just don't draw me."

I debated telling Charlie the details of Frank's offer, but I had vetoed my own decision before I'd even left the police station. Charlie, I decided, would be kept in the dark about my allegiances, as would Frank.

Frank was worried my friendship with Charlie would obscure my objectivity, and I understood his concern. But then I considered the legal terms of my proposed employment with the Cold Spring Harbor police. I was only hired to draw. Plain and simple. The idea that I would purposely falsify sketches to help Charlie was ridiculous. My sketches are executed in the presence of the police, who are listening to a witness's description while I'm drawing. If my pictures don't capture the description, the police are at liberty to discard them. It's not like I could turn a witness's description of Charlie into a completely different person. Using this logic, there was no room for me to play both sides of the fence. I can only draw what people tell me to draw.

Frank's real concern was that through the course of my employment, he'd reveal information to me that wasn't meant for Charlie's ears. Technically, a leak in the investigation wasn't my problem. From the minute Frank took the oath of service, it became his job to maintain the integrity of an investigation and if nothing else, he was the most ethical man I'd ever met. He wouldn't slip. My boyfriend had a poker face that even the most experienced Vegas high roller couldn't crack. However, I could appreciate how the proximity of the players created potential holes for Frank. Charlie and I lived together, and Frank was often at Harbor House with us.

My solution? I'd play in the gray.

My circuitous rationalization had come to me on the drive back from the station. I settled on a solution that kept me precariously balanced between good and bad. I'd help Frank by doing what exactly what he'd asked—drawing. I'd support Charlie by whatever means possible. I'd keep the two men at a distance so neither would feel compromised, and then I'd pull every last thread of my Freegan resourcefulness out of my recycled hat and figure out how to prove Charlie's innocence while making the Cold Spring Harbor police look like the heroes.

Easy, right?

Charlie rubbed his face. He was exhausted, but he didn't want to let Katrina down. Less than a day earlier, he'd crafted a lucrative business deal with a man who was now dead. The first to be found at the scene with the victim's blood on his shoes, Charlie was in a bind. I leaned forward and rested my head in the crook of his shoulder. He wrapped his arm around me.

"We'll get through this," I whispered.

"Why me?" Charlie moaned. "I've broken the rules my whole life and never been caught. Now I'm being accused of something I didn't actually do."

I took a second to consider Frank's actions at the scene of the murder. "Why do you think Frank spoke to Ricky before you?"

Charlie sat up straight and twisted his bottom lip. "Because he'll never get over the fact that I slept with you first."

I laughed. I couldn't help it. It was funny and Charlie thought so too.

"That's not the reason," I said as my laughter subsided. "He didn't need to speak to you. He knows you, and he knows you're innocent."

Charlie tilted back in his chair, his signature move. He was so good at it, he could balance for thirty seconds before tumbling forward. "Not to sound too cliché, but tell it to the judge," he said. "Without a real suspect, I'm the next best thing."

I frowned. At this moment, Charlie was his own worst critic. So convincing, in fact, that I started to think about his dinner invitation to the Fletcher house.

"I still don't get why you accepted the dinner invitation."

"It's called networking," Charlie rose from the table. "It's something people who work do."

There was nothing worse than a Freegan defector. I narrowed my eyes at his retreating back, watching him go upstairs to sleep. "Hey, if you're all about work," I yelled, "how about paying some real rent?"

SIX

"So who are we speaking with first?" I asked as Frank parked his car in front of a brand-new Green Acres home. As much as my conversation with Charlie had upset me the previous evening, I had called Frank first thing this morning and agreed to work with him. *There was no going back now*, I thought as I sized up the million-dollar home in front of me.

"Phoebe and Kevin Calhoun," Frank said. "They've been in their house for over a year. Husband works on Wall Street. Wife stays at home."

My first impression of the Calhouns' Green Acres home was not, surprisingly, all that bad. Fletcher had decent taste, something I had previously noted after spending two weeks in his own home when I painted his wife. New money and old mansions can make for a disastrous renovation mix, but Fletcher's home was impressive, with finishings that whispered wealth as opposed to screaming it. The Fletchers' kitchen in particular stood out in my memory because it appeared to be a room that was actually used for cooking, if not by Fletcher and his wife, then by a professional staff. Instead of twelve-foot slabs of granite countertops, Simon had installed worn butcher-block, apparently salvaged from a bakery in Europe. As for his wife, Jamie, she too, was no slouch in the looks department. Her features, regal, almost handsome, were easy to capture on canvas. Her face, like the Calhouns' home, was a series of angles softened by traditional elements.

The Green Acres homes, ten in all, were like a box of assorted Italian pastries, each one slightly different but equally as good. The Calhoun house had the lines of a 1960s split-level, but oversized windows and premium materials catapulted it into the realm of high-end architecture. The solar panels coupled with unexpected features, like a rain run-off system, gave the visitor a feeling that something special was happening in the cul-de-sac. I had to admit the Green Acres development had a magical quality—the same quality that had made Simon Fletcher famous.

"They're expecting us," Frank said as he rang the bell.

A woman about my age opened the door. She was short and bottom heavy with a mane of dark hair and misplaced highlights. The recognition was instantaneous.

"Get out," the woman yelled. "Don't tell me that CeCe Prentice, the biggest tree-hugger in high school, is a cop."

I looked at Frank and then back at the car. I wasn't interested in interviewing my high school nemesis, Phoebe Purcell. I guess she was Phoebe Calhoun now.

"You know each other?" Frank asked as he stepped into the house, purposely blocking me from making a hasty getaway. He shook Phoebe's hand while I held tight to my sketch book.

"Phoebe is a few years older than me, but it was a small school."

"So you're a cop?" Phoebe said.

"I'm a sketch artist. Detective DeRosa said you or your husband saw something, and I'm here to help."

"Right," she said, tossing her hair. "I remember. You were the artsy-fartsy type. What ever happened to that hippy guy you hung out with? The one with the blond curls."

Her poorly veiled reference to Charlie was insensitive at best, but's that exactly how I remembered Phoebe Purcell. She was a mean girl, and I was one of her targets. Charlie and I were three years younger than the all-powerful Phoebe and when we entered high school, she turned stealing Charlie into a full-time job. By the time she was a senior, she had plowed through the entire male population—including some teachers—and Charlie, with his trademark mop-top and blue eyes, must have looked like fresh meat on the first day of her senior year. Charlie and I had weathered Hurricane Phoebe, but her curvy body and tousled hair had definitely caught his eye. To this day, I wasn't completely convinced that something hadn't gone on between the two of them while he and I were dating.

"Charlie and I live together," I said, and then paused as Phoebe lifted her eyebrows. And then I added, just because I could, "Detective DeRosa is my boyfriend." Could I be blamed? Frank looked particularly handsome this morning, a fact that the heat-seeking Phoebe surely hadn't overlooked.

Before Phoebe could respond, Kevin Calhoun walked into the foyer. Pressed khakis, button-down Oxford, eyes glued to his phone screen. "Well, at least that's working," he said. "The camera picked up the two of you at the bottom of the driveway." He titled his phone to reveal a snapshot of Frank and me on the Calhouns' front steps. He looked back at his phone and asked, "Is the temperature okay? I can adjust it from my phone if you're uncomfortable."

43

Frank shrugged.

"I'm fine," I said.

Kevin's phone beeped. He turned the phone toward us again and what appeared to be a door icon flashed on the screen. "Door's not fully closed," he said brushing by us to secure the front door. I'd have loved to get a feel for Kevin's face, but at this point it was still turned down to his screen. I did get a good look at the bald spot on top of his head, though.

"Kids just went into the basement," he announced to Phoebe, his gaze still on the phone. My neck tensed. *This is modern living?* I thought. If that phone could take my blood pressure, it would crack the screen.

Kevin punched away at his phone while Phoebe waited patiently. "I just started the coffeemaker," he said.

I had about two more minutes of automated house living before I snatched Kevin's phone and threw it out the window. Maybe there was an app to open the window?

"Let's sit in the kitchen," Frank suggested. "Will you be comfortable in there?" he asked me. He could see I'd had it, and we hadn't even started yet.

"The kitchen will work, good light," I said as I took in the wall of framed family photos. Either every photo was taken during monsoon season or the Calhouns had invested in a wind machine to emphasize Phoebe's long locks. She did have beautiful hair, and if I had to be honest, they looked like a happy family.

We settled at the kitchen table, and Frank started with the basics. The Calhouns had just come back from their daughter's dance recital yesterday when the lights flickered.

"Let me tell you," Phoebe said, "if Fletcher wasn't dead, one of the neighbors would have eventually sued him. Half the shit in this house doesn't work. We're supposed to have a high-tech security system, but the damn thing doesn't record if there's no electricity. I'm just so glad I saw someone and that you're here to take my statement."

"So your solar panels feed the grid, not your homes directly?" I asked.

"That point," Kevin said, head still in phone, "wasn't made clear to us before we purchased."

"I thought we were getting money back," Phoebe added. "The whole idea was that this neighborhood was supposed to be self-sustaining, as in zero dollars."

Kevin squirmed. I don't think he liked when Phoebe talked money. He placed his hand on his wife's arm to get her to slow down.

She nodded blankly. Her only worry, it seemed, was that the maximum voltage on her hair dryer was met. I stared at Frank. He knew I had my limits. "You're good to start?" he asked. My pad and pencils were already on the table.

"So I see someone running across the street toward the neighbor's house," Kevin said.

"Did you get a look at his face?" I asked. Kevin motioned to Phoebe.

"I was standing there," she said and pointed to the window over the sink. "A head popped up out of the bushes. Scared the crap out of me. It was a kid, young, maybe fifteen or sixteen."

Now it was my turn to slow Phoebe down. The thing about being in your thirties is that you have trouble pinning down a young person's age with any real accuracy. "How do you know he was in his teens?"

Phoebe turned to Kevin, and he offered me his screen again.

"That's Adam," he said, pointing to the frowning photo of a teenage boy, conspicuously missing from the family wall of photos.

"My son from my first marriage," Phoebe added. "Let's just say I know young boys."

At least she had said it so I didn't have to. I swallowed my tongue and politely ignored the fact that "to know young boys," Phoebe must have given birth shortly after high school to have one of her own. Of course, I had a teenage daughter myself, but the similarities in our lives ended there.

Another glaring difference between Phoebe and myself was her apparent disinterest in detail. Hair color? Eye color? Height? She couldn't seem to remember a single thing about the young man in her bushes. She looked at her husband for help.

"Remember what we discussed last night," her husband urged, but Phoebe still drew a blank.

"Did he look like your son?" I asked. I hoped my direction would spark her memory.

Phoebe acted as if I'd smacked her. I guess I'd asked the wrong question. "Of course not," she said. "Why would Adam be breaking into a house?"

Kevin lifted his head from his phone. *You picked her*, I thought.

I turned to Frank. "I don't think I have enough to go on," I admitted, and then I had an idea. "Phoebe," I started, "if we had gone to high school with this kid, who would he have been?"

She snapped her fingers. "Walter Todd. This kid looked like Walter. Remember him?"

"Sure," I said and quickly sketched a drawing of a guy I hadn't seen in over ten years. "Walter ran track," I said as I remembered his wiry, athletic frame. He also smoked like a chimney, a boy of contradictions. One minute he was getting detention and the next

46

he was breaking school records. He also had a salient facial feature that made his face difficult to read—really bushy eyebrows. I filled in the brow by turning my pencil on its side and then I rubbed my finger hard on the paper. I turned my drawing to Phoebe.

"Yeah," she said. "This kid had Walter's eyebrows."

I heard a footstep behind me and instinctively turned. A lanky teenager in head-to-toe black slid into the kitchen. *Angry* was the first word that came to mind. That was followed by *disconnected*, *disgruntled*, and *borderline destructive*. I assumed that the explosion of teen angst and raging hormones standing in front of me was Phoebe's son Adam.

The teenager reached for a sugary box of cereal, tilted it toward a bowl, and then threw the empty cardboard into the sink. *Not a fan of recycling*, I thought.

"Shouldn't you be at the supermarket?" he asked his mom. "Getting me more cereal?"

"Don't talk to your mother that way," Kevin said. He nodded at Phoebe as if to say, *I'll take care of this*, but he might as well have been talking to a wall. Adam stuck his tongue out at Kevin and flipped it like a serpent. As he retracted his tongue, I understood why he was missing from the family photos: his demonic image couldn't be captured on film.

"The automatic shade on my bedroom window is broken," Adam said as he inhaled a mouthful of cereal. "And the dogs' GPS collar stopped working again."

Kevin flinched, and with his face finally directed away from his phone, I could see he was so angry at the ever-growing list of housing failures that he practically spit.

Adam tossed his bowl in the sink and then grabbed a can of soda from the refrigerator. "I thought bankers were supposed to make good investments," he laughed as he took a pot-shot at his stepfather.

I looked at Phoebe. She was mortified and her husband seethed. I wasn't sure if Kevin's anger was directed toward Fletcher or Adam, or both. Kevin titled his head toward Frank. "This is Detective DeRosa and his assistant," Kevin said. "They're investigating the break-ins."

I stood up and nodded to Frank, hoping he'd take my cue. I walked over to Adam, pad in hand.

"Were you home when the break-ins occurred last night?" Frank asked Phoebe's son. Kevin was about to interrupt when I turned my pad toward Adam.

"Ever see this kid?" I asked. I stepped quickly to the side so Frank could get a clear view of Adam's face.

Adam looked directly at his mother. Behind the black bangs plastered on his forehead, a set of hazel eyes searched for safety, or maybe an alibi. I turned to look at Phoebe. It was a slight movement, but she lifted her chin to the ceiling.

"I was in my room the whole night." He pushed past us, his soda leaving a trail of sticky splotches on the floor. "Your drawing sucks," he said as he left the room.

"Teens," I sympathized. "Such a tough age."

"I think we've got what we need," Frank said as he thanked the Calhouns. "We're going to shop this photo around to the neighbors. If you remember anything else," he said as he handed his card to Kevin, "give me a call."

SEVEN

FRANK SURVEYED THE GREEN Acres home.

"Nine more to go," he said. "Where should we start?"

"Forget the neighbors. Let's start with Phoebe's son," I said. "That kid was a train wreck."

"And we got the watered-down version. I'd hate to see him and Kevin go at it behind closed doors. Not a whole a lot of love there." Frank shook his head. "I'll have Cheski do some digging, call his school." He reached for my hand. "How much are you loving Gayle right now?"

I laughed at the image of my faux-punk daughter in her vintage garb and dyed black hair. There was no amount of black eye liner that could cover up the genuine sparkle in her eyes. She had every reason to be a defiant teen like Adam. She'd grown up in a nontraditional family, she'd lost a parent, and her entrance into the world was unethical at best. "I hit the jackpot with that one," I said. "I wouldn't wish Adam on anyone, even Phoebe."

"You're a saint," Frank chuckled.

"Do you think he recognized the guy from the bushes?" I asked.

"Hard to tell," he said, "but I'm not convinced he was in his room either. There was something going back and forth between him and his mother."

We did a sweep of the remaining houses on the block. Like the Calhouns, most of the families were about the same age with young kids. Like Kevin, they were all disappointed in the quality and complexity of the technology Fletcher had sold them despite their genuine interest in fully wired, eco-friendly houses. My favorite complaint was from a young mother who insisted that the toaster popped every time the television turned on. Across the board, all of the residents were particularly annoyed with the faulty security system. Neighbors had spotted people running through the neighborhood, although no one could confirm the face Phoebe had seen.

"Either our bushy browed guy is Peter Pan," Frank pondered, "or this was a group effort."

I pointed to the final house on the block. "I wonder if Adam has a bunch of delinquent friends," I said and then paused. "We don't have a gang problem in Cold Spring, do we?"

"If we do, then it's the first I'm hearing about it. In these neighborhoods, the biggest juvenile issue is cheating on the SATs," Frank said as he leaned on the doorbell. For good measure, he smiled up at the security camera that we now knew had been installed in the right-hand corner of every front door in the development.

A lovely retired couple, Dotty and George Fraser, greeted us at the door. Clearly the block's outlier, the Frasers didn't fit the neighborhood mold. With children over forty and twenty solid years of active retirement ahead of them, they were passionate about their newly sustainable life and thrilled they had made the investment in Green Acres.

"Does everything work?" George asked rhetorically. "Of course not. But now I've got a hobby. I almost look forward to things breaking."

"It's true," Dotty said. "Why don't you take them down to command central?"

George led us proudly into his basement and then proceeded to show off his handiwork. He had installed rack upon rack of stainless steel shelving from which hung enough tools to make a mechanic's knees weak. "I wanted to be an engineer as a kid, but my dad pushed me into finance. Now I love when stuff breaks. I have all the time and money in the world to tinker."

"So you're not mad at Simon Fletcher?" Frank asked.

"The guy's heart was in the right place, but he's not an engineer. He's an environmentalist, and this stuff is tricky." He picked up the casing for a remote-controlled thermostat and handed it to me. "The pieces work fine by themselves, but coordinating them is another matter and that's where Fletcher's plan fell apart." His glee was inversely proportionate to Simon Fletcher's failed mechanical plans.

Frank walked through George's workroom, randomly picking up and putting down odds and ends as he strolled. "So you've been experiencing the same flickering and occasional blackouts?" he asked.

"Yes sir," George replied. He walked over to his workbench and booted up a computer.

"Interesting," Frank said as he pointed to the computer. "I didn't expect a laptop on a tool bench."

George laughed. "It's not like building a lamp in shop class

51

anymore. All these home gadgets are programmed through a network." He motioned us to come forward and view the 3-D architectural drawings of his Green Acres home.

"I installed a backup generator on my own," he said, pointing to the rear exterior of his house. A square box was positioned toward the back. "The blackouts haven't been an inconvenience for Dotty and me."

Frank paused. "The other neighbors are angry."

"Oh boy," George hooted. "Are they ever!" He pulled a tray from a shiny red tool box. "The neighbors publish a quarterly Green Acres newsletter." He handed a sheet of paper to Frank. "This one was a keeper."

"'Meeting at the Calhouns' home,'" Frank read. "'Agenda, suing Simon Fletcher.'"

Finally. A distraction from Charlie. At least now we had printed proof that Simon Fletcher had detractors. The Green Acres homeowners had paid over a million dollars for their new residences and it appeared some were disgruntled enough to consider legal action. I had to assume that the neighbors had approached Fletcher with their complaints already. I wondered how that conversation had gone down.

"Can I keep this?" Frank asked. George took the newsletter and laid it facedown on a printer. "I'll scan you a copy."

Frank stared at George's computer screen and then he pointed to the generator. "That means your security cameras were working during the blackout?"

"There's a slight delay when the power goes out. I've got to start the generator manually. After I found a flashlight, it probably took me about fifteen minutes to get everything up and running again.

So except for that gap, we may have caught something on camera. I'll see what I can download for you."

Frank stopped grinding his jaw. "That would be great," he said, handing George his card.

George led us back to the front door and gave Frank a hearty shake. "Is it connected?" he asked as his face turned serious. "Fletcher's murder and these break-ins?"

"I'm not sure," Frank answered, "but I'm asking the neighbors to keep their doors and windows locked at all times."

The man gave us a can-do smile, and I predicted that within five minutes of our departure, George Fraser would purchase a few thousand dollars of additional security equipment, just because he could. "Oh, I'll be prepared when they come back." He winked and confirmed my suspicion.

EIGHT

It was a frigid Saturday morning as my mother, Gayle, Katrina, and I climbed into my preowned vehicle, a fancy new-fangled term for used. Although nothing could replace my Gremlin, a car I had rescued from the town dump and drove until it literally stopped, I had recently bartered a portrait for a hard-driven Subaru. With more miles than odometer place settings, my used Subaru drove like a dream. Even Baby Roon, strapped in his car seat, was as happy as a clam.

"Trina, are you sure you want to buy a new wedding dress?" I asked. "Wedding dresses are meant to be worn once. I'm sure we can find a used one in decent condition."

Katrina stuttered and I realized I was no better than Phoebe, the mean girl.

My mother swatted my arm. "Now is not a good time for your idealism," she reprimanded.

"I'm sorry," I apologized. "Please don't cry, Trina. Roon will let loose if you cry."

Katrina fished in her bag for a tissue and blew her nose hard, the cue for Roon to start screaming. *Please stop*, I thought. I loved Roon, but I had been unprepared for his chronic fussiness, which was even more difficult to handle now, given Charlie's predicament. Although Frank and I had made some progress in the previous days, we were still unable to place anyone else at the scene of the murder besides Charlie. Frank was spending the day gathering available security footage while I accompanied my best friend on a bridal dress shopping spree. Charlie was hard at work on the huppah, and I had made arrangements with Frank to stop by the station later. It wasn't all that easy keeping Charlie and Frank at a distance, but I was determined to work both sides of the case all while planning a wedding.

Gayle reached around the driver's seat to show me a photo of a simple white gown. "I think Katrina would look great in this," she said. Smooth. My daughter just saved my insensitive butt.

I stole a quick peek at the dress. "It's beautiful." I forced a smiled. "You're going to be a beautiful bride." I needed another adjective besides *beautiful*.

Katrina misted up again. "No, you're right. The guilt of buying a new dress is killing me," she wept. "My mother gave me a five-thousand-dollar gift card for this place. She won't come to the wedding unless I wear something with tags." Katrina pointed out the window. "It's there," she sniffled, pointing at a boutique bridal store called Le Mariage.

"Wow," I exclaimed as I looked at the luxury cars lined up like a dealership. "So this is where the one percent shops." Manhasset's Miracle Mile, a high-end shopping venue made famous by a Billy Joel lyric, stretched out before us.

"Yeah, we're gonna cruise the Miracle Mile," I sang. Katrina started to laugh and chimed in with a few more lines.

"I always park to the left of Barney's," my mother said.

Of course you do, Mom, I thought.

———

A mature woman who insisted we call her Miss Suzy greeted us at the door of Le Mariage with a tray of champagne and cookies. My mother shot me a worried glance. She really wanted a glass of bubbly, and I could have used one myself, but my mother's sobriety was paramount.

"We'll pass," I said politely, "but the cookies are perfect." I lifted the plate and we munched on sugary wafers while Miss Suzy gave us the grand tour of Le Mariage. On the second floor, we passed a pack of giggly girls in their early twenties oohing and ahhing over a teal tea-length dress. I nearly choked on my cookie. Bridesmaid dresses? There was no way I was leaving Le Mariage in a ball of itchy taffeta. Katrina and I hadn't discussed the wedding party details as yet, but I hoped she understood it would take a mile of miracles for me to purchase a dress that would definitely only be worn once.

"Oh, you'll wear that one again," Miss Suzy encouraged the chattering wedding party.

No you won't, I thought. *That dress, along with every other bridesmaid dress you purchase, will be banned to the back of your closet for eternity within twenty-four hours of the nuptials.*

Katrina must have noticed my alarm as she put her arm around me. "Don't worry, I planned on going down the aisle with just Roon and Jonathan," she said.

"What are you saying?" I replied. "I don't look good in teal?

Roon wailed and Katrina lifted him out of the stroller to drape him over her shoulder. Miss Suzy feigned a smile as Roon let out an enormous burp. "She's just lovely," Miss Susy drawled. The pink pajamas had struck again.

Katrina passed Roon to Gayle, who slung him on her hip like a pro. Then we proceeded to wade our way through racks of floor-length silks, chiffons, and lace. After five minutes, all the gowns, no matter how exquisite, were impossible to distinguish. "How can I tell the difference?" I yelled from behind a display of veils. "They're all white." The resemblance among the dresses reminded me of the Green Acres homes. Similar but different, and that got me thinking. Only three of the ten houses had had break-ins. Why those houses? They all shared common features, but the burglars had focused on just three.

At that moment, Katrina walked up to me with an armful of dresses. She held them out for comment and I noticed that all of her selections had rhinestone belts. I looked at the dress I had chosen for her. No belt.

A pattern emerged in my head, one that I couldn't contain. I needed to talk to Frank, but the pile of gowns in front of me also required attention.

I randomly picked one of Katrina's dress options. "This is the one," I said with false confidence. I waited until Katrina headed to the dressing room, and then I slipped out a side door to an alley. Safely outside, I searched for my phone and then remembered that I hadn't thrown it in my bag. I hadn't really figured out how to buy prepaid minutes, so I often left it at home. As I cursed my frugality, the side door opened again and Gayle stepped out.

"What's up?" she shivered.

"Nothing," I said as if I always hung out in back alleys in the middle of February. Too bad I didn't smoke. My presence outside would have been completely believable had I been a chain smoker.

Gayle smirked. "You're a terrible liar."

I pulled her to the side and inched the door back open. The heat was enticing, but I closed it again as I spotted Katrina searching the aisles for us wearing a white gown with a sparkly belt. It wouldn't be long before I'd have to explain the events surrounding Fletcher's death to Katrina. Four days had passed, and I wasn't sure how much longer my housemate would go without picking up a recycled newspaper.

"If you lend me your phone," I said to Gayle, "I'll explain everything later."

"I think I know the person you sketched in your pad," she whispered.

"That's impossible," I said. "You don't even know what's going on."

"If Charlie is in trouble," she said with a cracking voice, "I want to help."

"Charlie is . . ." I started.

"He's not fine," Gayle said firmly, and I could see the rising frustration of a sixteen-year-old when they know they're right, but the world seems to be working against them.

"Okay," I bargained. "Give me your phone and I'll explain everything when we get home. For now, your job is to find a dress for Katrina, and fast." I looked back at Katrina. "I kind of like the one she's wearing. It's white, it's long. What's not to love?"

Gayle laughed and handed me her phone.

"You really recognized the guy in my drawing?" I asked.

"I never said it was a guy," Gayle said, clarifying her earlier statement. "I'm not even sure you've drawn anything yet. But I did get you to agree to tell me what's going on."

The power of genetics. It was amazing how I had *not* raised a child exactly like myself. I shooed Gayle back into the boutique and then dialed Frank. He picked up on the first ring.

"It's me," I said through chattering teeth. "I've thought of something." Before I could explain my theory about the burgled homes, Frank cut me off.

"I have to take another call," he said. "I'm putting you on hold."

I considered hanging up again, but in this case, Frank had the advantage, as I really needed to speak with him. I counted to twenty knowing full well I might have to count to one hundred and even then I wouldn't disconnect the phone. When I passed ninety, I started to wonder who was more important to Frank than me. Who had Frank bumped me for? Someone with more information? A possible lead? As I was debating my position in Frank's queue, he came back on the line.

I took a stab in the dark. "The district attorney keeping you busy?" I fished.

Frank didn't answer and my heart sank. If the DA was hounding Frank, it would be that much harder for Charlie to fly under the radar. I had to remind myself that Simon Fletcher's death, a high-profile murder, would be a top priority in town.

"Hey," my voice shaky as much from the cold as the situation, "I'm thinking thieves don't pick houses randomly. I'm not an expert, but doesn't the above-average criminal pick houses that meet some type of thief requirements?"

"They do," Frank replied. "The pros will watch a house for months before they act."

"That's what got me thinking," I said. "What do the houses that got hit have in common? There's got to be a reason they chose some homes and not others."

There was silence on the other end of the phone. "And the Fletcher house," Frank added. "Cheski and I went back over Fletcher's house carefully and found an unlocked door near a service entrance by the kitchen. It's quite possible someone was in the house that night too."

"So the houses do have something in common."

"Actually, only one house has a dead body," Frank said. "How long will you be with Katrina?"

I cracked the door a notch to see Katrina shake her head and paw at her sample dress like it was made out of torn potato sacks. For someone who had been wearing milk-stained button-downs for the past three months, she was awfully picky.

"I'm in for the long haul."

"Come by the station tomorrow morning."

"I'll bring breakfast," I offered.

"It better come with a receipt," Frank responded, but I could tell he didn't want to hang up. There was an awkward silence.

"What?" I asked.

"Are you one hundred percent in about helping with this investigation?"

Any pause and Frank would doubt my motives. "I'm in," I volleyed back.

———

By the time I rejoined the dress selection—or rather rejection—Katrina had been through a dozen gowns that didn't please her for whatever reason.

My mother handed me the dress that I had originally suggested to Katrina. "Will you indulge me?" she asked.

"You want *me* to try this on?" The news about the district attorney had deflated my already low interest in gown shopping.

Gayle handed me a pair of heels. "Oh come on," she urged. "This will be fun. Katrina's getting burnt out and this will give her a break."

I took the dress from my mother and noticed that it wasn't a true white but rather a creamy shade of ivory. With no embellishments save for a row of covered buttons down the back, it was surprisingly light in my hands and so simple, it could have passed for an expensive slip. I held the dress up to my neck while my mother beamed. Had I subconsciously chosen a dress for Katrina that I secretly wanted for myself?

I figured the only way to find out was to try it on. I reached for Katrina's hand. "Let's do this together."

We waltzed into the dressing room while Roon pitched an awesome fit. Behind the dressing room curtains, we peeled off our clothes to the sound of his cries, and then I slid into a dress that cost more than my entire yearly food allowance.

"You're going have to take that off," Katrina said as she gazed at me in the mirror.

"That bad?"

"No," she barked. "It's perfect, but I'm not about to let you show me up in the first dress you've tried on."

I turned slowly and glanced over my shoulder. The buttons, nearly thirty in all and extending halfway down my back to my butt, were so carefully crafted, they should have been behind a locked case in a museum. "I never thought I could pull this off."

"Oh, you'll be pulling it off," Katrina joked, "but not before I take a picture." She snapped away and then, to please my friend, I took off the dress and put on one from her reject pile. The new gown bagged and pinched in all the wrong places. Whatever chest I thought I had floated unsupported behind the oversized bodice while the arms clung to me like a wet swim shirt.

"Now that is perfectly horrible," Katrina crowed. "Make sure you stand as close to me as possible."

We paraded back out of the dressing room, arm and arm, to the gleeful cheers of my mother and Gayle, who burst into applause at Katrina's dress. "Katrina," my mother beamed. "That's the dress. That's the one." And like the sky clearing after a torrential downpour, Baby Roon stopped wailing long enough to stare, dry-eyed at his beautiful mother.

Gayle high-fived Roon's baby fist to celebrate a Freegan first: the purchase of a brand-new wedding gown. I smiled at one of my dearest friends as she beamed at her son, anticipating her happily-ever-after with Jonathan, and thought about the original dress I had tried on. Maybe it wasn't the last time a Freegan would purchase a new wedding dress.

NINE

THE BARN AT HARBOR House, like many of the outer buildings, was in desperate need of repair. For someone like me, the barn's advanced age only increased its authenticity. I loved the chipped red stain and wilting sideboards. In a competitive real estate market where older homes were torn down and replaced by new ones, I felt an obligation to maintain our property "as is."

I swung the creaking barn door aside to find Charlie hard at work on the wedding huppah. The barn was freezing, but I had come prepared in a ski jacket and hat. Charlie wore a t-shirt and a thin layer of sweat.

"It looks good," I said as much about the huppah as Charlie himself. The canopy frame, maybe ten square feet, was built entirely out of reclaimed wood, giving it a warm and inviting glow. Charlie, my creative friend, had added a delightful twist by weaving an intricate display of vines through the beams. The effect was dreamy and enchanting and for a split second, I could see myself in a particular dress under the canopy.

"How are you planning on transporting it to my mother's yard?" I asked, as if Charlie had built a boat in a bottle.

He ground a screw into a corner notch "It's easy to dismantle," he mumbled as he pinched another screw from between his lips. "I made sure the four sections come apart. The vines look connected, but they're not."

"Masterful," I said as I approached the huppah. "Can we talk about Fletcher?" I asked, cutting to the chase.

Charlie put his hammer down and we sat cross-legged under the canopy.

"I'm just going to say what I'm thinking."

Charlie nodded. "Go for it."

"There's fifteen minutes missing in your story."

He nodded again but offered no explanation. We sat quietly for a few more seconds, and I decided to cross a line that I knew I was inching toward anyway. I revealed what Ricky, Fletcher's assistant, had told Frank.

"Ricky told Frank he thought there was something going on between you and Jamie."

Again, Charlie didn't offer a response. I frowned.

I had just broken Frank's trust by passing police information to Charlie, and Charlie had the nerve to stonewall. "This is stupid," I said. "I can't help you if won't talk to me." I waited a second and then added, "But I could help Frank, and you're losing points quickly."

"Fine, I'll play," he acquiesced.

"Where did the fifteen extra minutes go?"

Charlie reached into his pocket and threw a silvery square packet on the floor of the huppah.

"A condom. You used the time to buy birth control?" I was shocked, but I continued to slap the sorry pieces of Charlie's alibi together. "The general store near my mother's," I calculated. "You stopped there before you went back to Fletcher's."

Charlie hung his head, and I watched his shoulders rise and fall. "I didn't kill anyone," Charlie choked. "I didn't sleep with anyone. I didn't even get a dinner out of it."

I stepped down from the huppah and made my way to the barn door. It occurred to me that I could just walk away from this altogether. A few years ago, I was living completely off the grid with little to no interaction with the outside world. I was single and free, hiding in my eco-friendly bubble. In less time than it takes one of my paintings to dry, my idyllic life had morphed from full-time Freegan to employed criminal sketch artist. And in the most bizarre twist of fate, I was now dating a town cop, a prominent member of the same establishment I had rebelled against. Running away seemed like a good idea, but I couldn't give up on Charlie, despite the evidence mounting against him.

I turned back and yelled, "How long before Frank figures out that you intended to sleep with Fletcher's wife?"

"Hopefully longer than it takes us to figure out who really killed Fletcher."

I inched hesitantly back toward the huppah and closed the gap between Charlie and myself. "I'm not judging, but why her? Why Jamie?"

"She sent me signals." He shrugged.

"Is that all it takes?" I asked.

"Pretty much."

"Give me your phone," I demanded. Charlie tossed me his phone and I reread the message Fletcher sent. Let's keep this going. "What exactly were you *keeping going*?"

Charlie flipped the condom in the air and then let it hit the floor. "When I arrived earlier in the day, Jamie grilled me about Fletcher. What else was he working on? Why was he so busy?" Charlie paused and then continued. "On the way out, she asked me whether Fletcher seemed happy." He raised his shoulders an inch as if Jamie's last comment was self-explanatory.

"I'm lost," I admitted.

Charlie shook his head. "When a woman asks too many questions about their significant other, it means they're feeling vulnerable or dissatisfied in their relationship. So I gave her a hug."

I sighed at Charlie's male-centric version of relationships. "And you figured her insecurity would work to your advantage?"

"That was the plan," Charlie said. "An ice princess with a few fissures. She was as good a challenge as any."

"So when you left the house, Jamie was on your mind. That's why you assumed the text was from her and not Fletcher."

Charlie nodded.

"And you didn't think sleeping with the boss's wife would jeopardize your business deal?"

"My mistake," he said as he swatted the condom like a dead fly into a far corner of the barn. "And then I had to go and purchase one of the few items that you can't pick up used."

"You're gross," I moaned. "Who sold you the condoms at the general store?"

"Mrs. Kranz."

I clapped my hands. "That's fantastic," I said. "She's a hundred if she's a day, and she can't see two feet in front of her face." It was true. Mrs. Kranz had worked at the corner store since the Nixon administration. "That's got to buy you a few days."

Charlie clearly wasn't convinced that a geriatric eyewitness's faulty vision would be the key to his freedom. "You know what I'm wondering?" he said as he tapped a hammer on the ground. "Why Ricky told Frank he thought something was going on between me and Jamie. I'd never said two words to Jamie before that day, and I never touched her before that hug."

"He's a guy too. Maybe he saw the signals," I said wryly.

Charlie shook his head. "You're missing the point. If he overheard us, then he had to have been in the house, and I thought he arrived after me." Charlie punctuated his keen observation by slamming the hammer head down.

I returned to the huppah and sat shoulder to shoulder with Charlie, my confidence rising. "And you're sure you and Jamie hadn't been flirting on another day?"

"Believe me, that horse was a long shot. Ricky has no reason to suspect something between Jamie and me because, frankly, nothing actually happened."

"If you thought she was sending you signals, maybe she put out feelers to Ricky too. Maybe something happened between *Ricky* and Jamie."

"Or maybe he just took a shot in the dark." Charlie moved a pile of sawdust with his finger. I watched as he drew lines through the wood fragments. His sketch started to look a bit like the floor plan of a house. He grabbed from a pile of nails and placed two nails in the drawing.

"When I left, Jamie was in the hallway. She then walked to the back of the house. I think the master bedroom is in the back on the main floor." He took the nail and moved it to Simon and Jamie's bedroom. "As I was leaving, Simon came up from the basement. He's got an amazing office set up down there."

"Was he surprised to see you hadn't left?"

"He didn't see me, and I didn't really want to be seen since I had just hit on his wife."

"At least you're being honest now," I said. "Where did Fletcher go after he left the basement?"

Charlie thought for a second and then moved Fletcher's nail to the back of the house. "The master or the kitchen, both are down this main hall and that's where he was headed. He would have seen me if he walked into the great room or the dining room." Charlie pointed to the two rooms adjacent to the front door.

I handed Charlie a third nail. "Retrace your steps inside the house from the time you returned to Fletcher's during the blackout."

Charlie dragged the nail through the sawdust and made a line from the front door down the main hall. He stopped at the entrance to the great room.

"You ended up in the great room, to the right." I pointed. "What made you go there?"

Charlie looked up at the ceiling as he rolled the nail across his fingers. "It was dark. I knocked, but no one came to the door so I let myself in and I called out for Jamie."

"Wait," I said. "The door was open?"

"It was. That doesn't seem right." He paused. "Does it?"

"It's a little odd for Fletcher's house considering he built a fully wired development with security systems. You know what else is weird—when you told me what happened at the beach, you said you heard the front door open and then Ricky came up behind you."

"I did say that." Charlie looked worried. "If he came in when he said he did, he had no reason to suspect there was something between Jamie and me. I'm wondering if he was in the house, but shut the door to make it *seem* like he had just arrived."

"He'd have to be pretty clever to set that up."

Charlie agreed but insisted that someone else must have been in the house. "I couldn't have been the only one in the house," he said. "If it wasn't Ricky, someone else must have been there."

I pressed on. "Then what?" I asked.

Charlie's chest rose and fell with effort and I figured he was remembering the events of the night more clearly. I realized I hadn't extended enough sympathy toward my friend during what had clearly been a devastating event. Who wants to find a dead body in the dark? I wrapped my fingers around his free hand and squeezed.

"I heard Fletcher moan." He moved the nail into the great room. "I didn't know it was him. I'm not even sure I understood that it was a distressed person. I walked forward, maybe ten paces, into a pool of his blood."

"Oh god," I sighed. "He was still alive."

Charlie visibly shuddered. "This is crazy. Fletcher was brilliant, and he was so much more than just a tech guy; he was an environmental icon. I don't understand who would want to hurt him."

I was sure the district attorney was wondering the same thing, but I wasn't convinced Charlie's sawdust diagram would hold up in court. Conversely, I thought about the residents at Green Acres and their complaints about Fletcher's ability to deliver on his green-living offer. Maybe Charlie didn't know Fletcher as well as he thought he did. Maybe none of us did.

Charlie picked up Jamie's nail and moved it down the hall toward the great room.

"Did you hear Jamie behind you?"

"Hear her? She screamed like a banshee." Charlie picked up another nail. "I turned around to look at her and the lights went on." He drew a nail up to Jamie. "Ricky walked up next to us." Charlie stood up and walked to the barn door. He reached for the light switch and turned it off. I sat in the dark for a second and then he turned it on again.

"What do you see?" he said.

I looked around. "Nothing I haven't seen before," I answered. He flicked the lights again. "My eyes are a bit stunned, if that's what you're asking."

Charlie shook his head. "No. Something was different at Fletcher's when the lights went on. I remember thinking something was off about the setting when the electricity came back."

"Charlie," I said, "you were standing over a dead body. I think the medical term is shock."

Charlie swung around one of the poles while he worked his memory. "What's the chance that you can get into Fletcher's house?" he asked.

"Why? What would I be looking for?"

He walked up to me in a stride I had seen a thousand times. In a western movie, he would have left his horse tied to a post, swung open the saloon doors, and smiled at the local girls swooning behind him. It was classic Charlie, and I would have been one of those local girls, my prairie skirt covered in dust as he loped by me. With his charm meter set to full blast, I knew that I was about to give in to whatever request was coming.

"You see things others don't," he said as he squatted next to me. "It's not just faces. You're insanely observant."

I had to agree. My powers of observation were pretty damn good.

"There's something wrong in Fletcher's house," Charlie said. "I felt it when the lights went on and I know you're the only who'll find it."

I took my best defensive swing. "And why would I do this for you?"

"Because someone is setting me up, and it's going to drive you crazy until you figure it out. In fact," he said, "maybe someone else texted me from Fletcher's phone."

"That's possible," I said as Charlie drew me further into the case. I thought about the barn door I had almost walked out earlier. I didn't leave when I had the chance because he was right. This was the kind of stuff that got far, far under my skin. A bout of the chicken pox would have been preferable to watching a friend get screwed.

"There's got to be a clue in that house. A clue Frank is not going to see without you by his side."

"Frank and I are going back to the Green Acres homes tomorrow," I said. "I'll find a way to get into Fletcher's." I reached for my drawing pad and handed it to Charlie. "This is a drawing of a least one person spotted in the development."

Charlie studied the drawing. "He's got Walter Todd's eyebrows." I couldn't help but snicker and then I proceeded to tell him about Phoebe Purcell's involvement in the case.

"She was so hot for me," Charlie gloated at the memory.

I grabbed my drawing pad back. "You are *this* close to me ditching you."

"I'm sorry," he said. "What do you want me to do with this picture?"

"Based on what you've just told me about you and Jamie, you'll need legal representation and Kelly has some names. It won't take Frank long to figure out the condom connection."

Charlie cringed at the mention of legal support, since it highlighted the severity of his situation.

"Then I want you to show this picture to Gayle, but get Kelly's permission first," I added as an afterthought. "These kids are all about the same age, and she might recognize him."

"I can't involve Gayle." Charlie was almost offended at my suggestion. "I was only joking with her at Kelly's house."

"She already knows something is up," I revealed, "and if we don't give her a job to do, she'll go off on her own like she did last time." Last year my insatiably curious daughter had gotten herself so far entrenched in a murder investigation that she nearly out-copped Frank. She was either a constructive part of this mess or a loose cannon, and I preferred to keep her idle curiosity contained by putting her to work. I didn't mention to Charlie that at this point, our team needed all the help we could get, even if that meant employing my teenage daughter.

"One last thing," Charlie said as he reached for my hand. "I don't want to go to jail, but if Frank has enough to go on, he won't have a choice but to bring me in."

"I realize that," I admitted all too easily. The thought of my current boyfriend arresting my ex-boyfriend was a real mood killer.

"I know you're trying to play both sides of this case," Charlie continued, "but I already think you've told me too much. I'm worried your Mata Hari strategy will backfire, and I'll end up convicted and you'll end up alone."

Sure, I thought. *Now you get a bout of remorse? You couldn't have mentioned this internal conflict before you sauntered across the barn like Clint Eastwood determined to destroy my resolve?*

"I've considered the shrinking space between my rock and my hard place," I said, "but I don't know how else to help you. I love Frank." I hesitated and then added, "But I love you too."

Now it was Charlie's turn to smirk. He knew he had me. "You'll have to prove your love by sleeping with me."

"I think the most you can hope for now is a conjugal visit."

Charlie's face dropped. "I'm not going to jail."

"Then it appears I'll be lying to Frank."

TEN

FRANK CALLED AHEAD TO the Green Acres families whose houses had been broken into to alert them that we'd be walking the grounds of their homes. As Frank explained it to me, criminals searched for easy entry and exit. The best scenario for a burglar would be an entry point that provided ample cover.

"The other commonality," Frank said as we walked across the manicured lawn of the first homes that had been hit, "is the contents of the house. The thieves might have tracked recent purchases from a computer or electronic store. Maybe all of the homes in question purchased a new television or computer, making them a centrally located target. It's likely the homeowners all shopped at the closest retail outlet to this development. Sometimes the store employees are involved in the planning for a piece of the take."

"I can see how families on the same block, purchasing from the same store might be enticing." If I were a thief, I'd be targeting Le Mariage. Those bridal registries are like a check-list of high-end products for the organized thief.

"Then there's the jewelry angle. These guys will go so far as to follow women in order to case their jewelry. Women who sport the fancy stuff to the supermarket typically have an even better stash at home."

"I've heard of that," I said as I peered around a row of bushes. "What's that called?"

"The smash and grab. Robbers break a window, head straight to the master bedroom, grab the jewelry on the dresser, and run out before the alarm sounds. Those guys are tough to catch because they're in and out of a house in an instant, often before the security company is notified. Worse, they'll wait six months for the family to receive the insurance money and when the wife replaces her gems, they hit the house again."

"It's amazing how the criminal mind works," I said as I put my hand up to an exterior window and waved. The homeowner came to the window. "Did your security system detect me?" I asked as a woman in her mid-thirties opened the window.

"The motion sensor caught you immediately," she answered. "I'm convinced that if we hadn't had these blackouts, the robberies wouldn't have happened."

"What did they get?" I asked.

"A bit of cash, some jewelry. They went right for my dresser, but it's nothing I can't replace. I think they left when the lights came back on."

"Thanks," I said, and then I turned to Frank.

"I already know what you're thinking," he said. "Did the thieves target these houses because of the repetitive blackouts? The blackouts make the perfect cover."

"Exactly," I agreed. "Did Fletcher's faulty design make them a target?"

Frank turned slowly and studied the development. "Fletcher finished these homes a year ago. From what I can gather, the homes were sold a year before they were completed. The entire block moved in within weeks of each other."

"When did the blackouts start?" I asked.

"Six months ago."

"And the break-ins?"

"Residents reported items missing about two months ago, but that doesn't mean the break-ins didn't occur earlier. Small items like cash and jewelry are not immediately noticeable."

"Not like a missing giant-screen television."

"That's why we hadn't linked the blackouts to the burglaries," Frank said.

We continued along a row of bushes that ran against the house's foundation. When Frank stopped at a basement window, he turned and put his finger to his lips. I stopped and waited for Frank to motion me forward, and then I inched along the thickly mulched landscaping to get a peek into the window.

Two teenage boys were hovered over a coffee table in a nicely furnished rec room, a giant step up from my mother's dusty cellar. With recessed lighting, a game room, a bar, and a media center, this basement was a teenager's dream getaway.

Frank pointed to the two boys, partially blocked by thousands of dollars in gaming equipment.

"They didn't pay for that stuff working at a fast-food joint," I whispered. Frank suppressed a chuckle as we watched the two boys fire machine guns at each other on a super-sized screen.

Frank pulled back from the window. "Did you see their faces?"

"Hard to miss Mr. Gloom and Doom," I said, referring to

Phoebe's son Adam, "but the other guy's eyebrows are pretty tame. He's not the one from the sketch."

"No, but these kids tend to run in packs. There could be a bunch."

"I wonder where the other kid lives. You have to check into this," I said, but Frank was already calling Cheski. "Can't we just bust in?" I asked as Frank connected with the other officer.

I was about to interrupt their conversation when a hand touched my shoulder. *Please*, I channeled my guardian angel, *let this hand not be attached to the boy with the bushy-eyebrows.* I watched Frank's face soften, and I turned slowly to find George Fraser hovering over me.

"Hey George," I said, and then I pulled the man down as far as his senior limbs would allow. "Do you recognize those boys?" I asked, motioning to the window.

George, who apparently had forgotten the art of back-stage whispering, proceeded to give Frank and me an exhaustive dossier on the teens in the basement. Frank motioned downward with his hands and George lowered his voice.

"That's Adam," he said. "Lives next door to me."

"We know him. How about the other kid?" I asked.

"Two blocks over," George confirmed. "Those two morons think the wife and I are senile. They're constantly trying to make a buck off of me. Carry my groceries, shovel my driveway. The goddam driveway is heated, as if they didn't know. Piece of—"

Frank cut George off before the cursing kicked-in. "George," Frank said patiently. "I don't want to alert these kids to our presence. Let's meet back at your house in five."

———

There was no way Frank and I were going to grill George Fraser, but the reality was he had proven to be an endless source of information. The eyes and ears of Green Acres, George was a one-man neighborhood watch.

We gathered in the Frasers' kitchen while Dotty brewed a pot of coffee. A retired high school teacher, she was also no slouch in the information department either.

"Don't get me wrong," Dotty said. "I taught for thirty-five years and I love kids, but Adam is a bad seed, and the rich stepdad and indulgent mother don't make it any better."

"Yeah, what about the stepdad?" I asked. "What's Kevin Calhoun think about Adam?"

"He knows the kid is trouble," Dotty said. "But you'll never crack Phoebe. You might get something out of Kevin, but the problem is that he adores Phoebe." Dotty scrunched up her nose and I could see we both thought Phoebe was a handful. "When we first moved in, we found Adam wandering around our house as if it were the model home. Kevin was overly apologetic to the point I was afraid he'd beat Adam when he got the boy behind closed doors."

Frank raised his eyebrows. If Adam was in the Frasers' house uninvited, it would fit the profile of a burglar in training.

"You said you recognized the other boy," Frank said to George.

"Sure did," George said. "Name's Tobey. I've seen those two boys at the general store trying to rip off the old lady at the counter." He shook his head and then brightened. "I still owe you the security tapes. Maybe you'll see something you didn't expect."

That comment reminded me that I still needed to maneuver Frank over to Fletcher's house so I could find the equivalent of a needle in a haystack. Worse, Charlie couldn't say for sure if it even was a needle. I had nothing to go on, but I'd promised Charlie.

"Why aren't you questioning Adam and Tobey?" I asked Frank.

He might as well as have moaned at my question. "It's never that easy. I don't know why you think it's so easy for the police to bring people in on nothing, much less a teenager." He turned to George. "How about you, George? Your house has never been hit."

"I thought about that," George said. "We're home a whole lot, of course, and we don't leave cash lying around. Dotty, thank God, was never much for jewelry, and I turn my generator on when the lights go off."

"Don't get him too excited," Dotty said. "He'd love it if we'd been broken into. It would give him one more hobby—amateur sleuth."

Back off, George, I thought. *That's my job.*

Frank winked at me.

"So." I stood up, hoping not to look too anxious. "You mentioned stopping by Fletcher's?"

Frank raised his eyebrow. "I didn't mention it," he said, "but I'm supposed to meet Cheski there in twenty minutes."

"Right," I replied. "Cheski must have told me. I'll tag along, and you can drive me home later." I turned away from Frank, unable to hold my face straight much longer.

"I can drop you off now," he said.

"I wouldn't want to put you out," I said, my back still turned as I regained my composure. "Let's go."

ELEVEN

THERE MUST HAVE BEEN a sale on police tape because Simon Fletcher's front door was wrapped tighter than an Egyptian mummy.

Cheski stepped out of his car to join us.

"Is this your doing?" I said, pointing to the yellow strands of tape.

Cheski smiled. "You should see my Christmas tree lights," he said as he peeled back a layer and ushered us into Fletcher's house.

"You coming?" I asked Frank.

He shook his head and walked along the side of the house toward the service entrance. "You forgot to tape the side entrance," he called out to Cheski.

"I ran out of tape," Cheski said.

I'm not sure what I expected as I entered the crime scene, but Fletcher's house felt like a house of horrors on Halloween. The idea that someone had met a violent end in this very space was almost physically painful. My back immediately stiffened and sent uncomfortable messages to my neck. The notion that Charlie was implicated in this devastating murder was nearly impossible to process.

I watched as Frank made the rounds of the house, and I realized I didn't have much time to uncover Charlie's thin description. All I had to go on was that something wasn't right. Something had changed between the time Charlie had left the house and the time he returned for his dinner invitation. As I had reminded him earlier, a dead body seemed significant enough to trigger his reaction, yet he insisted there was something else askew in the Fletcher home.

I walked into the great room, where Fletcher took his last gasp of air. The room, large by design, now seemed cavernous and devoid of life. A lovely bay window, facing west, had proven to be an ideal spot to paint Jamie, and I remembered the setting well. My portrait of Jamie now hung over the fireplace, an impressive showcase for the lady of the house. It had originally been displayed in the couple's bedroom. I wanted nothing more than to admire my own work, but I wasn't able to appreciate the artistry on this day.

I moved forward quickly, sidestepping the spot where I assumed Fletcher had fallen. A sturdy coffee table sat next to a reading chair alongside the fireplace. I removed a stack of books from the table and pushed the squat piece of furniture in front of the hearth. Then I placed my foot on the table and lifted myself up, my palms on the mantel.

"What the hell are you doing?" Frank yelled. "This is a crime scene."

"It's a crime scene all right," I said without turning my head. I reached up and placed my pinkie finger on Jamie's portrait. Then I slid my finger along the base of the painting from left to right until the smooth finish changed consistency.

I heard Frank's anxious footsteps charge toward me and for a split second I wondered if he'd kick the end table out from under me. I turned and jabbed my stained finger into the air.

"This isn't my painting," I said calmly.

Cheski rounded the corner like a pit bull protecting its yard. I held my pinkie out and used my other hand to point over my shoulder. "That's not my signature," I added as I waited for the two men to approach the fireplace. "I didn't paint this picture," I said again.

Frank stopped. He was as confused as I was. "What?" he asked.

Cheski took my free hand for support as I jumped off the table. Then he grabbed my pinkie and smelled it. He turned to Frank and said, "It's not strong, but it smells like paint."

True to form, Frank's jaw rotated harder than an industrial kitchen mixer, and he proceeded to climb on the end table to inspect the portrait himself. "I don't understand what you're telling me," he mumbled as he inched toward the painting. I used his momentary processing gap to head off on a quick spin of the house. With Cheski trailing behind me, I headed to the main floor master bedroom.

I looked to Cheski to see if he'd stop me, and he just shrugged. This case had now taken such an unexpected turn that entering the bedroom seemed relatively benign.

It wasn't the first time I had been in the Fletchers' bedroom. Heavy on woodwork, it had the same old-world charm as the great room. Angled next to the king-sized bed and resting low on a waist-high antique easel was a dramatic painting of Long Island Sound during a winter squall. I recognized the water landscape

82

immediately, although I had previously seen it displayed above the fireplace in the great room, where the portrait I hadn't painted now hung.

Frank caught up with me as I leaned over the easel to eyeball the landscape. "Don't touch it," he yelled. Instead I used my nose and sniffed.

"This one is dry," I said, as if I had any idea how these paintings were even involved in the case. Frank and Cheski came over to check out the canvas. I stepped back, turned, and walked into the master bath. I searched out the bathroom garbage can, which was more elaborately decorated than a Faberge egg. I picked up the colorful bucket and marched it out to Frank and Cheski.

"Take a whiff," I said, shoving the garbage pail filled with tissues and basic bathroom paraphilia under their noses. Frank and Cheski blanched, so I carefully lifted out the unrelated items—razors and a home waxing kit. "I think we can ignore the homeowners' obsession with hair removal," I said as I moved the pail forward.

Cheski leaned in. "Nail polisher remover," he said. "I've got three daughters."

"Yup, it's acetone. You can use it to clean cheap paint from your hands," I said.

Frank nodded. Now I had his attention.

"My portrait originally sat on that easel." I gestured. "When I was here last, the landscape hung over the mantel. Now the paintings have been swapped and someone forged my painting. Given the fact that the portrait is still tacky, it had to have happened recently. Whoever mounted the painting probably got some paint on their hands, hence the nail polish remover."

Frank was not happy. "When did you finish securing the house?" he asked Cheski.

"We got the call about Fletcher shortly after seven p.m. The labs guys were here all night. I came back the next morning and cordoned off the front door."

"We've had patrols." Frank hesitated. "Right?"

"Mostly at night," Cheski said.

"So it's not inconceivable that someone entered the side door and came in the house in the last two days."

"Once the evidence is collected," Cheski said, "it's usually not an issue."

Until there is an issue, I thought.

Frank took the garbage and handed it to Cheski. "Mark it as evidence. Tape off this room. Have forensics come back and sweep the portrait for fingerprints and make sure they go as high as the mantel in the great room." Then he pointed at me. "You," he directed, "back in the great room." He turned to Cheski. "We took a picture of Charlie's hands?"

Cheski nodded. "Clean," he responded.

———

Frank and I stood facing the mantel. "It's a big painting," he said. "Shouldn't we be able to smell the paint from a distance? When you're actively painting with oils, your studio has a strong smell."

"That's true," I agreed as I took in the whole painting. "I'm wondering if only the bottom right quadrant has been doctored." I took a few steps back and looked at the dry parts. Then I narrowed in on the top half. "Yeah, I think I'm half right," I said, questioning my earlier conclusion.

Frank frowned.

"Maybe this is my painting, but someone has touched up the bottom corner where my signature is. Forget the rest of the portrait for a second," I said, indicating the bottom right corner. "That's not my signature, and this area here," I said as I made a circle the size of a pizza, "someone else painted this area. The strokes are longer than mine, as if the artist was in a rush."

Frank and I looked from the mantel to the bedroom, mentally switching the two portraits. Is it possible Charlie recognized the swap? Not inconceivable, yet there was no way Charlie would have known my painting had been altered. Maybe something else about the room had also changed, and Charlie had picked up on it.

Before I start a painting, I take a stack of photographs just to get a feel for the subject and the setting. I had taken photographs of Jamie sitting by this window before I put my brush to canvas. I wondered now if those old photographs would reveal anything else about the room. I wondered if I had even kept the photos. If I had, they might offer a clue. We knew the paintings had been exchanged, but we weren't sure why. Maybe my photographs of Jamie in the great room would reveal something.

Frank couldn't take his eyes off Jamie's portrait. "Question," he said. "How good is this forgery?"

That was easy to answer. I'd seen a lot of art, most of it destined to be sold at a mall or flea market. That wasn't the case today. "I don't know who did this, but they're fast, and they're good. Here"—I pointed to the outer limits of Jamie's skirt—"they had to match my colors, and you need a really keen eye to make the transition seamless."

"So we're dealing with a legitimate forger." Frank scratched his face.

I nodded. "Our universe just shrunk considerably."

"If only we understood why the paintings were swapped in the first place and then this one touched up. Could it be unrelated to the case? Maybe Jamie didn't like your version."

"My version was fine." The retouching had nothing to do with taste. Something bigger was going on, something dramatic enough for Charlie to pick up on. I wanted to defend my assumption, but I also didn't want Frank to know I had discussed the case with Charlie. "I know of a guy, out east, by the beach. He's an old-timer, a real portrait artist."

"You think he did this?"

"No, but he might know who did."

"Is there some underground world of illegal art I don't know about?" Frank chuckled.

"Actually, there is," I said.

Frank realized I was serious. "When can you see him?"

If this was the break that cleared Charlie, I'd commission a flying carpet to transport me out to the east end of Long Island, but in February, the roads to the beach would be empty. "I can make it under two hours." I hesitated. "Let's say three, to be fair."

Frank's phone rang, and I could tell just from his face it was the district attorney. Charlie's window of freedom was about to close, and I felt the pressure mounting. My boyfriend looked up at me kindly before answering the call. *Take Cheski*, he mouthed.

I pulled Cheski aside in the front hallway. "I promised Katrina I'd go the printers today and look at wedding invitations. I need a half hour."

Cheski grinned. "If we need to make up time, I'll use the siren."

We were about to leave via the side door when a voice called from the foyer.

"Hello?"

It was Ricky, Fletcher's assistant.

"So much for a ream of police tape sending a message," Cheski said as he marched forward, his finger extended accusingly. "You can't cross the police line. I'm going to have to ask you to step back outside."

Ricky's eyes darted around the room. "I've got paperwork to pick up. There's only so much I can get done without access to the office or our files." Ricky continued into the house, but Cheski held firm.

"I'm serious," he said. "You can't enter the house. This is an ongoing investigation."

"You've had four days." Ricky was polite, but insistent. "I realize this is a private home, but it's also command central for Fletcher, Inc. At the least, I need access to Simon's schedule so I can alert his clients." Ricky made an attempt to walk around Cheski. Despite dropping a few pounds on his organic diet, Cheski was still built like a fire hydrant and Ricky's anemic frame was no match.

"No deal," he reiterated. The two men held their stance. I walked up to Cheski and whispered in his ear. Ricky was holding a pile of Fletcher's mail that he must have picked up from the mailbox by the street. He eyed another stack of mail on a hall table.

"I'd like the mail on the table," Ricky said.

Cheski reached out and took the mail from the young man's grasp.

"Thanks for coming by to drop off the mail," Cheski said.

Ricky hesitated. He didn't want to leave. "This is my boss's mail," he said. "It's part of my job."

"Is your name Simon Fletcher?" Cheski asked as he leafed through the envelopes. He held up a postcard and stretched out his arm out the way people do when they refuse to wear reading glasses. "Aha," he said. "Here's one with your name on it." It was coupon mailer for a local yogurt shop. "Twenty percent off until tomorrow," he said as he placed the banded stack of mail on a hall table. With his hands free, he hustled Ricky to the door. "You better hurry before the yogurt machine runs dry."

Ricky returned to his car and waited.

"He's not budging," I said, looking out the window. "This is unbelievable. Do you think he'll just come back in after we leave?"

"Apparently, he won't be the first," Cheski grumbled.

TWELVE

CHESKI DROPPED ME OFF two blocks from the printers so Katrina wouldn't see the cop car. I jogged over and met her already knee deep in ivory-colored paper options.

"Hey, Ce," she said. "I'd like you to meet Mary. She's a professional calligrapher, and she might do the envelopes for me."

I shook Mary's hand and kissed Roon's sweaty forehead. Stuffed deep into his snow suit, I couldn't remember a day when this poor kid was actually comfortable. I unzipped his suit down to his belly to give him some air and wouldn't you know it, the kid cried.

"He likes to be warm," Katrina said as she rezipped him. I couldn't win with this baby.

I grabbed a chair at the table and prayed that Katrina had narrowed down her invitation choices.

"So you've got fifteen different font styles I can choose from?" she asked Mary. *Fifteen*, I groaned inwardly. *I'll be here all day.* I politely took Mary's sample sheet and reviewed the lettering options.

"Unless you're a Celestine monk, it's sort of a lost art," I said, admiring Mary's perfectly formed letters. It was amazing how she was able to maintain consistency across fifteen different versions of the alphabet. "These are wonderful." I pointed to a classic font, and Mary dipped her pen in ink. With great concentration, she wrote out Katrina's name and the address of Harbor House on a starkly white envelope.

"It's my personal favorite," she said as she turned the envelope towards us.

Katrina was excited by the finished product. It was crisp and clean with the fewest number of flourishes. "I want to avoid a Disney feel," she said and then added, "I think this style might work."

"It's classy," I agreed, and then I turned my attention to Mary. "I'm still amazed you can replicate the letters with such consistency. Just out of curiosity," I asked, "is it muscle memory or are you seeing the letters in your head as you write?"

Mary tapped the excess ink off her pen and dried the tip on a lint-free cloth. "Katrina mentioned you were an artist." She smiled, happy to talk shop. "At this point, a lot of it is muscle memory, especially when I'm working with one of my favorite fonts. But I'm pretty good off the cuff too."

"You ever study handwriting samples?"

She smiled again. "Katrina also mentioned your boyfriend was a cop and yes, I have done some trial testimonial that involved handwriting. It's great work when I can get it."

Katrina rolled her eyes. "Can we get back to my wedding?"

We spent the next twenty minutes evaluating nearly identical shades of ivory paper. Even with my trained eye, it was difficult to distinguish between the seemingly endless varieties of white.

Suddenly I was back at Le Mariage under a pile of interchangeable wedding dresses. Only Eskimos, who have multiple words for *snow*, should be subjected to this many shades of white. For the first time in the last year, I almost begged Roon to break the monotony of invitation shopping with his cries. Desperate to wrap up our outing and pick up the trail of the art forger, I leaned over and babbled nonsense at Roon. His little face scrunched up, and his bottom lip began to shudder.

Bingo.

"Trina, I think he needs to be changed," I said as I pinched my nose. "Why don't you let us artists settle on the final shade of white."

As soon as Katrina left for the ladies' room, I put my finger on one of the samples. "This one is fine."

"As are all the others." Mary shrugged. "Part of the job is allowing the bride her time even though I already know that ninety percent of women will choose the font Katrina picked."

"Patience is not my thing, but you seem to be very good at it," I said. "Listen, my boyfriend, Detective DeRosa, is working on a check-cashing scheme, and it got me thinking. How hard is it to forge a signature?"

"Harder than you think." She gave me a scrap of paper and asked me to sign my name. She looked at it for a few seconds and then offered her own rendition of *Constance Prentice.*

"Not bad," I said.

"But you know that it's not your own signature."

"You're right. I can tell it's not mine, but a bank teller or a bank machine wouldn't."

Mary folded the sheet and threw the evidence out before Katrina returned. "And that's why it's a common crime."

Unless you're forging art, I thought. That's a whole other level of signature forgery and even Mary, a calligraphy genius, was hard-pressed to perfectly replicate my signature. The forger who had touched up my painting and re-signed my signature was at least as good as Mary, most likely even better. Had I not climbed up to the mantel, I'm not sure my falsified signature would have been the first thing I noticed.

Mary pointed out the window of the print shop. "That cop car has gone by three times already. I'll tell Katrina your boyfriend stopped by to pick you up."

"I owe you one," I said as I grabbed my coat.

THIRTEEN

THE NORTHERN STATE PARKWAY in the middle of winter proved to be a pleasurable route on an off-hour. The road to Long Island's Hamptons was clear for miles, since the low-lying underpasses couldn't accommodate the commercial trucks that typically congest the other major thoroughfares. We turned south toward the Robert Moses State Park and then hooked a left on Route 27 with the ocean on our right.

While I was at the print shop, Cheski had done as I had asked and picked up my mother.

The man I was hoping to interview was the legendary Dominic LaSalle and my mother, the semi-retired artist Elizabeth Prentice, was my carrot. A recluse of sorts, in his early seventies, Dominic was famous for painting the Hollywood greats. Jane Mansfield, Elizabeth Taylor, and Grace Kelly had all sat for the fabulous LaSalle. He took his shingle down in the late sixties and headed out east to establish the only public art studio in the now star-studded Hamptons. In the early days, before the onslaught of wealthy financiers and starlets, the east end of Long Island was a simple fishing town, a perfect venue for a burnt-out artist in need of a breather.

The LaSalle studio was nothing more than an old landed barge nestled comfortably in a perfectly protected bay across the highway from the ocean. Unless you really dug art, like my mother and I, the average tourist could drive right by the studio, never giving the rundown barge a second thought. But for the past forty years, Dominic LaSalle had offered his studio to artists in search of space with rent so low even a Freegan couldn't complain.

Cheski drove while I filled my mother in on the details.

"Mom, I know you were friends with Dominic LaSalle back in the day."

"I was," my mother replied hesitantly, as she tried to process everything I had just told her. Although she had heard her neighbor Fletcher had died, she didn't know the details and now was visibly upset to learn that Charlie was a suspect. Like me, my mother fully appreciated that Charlie was the last connection we had to my brother. It was our job, the three of us, to keep Teddy's memory alive, and that would become progressively harder if Charlie was behind bars.

"Cheski and I can't bumble our way into LaSalle's studio and grill him about art forgery. I know *of* LaSalle, but I've never met him, and if I understand correctly, he's a bit of an eccentric."

My mother laughed. "Aren't we all?"

Cheski passed me a bag of fresh celery. "No, we're not all eccentrics, but you Prentices are about as off-beat as a deaf guy singing *The Star Spangled Banner*. I can't wait to meet this LaSalle."

"Hey," I interjected. "We're not that crazy."

"Crazy and eccentric are two different things," Cheski mused. "That's why Gayle fits. Peas in a pod, the Prentice women."

I glanced at my mother. I was glad we "fit"—my mother, Gayle, and me—but I wanted Charlie in that pod with us. "Step on it," I said to Cheski.

We sped through the high-end historic towns of South Hampton, Watermill, and Bridgehampton. The antique stores and clothing boutiques were closed for the season and except for a few off-season tourists, the streets were empty, allowing us to make good time. With every mile, the population dwindled until we reached the town of Amagansett. It was so empty, we could have driven with our eyes closed.

"It's beautiful out here," I said as I admired a row of cottages with hedges twice the height of the homes themselves. "But even I'd get stir crazy out here in the winter."

"You'd probably starve," Cheski laughed. "I'm guessing the Dumpsters don't see much action in the winter."

"Lonely and hungry," I agreed. "Not the life for me." As a Freegan, we knew our enemy, the gluttonous consumer. We didn't like them, but we needed to live near them; the more they discarded, the better our lives were.

"How does Dominic get by out here in the winter?" I asked my mother.

My mothered smiled as she remembered Dominic LaSalle. "He lived so large in his hey-day that he could survive for decades on memories."

My life should be so pleasantly interesting, I thought.

"You did meet Dominic, once," my mother continued. "I brought you and Teddy out here for an art installation when you were toddlers."

"Let me guess," I said. "Teddy was well-behaved, and I was hanging from the rafters."

"Don't be so quick to put yourself down," my mother said. "Actually, you were mesmerized by the paint colors. Dominic sat you on the floor and you literally rolled in the paint." It was happy memory for my mother.

I held her hand and said, "Thank you for helping today."

———

It was past four when drove across the sandy parking lot to the entrance of the barge. Dominic LaSalle was perched on the decking, and he appeared to be locking up the studio's front door for the day.

"Move it, Mom," I urged.

My mother climbed out of the car as if she hadn't a care in the world, but we all knew she could put on a good show. We were here to get information from Dominic LaSalle, and she took her role in this investigation seriously.

"Yoo hoo," she called out. "Dominic, dear. It's me. Elizabeth."

My mother blew air-kisses that floated, *Fantasia*-like, and then she held out her arms in a welcoming gesture. Dominic squinted and for a moment I panicked. What if he didn't recognize my mother?

I watched as my mother, heavy on the charm, reconnect with Dominic as the frigid sea air lifted both their thinning hair. After a few minutes strolling down memory lane, she motioned for us to come, and Cheski and I dashed across the sand and into the barge.

The interior of the barge was surprisingly warm and despite the sun's low position on the horizon, the art room was flooded with natural light. I couldn't tell if the glow was the sun's reflection off the bay or merely being in the presence of a great painter. Regardless, the venue begged me to paint, and I assumed that was exactly what Dominic had wanted when he picked this location.

"This is magnificent," I said as I shook Dominic's hand. "I'm CeCe Prentice, Elizabeth's daughter."

Dominic took a step back. "I know who you are."

I looked at my mother. Had I screwed up already?

My mother smiled. "Dominic informed me that he's recently lost some commissions to you."

Dominic laughed and tossed his wiry braid of gray hair over his shoulder. "You're my up island competition." *Up island*, a term reserved for full-time residents of the east end or rather *The End* as it had come to be known, because New York State literally ended a mere ten miles to the east at Montauk Point.

"I used to be the only game in town, but with the traffic now, I'm losing business to you and your desirable, mid-island location."

"Seriously?" I said, secretly flattered.

"Yep. At first, I was a bit peeved, but then I heard the last name Prentice. I remembered Elizabeth had a daughter." Dominic beamed at my mother, and I realized that something more than painting had occurred between these two.

"So did my mother tell you?"

"About the forgery?"

"Yes." I hesitated. "I think I've been ripped off."

"I'm not surprised," Dominic said as he offered us a seat at a long work table. "Happened to me years ago, and I took it pretty hard. The thing about portraits is that despite the artist's attempt to replicate the subject's face, there's still a smidgen of room to add the artist's signature flair." He paused. "Mine is the eyes."

"I'm big on *expression*," I said as I remembered Jamie's face.

Despite my genuine effort, I couldn't capture the emotion behind her countenance. It had been frustrating at the time, but as I reminded myself, it didn't bother Jamie. I wondered how she now felt about the doctored portrait.

"But," Dominic continued, "a good forger can mimic a style you've spent years perfecting. It's quite annoying."

I nodded. "Here's the thing. This artist is not just good, they're fast. Really fast. Like McDonald's drive-thru fast."

Dominic took a sheet of note paper and a charcoal pencil off the work table and jotted down a name and number. "I think this is your guy."

"How can you be so sure?" Cheski asked. I wished he had left out the word *so*, as it put Dominic on the defensive.

Dominic tossed his ponytail over his shoulder again. "The studio received a call three days ago. A man requested a portrait artist, someone who could be discreet."

"Is that a typical request?" Cheski asked.

"If you want a portrait of your mistress painted while your wife is out of town," Dominic answered. "It definitely raises an eyebrow and that's why I remembered it. This guy had no problem paying for speed."

Dominic looked at Cheski as if to say, *good enough for you?*

Cheski smiled. "Works for me."

Dominic pointed to the reception phone. "My assistant answered the phone, and she gave the caller this artist's number on my recommendation."

I looked at the name on the paper. Kwan Ko. "I think I know this address."

"You know the art supply store on Delancy, north of gallery row?"

"Very well," I said. Every art student in New York City had purchased supplies there in college.

"He rents a room upstairs," Dominic said. "Painted his way out of North Korea on favors and falsehoods. He's your best bet."

I looked at Cheski and frowned. It would take over three hours to get to back into Manhattan.

"We gotta hustle," Cheski said as he made for the door.

"Mom?" I said.

"I think Dominic and I would like to catch up."

Dominic smiled. "I haven't driven up island in years, but I'd be happy to bring you home," he offered and then paused. "Tomorrow."

FOURTEEN

I LEFT MY MOTHER and Dominic LaSalle staring off into the horizon. What could I do? My mother hadn't been happy for years, and it wasn't as if she had a curfew. Did I really care if she spent the night with an old flame?

"Your mother has got more going on than you do," Cheski said as he rolled over the railroad tracks and onto the highway.

"I appreciate your candor," I replied. "Are you going to chew my ear off about this for the next three hours?"

"I'm just saying," Cheski said, "this thing between you and Charlie and Frank is getting weird."

I picked up the depleted bag of celery. "I can't have this conversation over wilted vegetables." I pointed to a lonely roadside restaurant. "Pull over and we'll see what we can rustle up."

Cheski parked behind the restaurant near the Dumpster. "Here's your warning: If you touch that lid, I'll arrest you. Keep your seatbelt on, and I'll get us some burgers. If it makes you feel better, I can expense this meal."

The car's temperature dropped quickly as Cheski trotted off in search of food. My breath filled the small space and within minutes the windows began to fog. I wrote my name in block letters on the inside of the car window, an activity I had loved as a kid. Then, with my hand in a fist, I stamped the window making the shape of a small left foot. I used the pad of my index finger to form five toes on a foot no larger than Baby Roon's. When I looked through to the passenger mirror, my name and foot appeared backwards, so then I wrote my name in reverse and created a right foot to match the left. Or maybe it was a left foot to match the right. As I scrawled on the window, I realized that looking in or out produced the same, but different images. I thought about Charlie's case and his perspective of the events. They were limited to his view. He could only tell his story from his position inside the house, but I wondered what the events looked like from the outside looking in. I thought back to the night of the murder. I looked out the basement window and saw a trespasser. Was it a robber in search of another hit or a murderer on the run? Or both?

And what about Charlie's story from his position inside Fletcher's home? He sensed something was off, and as it turned out, he was right. The problem was that we weren't sure why my painting had been painted over. I kept circling back to my photos of Jamie taken at the time of her portrait. I had come to the Fletcher home a few days before Jamie's sitting, and I took photos of Jamie in a few locations and a few positions. Other than Charlie's memory of the night and my cursory visit, the only other access I had to the murder site were my preliminary photos of Jamie in various rooms of her house.

"Can we stop at Harbor House before we head to the city?" I asked Cheski as he jumped in the car with a bag of hot food. It was already six and we wouldn't hit the city until after nine, but I needed to dig up my old portrait photos. Maybe the room where Fletcher died looked differently through the lens of a camera. Maybe my photos held a clue.

Cheski bit into his burger with such gusto, I could hear my stomach growl. "Those celery sticks were making me sick," he said through a mouthful of ketchup. I took a bite of my own burger, and it was beyond delicious. "I don't know what they fed this cow, but he probably ate better than I do." I wiped my mouth and added, "What do you think? Can we stop by the house?"

"I think we're going to call it a night anyway. If our buddy Kwan is the forger, we don't want to show up at his door at like midnight. He'll realize something is wrong."

"What if someone tips him off tonight?"

"The only other party that knows something is up with your painting is Dominic, and I'm going to guess he's occupied for the next few hours," Cheski said.

"That's my mother you're talking about," I laughed.

Cheski smiled. "Can I ask you something?"

"Sure."

"Frank's a good guy."

"That's not a question, but I know where you're going with this," I said guiltily. "You're worried my old feelings for Charlie might surface."

"He's the underdog," Cheski said. "He's vulnerable and you want to help him. It's only natural, but what you need to remember is that Frank is the only one with the authority to help Charlie."

My throat constricted and I started to cough. Cheski whacked me on the back and my eyes started to tear. "You okay?" he asked.

I grabbed a napkin and spit my burger out. Before I could stop them, the tears came faster than the tissues.

"Hey," Cheski said, handing me a bottled water. "I'm not trying to accuse you of anything. I get why you want to help Charlie. Hell, I want to help Charlie. I just think you and Frank make a decent couple."

"It's not that," I blubbered. "I'm not sure Frank can help Charlie."

"Look," Cheski said as he put his burger down. "We've got nothing hard on Charlie and everyone knows it. All Frank needs is another viable suspect and that's just a matter of time."

I shook my head. "There's other stuff. Stuff Frank doesn't know," I wept as I thought about the condom Charlie had purchased. As soon as Frank figured out that Charlie intended on sleeping with Fletcher's wife, the case would get messy.

"He's not guilty," I cried to Cheski, "but I'm afraid he's going to look guilty if I can't move this along and all I've got is my painting as evidence that something is wrong."

"You have to tell me what you know," Cheski said flatly.

So I did.

———

Cheski tossed the rest of his burger in the bag and then spent the next five miles cursing Charlie's decision to sleep with the boss's wife.

"He didn't actually sleep with her," I reminded him. "It was premeditated, unconsummated sex. It never happened."

"But Ricky knew something was going on between them," Cheski countered. "He told Frank as much on the day of the murder."

"It's impossible," I explained. "There was nothing going on prior to that day."

"Maybe Jamie thought Charlie was hitting on her and she told Ricky," he said. "Maybe Jamie thinks Charlie did kill Fletcher."

I nodded quietly as we pulled into Harbor House. I could see Katrina through the window nursing Roon. She rose quickly and headed to the front door.

"Why didn't you tell me?" she yelled as she placed Roon in a bouncy chair. "They took Charlie to jail. Jail, for god's sake. I don't understand this at all," she yelled as she buttoned her shirt. Her frazzled hair looked as though Roon had regurgitated milk on her head. I had a hard time envisioning Katrina as she had looked a day earlier, lovely in her wedding dress.

"What the hell's going on?" she continued. "Simon Fletcher? Why the hell would Charlie kill Simon Fletcher? I didn't even know Fletcher was dead." Roon started to screech and Cheski, in the most endearing gesture I have ever witnessed, picked the baby up with such composure that it was obvious he had spent many a night calming his own children.

He raised an eyebrow. "A pink blankie?"

As Roon's cries turned to whimpers, I led Katrina to the couch and explained what had happened over the last few days.

"I'm going to get married under the huppah that Charlie started, and that means he needs to finish it," she said calmly. "I think we can all agree Charlie thinks with his zipper, but he didn't kill anyone."

"I know that," I said as I made a mental note to call Kelly. It no longer mattered that I had told Cheski about the condom. Frank had probably already figured it out, and now it was time to get Charlie the legal representation Kelly had promised he'd help arrange.

FIFTEEN

KELLY, CHARLIE, AND I sat across an expansive desk from Osbaldo Rivera, Esq, in his office on the thirty-fourth floor of the Empire State Building. Charlie was out on $250,000 bail, which he drew, without hesitation, from his own bank account.

"Freegan means I get things for free," he said to me as he wrote the check. "It doesn't mean I don't charge for my own services." And charge he did, because it appeared he also had plenty of money to cover Mr. Rivera's $50,000 retainer.

"I like tech money." Osbaldo smiled as he slid Charlie's check into a folder. "New money, no strings attached, and easily replaceable in a booming tech market. You write a few more apps and you'll never miss this cash."

"I'm not sure what my computer privileges will be in prison."

Osbaldo laughed broadly and as he raised his hands in the air to clap I caught a glimpse of his pearl-encrusted cufflinks. With his jet-black hair cut to precision, I couldn't detect a single gray hair although I figured the criminal lawyer to be in his mid fifties.

To complement his tanned complexion, he wore a slim cut suit with a tapered pant leg. And in a fashion statement I would never understand, he finished off his attire with expensive wingtips and no socks. His choice of footwear spoke volumes. Osbaldo Rivera, high-end attorney, was out and proud.

"So how do you and Kelly know each other?" I asked.

Osbaldo pointed his finger at Kelly. "This one got himself into bit of trouble in Mexico."

Kelly shrugged. "Spring break, 1987. Osbaldo was an off-duty local cop and I was almost through law school when I got caught in a scuffle at a disco." Kelly paused. I would have loved to be a fly on the wall at the Mexican disco where Kelly and Osbaldo were partying. "Some people," Kelly continued, "not Osbaldo, thought I might have been carrying drugs."

"So I cut him a deal," Osbaldo said. "I spring you and a few years from now, you get me in to the US legally." He leaned back in his chair. "Kelly delivered on his end of the bargain. I got into the US. I applied to law school, worked my tail off, and now I'm rich."

I glared at Kelly and fought the urge to jump to conclusions, but my first impression concerning Osbaldo was *slippery*. Maybe that's because Osbaldo had just told us he had been an officer of the law who cut deals with American college students. And, if I understood correctly, cutting deals was what Osbaldo was now selling us. The problem was that I didn't want Charlie to get a deal; I wanted him to be proven innocent.

I shook my head slightly.

"Trust me," Kelly said, and then he turned to Charlie. "The burden of proof is on the prosecution and most defense lawyers will sit back and let the prosecution build the case in hopes the holes will form themselves. That's not how Osbaldo does business. He loves a challenge."

"I do." He nodded. "And that's why I'm going to read this crime from as many angles as possible. If this thing goes to trial, I'm going to create enough reasonable doubt that the jurors will start to question how the case even made it past the grand jury. I deal in volume, so much volume that the average juror will simply doubt their own decision-making ability. The prosecution will immerse themselves in every last fact, and I'm happy to go the distance when it comes to facts. However"—he paused—"I need more than just facts. I'm looking for the hunches, the theories, the suppositions, the innuendos, and the gossip."

"You're seeking distraction," Charlie confirmed, "the disruption."

"That's correct," Osbaldo said. "Because if you believe in chaos theory then you understand that patterns emerge in chaos. To find alternative solutions, as in this case, you need to create the chaos; that's what I'm good at."

I looked at Charlie. Osbaldo was speaking his language. "Now you got yourself a deal," Charlie said as the two men shook hands.

I stood corrected. Kelly had picked the perfect lawyer for Charlie.

———

We spent the next two hours re-creating the timeline from the point Charlie left Fletcher's home to the time he returned and the police arrived. I was immediately impressed with Osbaldo's patience and interest in the details. He had Charlie tell his version of the events over and over until I could recite the night of Fletcher's murder in my sleep. The repetition, almost mind-numbing in its sameness, was still somehow intriguing even on the tenth telling. Osbaldo's method was mesmerizing.

"One more time," he said. "You parked your car and entered the house."

"Yes," Charlie said, keeping pace with Osbaldo's commands.

"And the lights?"

"Were out. A blackout."

"You walked forward. What part of you sensed something first?"

"I heard a moan."

"Stand up," he instructed. "Put your hand out and point to the moan."

Charlie lowered his hand toward the ground and smiled. "I guess I sensed someone was on the ground."

"What did you feel next?"

"My foot squished in the carpet."

"Did you slow down?"

"I think I rolled backward a bit."

"Put your hand out again."

This time Charlie reached out at waist height.

Osbaldo nodded. "That's good. You knew something was wrong and you reached in front of you so you wouldn't trip." His excitement increased and he stood up from his desk to face Charlie.

Charlie understood where Osbaldo was going and continued with this train of thought. "I pointed my toe and kicked forward a bit."

Osbaldo jotted some notes down. "We'll see if the blood stain on your shoe matches that action."

"Why is this important?" I asked. "Does he really want to be accused of kicking a dead body?"

Osbaldo shook his head impatiently. "If he killed Fletcher, he'd know exactly where he'd left the body, and he wouldn't have to test the waters with the tip of his foot. If the shoe fits, as they say, we've just created a distraction."

"Oh, that's good," I admitted and then I stopped as an explosive thought filled my head. Not sure of my role, I raised my hand and Osbaldo gave me the cue to speak.

"Ask it in a question. Don't lead Charlie," Osbaldo instructed.

"Why did you use your hand and foot?" I asked Charlie.

He paused. "It was dark. I guess I couldn't see Fletcher on the floor."

"What happened next?"

"I heard Jamie scream behind me."

"How far behind you?"

"Maybe ten strides," Charlie said slowly, and then his face crumbled. "Oh my god, how could she have known Fletcher was dying on the ground from behind me when I couldn't see him from two feet away?"

Osbaldo beamed. "I bet that was the best fifty grand you've ever spent."

"Now what?" I asked.

"Kelly and I are going to dig so far back into Mrs. Fletcher's background, we'll be able to tell you what she had for breakfast on her first day of kindergarten. And as for you," Osbaldo said to Charlie, "I want to review your business contract with Fletcher. At this point, the prosecution's motive is slim. You were having an affair with his wife and either you or the two of you plotted to kill Fletcher so you could be together."

Kelly's face cracked and I could see he was politely suppressing a smirk.

"What?" Obsaldo said.

"I was just thinking," Kelly answered, "that everything in Charlie's history would argue against that logic."

"Oh yeah," I chimed in. "Charlie's been with hundreds of women." I leaned over to peck Charlie on the cheek just to ensure there were no hard feelings. "He'd kill someone to get *out* of a permanent relationship," I said.

"But there's no way in hell," Charlie continued, "that I'd kill someone to *secure* a permanent relationship."

Osbaldo laughed. "I can see the witness stand now. Dozens of bombshells testifying about how Charlie dumped them."

"That leaves the business deal," I said. "How would Charlie benefit from the business deal if Fletcher was dead?" I asked. "They were both going to make money."

"He has to make sure that a transfer of ownership upon the death of a partner isn't motive in and of itself," Charlie said and then added, "I think we'll be fine on that account, but I didn't read the fine print. These apps have a short shelf-life. The revenue stream tends to peak and drop within a few years. I can't be sure we added a transfer of ownership clause in the event of death because the lifetime of the product is so short."

Osbaldo stopped. "Then I have to assume that upon Fletcher's death, his assets would go to his wife."

Kelly nodded. "We really need to start looking at Jamie."

"Three days," Osbaldo continued. "Then we reconvene."

SIXTEEN

FRANK'S HEAD WAS so low to his desk I thought he might be sleeping. I walked around the desk and wrapped my arms around him. "I'm sorry," I said. "I'm so sorry. I feel like I can't make this right again."

Frank kissed me hard. I had forgotten what it felt like to be desired. Had we not been in a police station, I could have easily been persuaded to remove a few choice articles of clothing. Frank pulled back and looked at me. "Did you know about the condom?"

"No," I lied too easily, "but I'm not surprised. Charlie gets around," I said, hoping to put the "player" defense in Frank's head. "I can't, however, see him wanting Jamie for anything more than a notch in his belt."

Frank remained silent, so I pulled the photos of the Fletcher's great room out of my bag. "I thought these might help," I said, spreading them out on his desk as I explained the context. "We know my painting was moved, but we don't know why or if anything else changed. These photos capture the room two years ago."

"Cheski is bringing Kwan Ko in now, so we may find out more about your painting in the next hour."

"That's fantastic," I said. "Do you have the crime scene photos so we can compare?"

Frank opened a folder and hesitated. "Sit down. These are hard to take standing up."

He was right about that. Fletcher's head, or what was left of it, had literally split in half. I gagged and covered my face. By the time I opened my eyes, Frank had placed a Post-it over Fletcher's body. "What hit him?" I asked, careful not to say *who*.

"I think it was a baseball bat," Frank responded flatly. "We've been combing the neighborhood for days. So far, nothing." He stopped. "Did Charlie own a bat?"

"I hate you," I said. "And no, he didn't own a bat. We used to have an old hockey stick at Harbor House, but no bat."

We chose two pre- and post-murder photos and laid them side by side. In my original photo, the water landscape hung above the mantel as I originally remembered. The photo of the murder scene, however, was taken at a downward angle, so the mantel was not in view.

"Damn," I said. "We can't tell which picture was hanging above the mantel on the night of the murder."

Frank ran his finger across the before picture. "It's the rug. The rug is different in these two pictures."

I looked closely and confirmed Frank's observation. "They're both tan, but the original one has a decorative border." I pulled the murder photo up to my face. Maybe Charlie noticed the rug exchange. "Look, see this indentation in the rug. You get that when a piece of furniture has been on the rug too long, but there isn't a chair or table near the indentation in this picture."

"You're right," Frank said. "Like your painting, this rug," he said, referring to the rug Fletcher was lying on, "was somewhere else in the house before it ended up in the great room." Then he tossed the photo aside and it slid to the floor.

"What are you doing?" I said, bending over to retrieve the photo. "This is good stuff."

"It's useless."

"Not to Charlie, it's not."

"Look," he reasoned. "It's interesting and it makes for a great story, but in reality, who cares about the floor coverings?" he said. "There's nothing concrete for me to work with here. Homeowners rearrange their furniture all the time. There's no crime in that. You tell me, what does this prove?" He moaned, and I could see he was frustrated. "So the Fletchers redecorated. It's a homeowner's prerogative."

He had a point, but we still didn't understand why the paintings and rugs had been moved.

Cheski poked his head in and broke the tension. "Kwan Ko is here. I've got him in interview room one. He came voluntarily."

Frank stood up abruptly and turned to me. "If there's something here, this is our only chance. I'm not convinced the rug and painting are connected."

I exhaled slowly. Frank had just cranked up the pressure.

"I want you to watch every move of this guy's face, no matter how infinitesimal. Watch his eyes, check the tilt of his head, and jot down anything you can capture. It's your painting. You're the only one in a position to identify a discrepancy in his story."

I nodded and we filed out and into the adjoining interview room to watch Kwan on camera.

The elusive artist appeared exhausted. His hair stood on end and the bags under his eyes looked like they had been surgically implanted. Apparently painting forgeries on a tight timeline was bad for the complexion.

Frank placed a blown-up photo of Jamie's portrait on the interview table. "You painted this within the last week."

Kwan nodded. "It had been damaged."

"Excuse me?" Frank said.

"The right half and bottom corner were ruined. Some type of accident. I didn't ask questions. Just paint." Kwan pointed to the picture. "Easy lines, this lady," he said referring to Jamie's bone structure.

"Was the canvas torn or cut?"

"Splattered," Kwan answered matter-of-factly. "I paint over stains. Good work. I'm a professional."

Splattered. Splattered with what? But I knew. Fletcher's blood was on Jamie's portrait.

"Who paid you?" Frank demanded. Kwan was taken aback. I didn't think he knew it was blood and technically, he hadn't done anything wrong. He came to the station willingly and had honestly answered Frank's questions. Kwan rose from his seat when he realized his rights were challenged.

"I'm sorry," Frank said. "Please sit."

Kwan resumed his position and Frank continued to speak. "You seem to be a very good artist, but we believe the stains you covered were blood marks connected to a murder." Kwan's face registered fear and I could tell he'd run for the hills before he ended up on a plane back to North Korea. "Who commissioned your work?" Frank asked, and I admired his change of tone.

Kwan shook his head. "The painting was in my lobby. There was an envelope with cash and a due date. I did the work and returned it to my lobby."

Frank rubbed his face. "No doorman?"

"No, just buzzers, but anyone gets in. Just press apartment buttons, and someone hits their buzzer." Apparently even a blood-splattered painting doesn't stop traffic in Manhattan.

Cheski led Kwan outside, but before they left Kwan turned to Frank. "The original artist," he said with a smile. "Pretty good."

Wonderful. I had just received a compliment from North Korea's most famous art forger.

Frank and I watched as Cheski drove Kwan back to the city. "So your painting and the rug were moved," he said.

"From the bedroom to the great room on the night of the murder," I said. "A swap of sorts. What do you think it means?"

"I think Fletcher was killed in the master bedroom and someone moved the body to the great room. It was probably easier to pull the body on the rug and then move the great room rug to the master. Your splattered painting was then mounted high above the mantel to avoid detection. It was touched up over the next few days so no one could spot the blood at a later date."

"So the murderer doesn't want us to know that the murder took place in the bedroom. But why?"

"Because a master bedroom is private. It's not open to everyone."

I sighed. "But now you think that Charlie may have been in the bedroom with Jamie. Fletcher catches them and Charlie takes a swing at Fletcher."

Frank nodded. "It's one option."

"It's not any option." I was furious. "It just didn't happen like that. Charlie's hands would have been red from swinging a weapon you can't even find. Who's to say Jamie didn't kill her husband and then text Charlie to set him up?"

"And drag her husband into another room? It's physically impossible. Plus, you said whoever called the art studio to get Kwan's contact information was a man."

I was angry now. This is not what I planned, yet I had done everything in my power to make things right. "Did you ever consider that these burglars go straight for the master bedroom to get to the jewelry? You know there were break-ins that night. Why does it have to be Charlie?" I yelled as I headed for the door. "I can't do this now. It's like you're begging me to break up with you." There, I had said it.

Frank called out behind me. "Hey, I meant to tell you that George Fraser is in the hospital as of yesterday. Minor heart attack."

When it rains, it pours, I thought.

SEVENTEEN

THE SUBARU WAS SHORT on gas so I stopped at the one gas station where the attendant didn't think I was nuts. Chris Peters and I had gone to high school together and although he wasn't a Freegan, he was about as cheap as it comes.

"Hey Ce," he said as he pulled a shallow bucket from under a bench and handed it to me. "Here you go. The guy at pump five was in a hurry. You'll get a few more drops out of that one. Then I'd try pump two."

I walked over to the pumps and placed my bucket on the ground. I disengaged the handle and tilted the tube up with the nozzle down. I shook the tube and a good size burp released a bubble of gasoline, followed by a few drops. I moved down the line repeating my maneuver until I had a few cups of gasoline, which I then transferred to my car using a funnel. Chris was nice enough to store the bucket and the funnel for me since it stunk up my car something awful. The entire process was painfully tedious, but it was free and I liked free.

"I heard a bit of gossip about Charlie," Chris said as I returned the bucket.

"Whatever you heard," I said, "it's not true."

Chris handed me a fully wrapped granola bar. "Some guy bought this for his kid and then realized it had peanuts. He tossed it, and I saved it for you."

"Thanks," I said as I unwrapped the intact bar and took a bite. "Can I ask you for another favor?"

"Sure thing."

I unfolded my drawing pad and showed him the picture of the teenager Phoebe thought she saw at her house. "I know a lot of young kids from the neighborhood hang out here. Do you recognize this guy?"

"By the looks of those eyebrows, I'd guess Walter Todd has a kid."

Man, those eyebrows were getting a workout in this case. "So you've never seen this kid?"

"Nope."

I explained the break-ins at Green Acres and I mentioned the connection to Phoebe Calhoun. "Now there's I kid I know," Chris said.

"Phoebe's son Adam?"

"He'd be lucky to land my job pumping gas. That dude and his band of vagrant friends, they're a bunch of delinquents. They come in here at night, no money, trying to pinch candy and sodas. I don't have time for that shit anymore."

"But not this guy?" I pointed to the drawing again.

"Never saw him," Chris said as he shook his head. "I'll call you if I do."

———

Next I drove over to Green Acres to check on Dotty Fraser. It upset me that George had had a heart attack and I wondered if the stress of the break-ins followed by Fletcher's murder had finally worn down George's enthusiasm.

Dotty answered the door on my second ring.

"Hey Dotty," I said offering my hand. "I heard about George."

"I just got back from the hospital. He's sleeping so I thought it would be okay to take a break," she said as she invited me in.

"You sit," I offered. "I'll make you something to eat."

"Actually, that would be nice."

I rummaged around the kitchen and found enough fixings for two grilled cheese sandwiches and a small salad. There was an open bottle of red wine and I figured what the hell. Dotty looked like she needed a drink.

"So what happened?" I said, biting into my sandwich.

Dotty sighed. "All the typical symptoms. His hand hurt, he felt sick. The doctor said it was minor and maybe brought on by stress."

"I worried about that with all the nutty stuff going on here."

"No breaks in the case?" Dotty asked.

I considered telling Dotty about my forged painting, but it wasn't worth it. I didn't need her having a heart attack too. I shook my head. "So when did it happen?"

She took a bite of her sandwich and a small sip of wine. "We were watching the security footage that the detective asked George to copy. You know, the period of time when the rest of the neighbors blacked out and George started our generator?"

"Did your cameras catch anything?"

119

"The only thing we saw was Phoebe Calhoun walk out her front door and down her driveway."

I thought about it for a second. If Phoebe thought she'd catch the kid who'd been hiding in her bushes, then she certainly wasn't afraid of the teenage boy. I wondered if she knew the young man. "What did she do next?"

"Her hands were across her chest at first. It must have been under forty degrees, and she didn't have a coat on. Then it looked like she was calling out for someone. Her hands went like this." Dotty made a megaphone shape around her mouth. "Finally she stomped back into her house and slammed the door."

Adam, I thought. She wasn't looking for the kid from the bushes. If she was yelling for someone, it was because her son Adam wasn't, as he had said, in his bedroom during the blackout.

"The disc is in the basement. Maybe you could take it over to the detective. And can you get George's laptop? He's insisting on using it at the hospital."

"What did the doctor say about the computer?" I imagined George staying up late surfing the net.

"No computers," she responded. "Just rest."

I shrugged. "Don't bring him the computer. He'll have plenty of time to tinker when he gets back."

I cleaned up Dotty's kitchen and headed down to George's workroom.

Nice digs, I thought again as I made the rounds of the basement. Organized, clean, and modern. George the task-master was on top of things, and I wasn't surprised to find a disc clearly labeled with DeRosa's name on the desk. And talk about organized—George's desk looked as though he had raided a big-box office supply store. What I loved was that this guy actually used all of his gadgets. I could see that his bins were filled and his pencils were sharpened, the shavings neatly piled in the can next to his desk. I wasn't a fan of overconsumption, but if you're going make a purchase, you might as well put it to use, and George had done just that. The best part about his setup was that he had a good old-fashioned desk calendar—the large kind that lays flat on a desk like an oversized placemat. If I had a calendar, which I don't, I'd have the same one. This way, you can see your month from a bird's-eye view. I have a rule about calendars that prevents me from actually purchasing one. If I have so much going on that I need to write it down, then I have too much going on. I only schedule what I can remember.

According to his calendar, George Fraser was a very busy man. I couldn't decipher his coding system or his chicken scratch, but it seemed his action-packed days had a little star in the middle. Maybe those were George's favorite days, the days where he was busy from morning until night. He seemed like that type of man. I looked closely at the calendar. There was a star the day Fletcher was murdered. That was unfortunate. I don't know what made me think about it, but I jotted down George's starred dates going back about two months. There were six in all and that included the day Fletcher died. If George stayed at the hospital a few more days, I might stop by and visit. Maybe his coded calendar would make for a good conversation starter.

I said my good-byes to Dotty and gave her the house number at Harbor House in case she wanted to talk, then I made my way back to my car. I started the Subaru and watched as the Calhouns' front door opened and, to my show-stopping surprise, my daughter sauntered out the door and down the driveway.

I honked and Gayle's head popped out from under a man's top hat. She looked like an extra from a bad eighties music video with her army boots and heavy overcoat. Of course, it's possible I was being too critical. Maybe I was simply furious to find her exiting the Calhouns' house when she had no reason to be there in the first place.

I rolled down the window. "What the hell are you doing here?"

EIGHTEEN

GAYLE TURNED AWAY FROM my car and started to walk toward the main road. Technically, she had no obligation to suffer through my reprimand since I wasn't her legal parent. *Semantics*, I thought as I rolled my car alongside her.

"Gayle," I stammered. "Get in the car now."

She shook her head.

"We gave you a job," I said. "To look at one of my sketches. That should have been enough."

"I did look at the sketch."

The car inched along, and I realized how hard it was to drive at exactly one mile an hour. "Look, my leg is getting tired. Can't you just get in?" I stopped the car, and Gayle came around to the passenger side still not looking me in the eye.

"Why were you at Adam's house? Do you know him?"

"He's a jerk," she said as she removed her hat and shook her shiny black hair out. "That kid is whacked. A total emo."

"What's an emo?"

"Like super emotional, 'the world is against me' kind of crap."

"What about the kid with the eyebrows? The one from my sketch."

"I don't know him. No one knows him. I don't even think he exists."

That comment brought the Subaru to a complete halt. "What do you mean, no one knows him?"

Gayle shifted in her seat to face me. "I took a picture of your drawing and shopped it around school. No one knows this kid. I spent the last few days working my way into Adam's freak show of a clique and pretended to make friends. That's how I got into his house today." She shuddered with disgust.

"Everything you just said is really wrong. How could you have approached Adam without Frank's permission?"

"Sorry, Mom," she mocked. "Maybe you'll like this next part better." She inched toward me and pretended to whisper in my ear. "I think Adam and a few of his friends have been breaking into people's houses."

"Are you sure?" I asked. "How do you know?"

"I don't know for sure, but they were joking about this game they call Hide and Creep. I think the idea is to get into someone's house and then get out undetected."

I turned onto the main road and drove to the general store so we could officially pull over and talk. "Are they stealing stuff?"

"I think one of Adam's friend's swipes stuff for fun, but the entering and exiting seems to be the main attraction. These guys already have as many toys and gadgets as they want without stealing anything. The thrill is getting in and out, unseen."

"How do they know who wins?"

My wise-beyond-her-years teen rolled her eyes. "They're not

that sophisticated. I think they literally break in, run around a bit, and come back out before they're caught. Then they sit around and bullshit about it as if they were darting around wartorn buildings in Iraq."

I thought about the way Gayle described Adam and his friends, and I remembered that the Frasers had found Adam in their house when they first moved in. How long had he been playing this game? I wondered if Phoebe knew what Adam had been doing with his friends. Is that why she was looking for him on the night of Fletcher's murder? I wondered if the kid running across my mother's lawn was a friend of Adam's and had planned on breaking into my mother's house. That thought was upsetting because, knowing my mother, she'd pull the trigger on a Prentice heirloom pistol if she came across an intruder in her house. In that scenario, a game of teenage hijinx could end very badly.

Then I wondered if Adam's game had already ended badly. What if Adam and his friends had broken into Fletcher's house and it had gotten physical? But why would a gang of teenagers move a body and hire an art forger? It didn't fit.

"How many kids do you think are playing?"

"Definitely Tobey. There may be three or more kids playing that live nearby."

"But not the bushy eye kid?"

"I'm telling you," Gayle said, "if that kid exists, he's not from around here. I spent hours on Instagram trying to locate Adam's friends, and I couldn't find anyone who looked like your picture. I even looked at Adam's stupid photos from sleepaway camp. It was an eyebrow-free zone."

"Shit," I said, thinking back to the cue I used to prompt Phoebe. "I basically told Phoebe to describe anyone we went to high school

125

with in order to spark her memory. She must have made up a face just to get me off of Adam's trail." I wondered if she and Kevin had called the police station to purposely report a suspect that looked nothing like Adam, but when put on the spot to describe who she saw, she choked. Maybe that's why she was so upset when I suggested the suspect might look like her son. Of all people, I wouldn't put it past Phoebe. I wrapped my arms across my chest. "Did you meet Adam's mom? Does she know what Adam is doing?"

"I'm sure she does," Gayle said. "While I was there, she told him she was going to the store, and then she asked him to stay in the house. She kept repeating it. *Stay in the house, stay in the house.*"

"She knows," I said. "That's why she tried to get me to draw a suspect that didn't look like Adam. And I was stupid enough to spark her false memories by suggesting someone we both knew." Maybe I was too naïve for this job.

"Sounds like she got you," Gayle said.

Foiled by Phoebe again, I thought.

"So what do you and Frank have so far?" Gayle asked. "Is Charlie really in trouble?"

I explained the scenario with the paintings and the rugs and I also, reluctantly, described the issue with the condom. Gayle agreed that Charlie's purchase of the condom and the murder occurring in the bedroom did not look good for her dear Uncle Charlie. As we had also recently discovered, the contract he had signed with Fletcher also worked to his disadvantage; full ownership would revert to the other signer in the event of a partner's death. With Fletcher dead, Charlie had sole ownership of the app.

Gayle pointed to the general store door. "There's Charlie," she said as she rolled down her window. "Hey you," she yelled. "Did you run out of condoms?"

126

Charlie jumped into the car. "It's freezing and you're mean," he said to Gayle.

"How did you get here?" I asked.

"I hitched," he said as he twisted the cap on a bottle of soda.

I shook my head. "I'm excommunicating you from the Freegan community. You're buying a single-serve soda? I think you're cracking. How could put your face in front of Mrs. Kranz again?"

"I had to get out of the house." Charlie guzzled the soda. "Is it just me or does that baby cry nonstop?"

We all agreed that Roon was a colicky ball of fuss and Katrina was most likely or was soon to be deaf.

Charlie chugged his soda and handed us a bag with a bunch of junk food in it. I tore open a bag of Fritos and munched away. We filled Charlie in on Gayle's information; he seemed pleased.

"This is the chaos Osbaldo is looking for," he said. "We've got a bunch of teenage boys well practiced at breaking into neighborhood houses and they're conveniently out on the prowl on the night of the murder."

"And we know Phoebe was outside calling for Adam that night," I added.

"I'm going to think like the teenage boy I used to be," Charlie said.

"Run for cover," I said to Gayle.

Charlie ignored me. "They know the neighborhood has an electricity problem that makes it the perfect location to play their game. The game starts when the lights flicker. Once the lights are completely out, they start roaming."

"Maybe that's why one of the boys was headed toward my mother's house. One of them may have actually been trying to get in. And that means another one of them could have been headed in the opposite direction toward Fletcher's house."

Gayle frowned. "Adam and his friends are way too wimpy to kill someone. I don't think that's their gig."

I had to agree. "These kids are just playing a risky game of hide-and-seek."

Charlie nodded. "But what if they saw something? Frank hasn't spoken with them yet, am I right? With three or four kids combing the neighborhood, someone must have seen something."

I thought about how quick Adam was to dismiss my drawing. Of course he hadn't seen the bushy-eyed boy, because the bushy-eyed boy was a figment of his mother's imagination. But maybe he'd seen someone else.

"You need to call Osbaldo," I urged Charlie.

"I think I'm pretty motivated in that regard," he said. "You need Frank to talk to these boys."

Gayle piped up, and I could see where this was going. "I can ask them," she said, and I realized it was useless to argue with her.

The ignition turned over quickly despite the cold. "Let's go see if we can make Baby Roon laugh." I gathered the garbage and crammed it in the car's side pocket when I caught a glimpse of George's security disc.

"Correction. I'm dropping you guys off, and then I have to bring the security disc to Frank," I said as I turned to Charlie. "It's one of the few pieces of evidence that works in your favor."

NINETEEN

FRANK'S HEAD WAS IN the same place as last time I was at the station—glued to his desk. "Your neck must hurt," I said as I slid the disc across the desk. "Based on what Dotty Fraser reported, you can see Phoebe Calhoun in her driveway calling out to Adam on the night of the murder. That means he probably wasn't in his bedroom. And according to Gayle, who's been snooping around at school, she thinks Adam and his friends are playing a game of break and run. They call it Hide and Creep."

"Did they specifically tell Gayle they've been breaking into houses?" Frank asked.

"I don't think they went that far," I said.

"That's the issue. No one's actually seen anyone breaking in, and unless Adam told Gayle, I can't just haul him in."

"Since when it is it against the law for a cop to ask questions?"

"I tried to talk to Adam, but Kevin Calhoun, of all people, went ballistic. New York State juvenile laws are unusual. We're one of the few states that consider a sixteen-year-old an adult. That means I don't need a parent present for questioning. However, when a kid is on the cusp, like Adam, and we don't have substantial evidence, we try to be flexible." Frank sighed.

"He doesn't like his stepson, but for some reason," I said, "he likes his wife, and he probably feels like he has to protect Adam to make Phoebe happy."

"He likes Phoebe because he's getting something out of that relationship. He's short, nearly bald, and chunky. Phoebe, despite her flaws, is still a looker."

"Did you say hooker?"

"Very funny," he said, offering me a seat.

"Where are *we*?" I asked.

"We are in the middle of an investigation with only one suspect and no serious candidates on the horizon." He paused. "I don't think Adam and his friends killed anyone. And since no one has actually seen Adam and his friends breaking into a house, I don't have enough probable cause to officially investigate the kid. That makes it difficult to move forward."

I repeated my question. "Where are we?"

Frank raised an eyebrow. He wasn't getting it, and he continued to talk about the investigation. "Well, then there's Jamie Fletcher. I haven't established motive, which makes it difficult to accuse her of murder, nor could she physically have moved Fletcher from the bedroom to the great room."

It was my turn to put my head on the desk. "I mean where are *we*?" I repeated. "As in you and me, like a couple."

"To be honest, I'd like nothing more than to tear your clothes off, but I'm feeling like the bad guy right now."

If I was going to be honest—and I wasn't—I was feeling like Frank *was*, in fact, the bad guy.

"I could stay at your place tonight," I ventured.

Cheski poked his head in Frank's office. "You can't stay at Frank's tonight," he said, "but you can stay at the motor lodge off I-95 outside of Guilford, Connecticut, near the Rhode Island border."

"You found the first Mrs. Fletcher?" Frank said with a smile.

"Yes, I did," Cheski said proudly, "and she agreed to meet with you if you can hustle up there. It'll take you a few hours and that's if it doesn't snow."

"I'm coming?" I asked.

"Your chariot awaits," Frank said.

———

The former Mrs. Fletcher lived in a picturesque Dutch Colonial about a half mile north of Long Island Sound in the town of Guilford. I had always been intrigued that the Sound provided miles and miles of coastal beauty along both New York and Connecticut's shores. The states were so different in their population yet they shared this wonderful natural feature that had provided millions of families with pastimes that included boating, swimming, and endless summer days at the beach. From what I could tell in the dark, through the sprinkling of snow that had started to fall about an hour into our trip, the town of Guilford didn't disappoint. The center green, flanked by picture-perfect Victorians, boasted "the third largest collection of historical homes in New England."

Frank grunted. He had spent the better part of the trip thinking about the case. Periodically he'd throw me a bone, although I felt as though he'd hit me over the head with it.

"How long has Charlie been working with Fletcher?"

"About six months, but he met Fletcher through me when I did the portrait two years ago. He helped transport the painting for me."

"So he'd been in the bedroom before?" Frank said, referring to the original spot for Jamie's portrait.

I turned to Frank and stared down his profile. His jaw was rotating and his hands gripped the steering wheel like the safety bar on a rollercoaster headed for the big drop. I had to remember that Frank was perpetually primed to pounce. There was no on or off switch or state of rest for Detective Frank DeRosa. His baseline wasn't a line at all, but an ever-rising series of peaks.

"That's a good question, but the answer is no. Jamie hadn't purchased the easel yet; we propped the painting up on a sideboard in the dining room. I was invited back later when the easel was purchased and the painting was moved to the master bedroom. It was just me. Jamie sought my advice about proper lighting."

"And she didn't show any interest in Charlie at that point."

"None," I said.

Frank nodded and then released one hand to point to a yellow house with gray trim. Mrs. Fletcher, who now went by Mrs. Ruthie Brown, met us at their front door with her second husband Roger. Like most Dutch Colonials, their home was high on charm. It had a nice balance of sea themes, like the occasional framed starfish hung above a sturdy piece of American Colonial furniture. We settled in a chintz-covered sunporch on the far left of the house. It had a lived-in, casual feel, as did its owners.

"It's really coming down now," I said as I watched the snow accumulate on the bushes.

"Miserable winter," Ruthie said, pouring herself a glass of wine.

"Thanks for seeing us," Frank said and accepted a glass of water. "I'm sorry for your loss."

"Yes, it was a bit of a shock," Ruthie confessed, and she looked genuinely distraught although well-preserved. I guessed her age to be close to Simon's, maybe sixty-eight or sixty-nine. "People can say what they want about our divorce, but there was no animosity between us at the end."

"And when did you divorce?" Frank asked.

"Twenty-five years ago," she said and then turned to Roger and smiled. "We've been married for twenty years."

He squeezed her hand. "We're very happy," Roger added, as if I couldn't already spot their undying devotion.

"Did you know Jamie Fletcher?" Frank continued.

"Of course. Simon snapped Jamie up right out of college. He'd been on the environmental lecture circuit, and he hired Jamie as his assistant." Ruthie bounced her head around as if to say, *and you can see where that led.* Yet, she didn't seem perturbed by the notion that her husband had had an affair.

"You must have been hurt," I prompted.

"It was inevitable," Ruthie replied and then turned again to her new husband. "Jamie was the right choice for Simon. It had nothing to do with me," she laughed softly. "Years of therapy and that's what I've learned. Jamie and I made peace years ago."

"So you spoke with Jamie about the affair?" Frank asked.

"I did," she said, "but it was almost unnecessary. Jamie's issues seemed minor compared to the break-up of my marriage. Obviously, picking a *man* twenty-five years older is a red flag."

Frank took a sip of water, most likely to give Ruthie a chance to keep talking, but she stopped. "Any children?" Frank asked.

She smiled. "It was too late by the time I met Roger."

Frank was too polite to dig any further. What he really wanted to know was whether she and *Simon* had considered having children.

"How did you meet Simon?" I asked.

"We met in college. I was studying to be a social worker, and he had enrolled in an environmental studies program. I guess we thought we were going to save the world, but as it turned out we weren't even enough for each other."

"But you stayed married a long time, almost twenty years," Frank noted.

Ruthie shook her head. "Oh believe me, I know exactly how long I was married and let me tell you, it isn't easy being married to man with an ego the size of Texas."

"And the newer, younger wife fed that ego," I added.

"It fed something," she said and then added, "Let's just say that Jamie and I are polar opposites."

"You're just built differently," Roger said, and they both chuckled.

I studied Ruthie's face closely and concluded that she was nothing if not believable. Her eyes never fluttered, she held her composure, and she never once appeared to search for answers. "Do you think he's made progress saving the world?" I asked.

"Now that's a great question," Ruthie said as she warmed up to her wine. "In the early years, Simon was true to his cause. It was the 1970s and the oil crisis and the recession proved to be a popular platform for people like Simon. But at that point, media was still rather simple and the whole movement toward a person as a brand hadn't been invented. It wasn't until the eighties and"—she paused and laughed—"that Jane Fonda came onto the scene with her exercise videos. That was when the shift happened, and Simon was a perfect candidate to be a lifestyle brand."

"Would you say that's when he became a celebrity environmentalist?" Frank asked.

Ruthie nodded. "That's when the speaking engagements started in earnest, and he seemed to require an assistant. It was his period of reinvention from an academic to a public persona."

Frank took one more sip of water and asked, "As his popularity grew, did he develop detractors?"

Ruthie's face grew serious. "Simon was an extremely focused man with very big ideas. He was frustrated by small people, conservative thinkers, and rule players."

"He made the rules," Frank said.

"It's not that he was above the rules. It's more that he wanted his own set of rules," Ruthie finally admitted. "I wouldn't be surprised if that's what got him in the end." Then Ruthie looked at me. "May I ask why you're here?"

"Me?" I said, and I realized I hadn't come up with a cover for this excursion. "I painted a portrait of Jamie a few years back," I replied. "The portrait has now become a piece of evidence in the case." I slowed down and gave myself time to flesh out my story before I revealed too much to Ruthie and Roger. I took a deep breath and continued. "I was wondering if Simon ever commissioned a painting of you and if so, who the artist was."

Frank nodded at my line of questioning.

"My wife doesn't need an artist to validate who she is," Roger said. "She's beautiful from every angle."

Roger was quite a find, I decided. "Did Jamie need to be validated?" I asked, using his words.

For the first time I could see that Ruthie had trouble answering a question. She sighed and said, "Jamie doesn't have a lot of confidence, but she hides it well by putting out an air of stoicism."

I had to agree with Ruthie's assessment based on my own personal experience. Jamie's lack of warmth may have been her cover.

———

I looked out the window a half hour later. We'd continued asking Ruthie and Roger questions, but nothing helpful came up. "This is going to be a tough drive."

"You'll stay here," Ruthie insisted. Frank was about to balk until he evaluated the drifts of snow that had mysteriously accumulated in the short hour we'd been at the Browns' house.

"These country roads are horrible in the winter. You can have our old master upstairs," Roger said and then paused. "You are a couple?"

Frank nodded. "We are." It wasn't a marriage proposal, but it was enough of a commitment for me at this point. I smiled.

"Ruthie and I converted the den to a first-floor senior living arrangement last year." Roger and Ruthie laughed again, and part of me really wanted to stay in their happy home. It was as if everything was an inside joke between these two and if I stayed long enough, they might let me in on it.

But not Frank. He had other ideas. Ideas that I surmised included getting lucky at the local motel.

The four of us stood by the window and watched as a plow came barreling down the street and slid into a snow bank. Frank grumbled, "I guess we'll take you up on the offer."

———

The top-floor master bedroom was magazine quality. There was an old fireplace, sloped ceilings, and an antique bed covered with a handmade quilt. Spending the night seemed a bit awkward, even more so when Roger suggested a late-night board game, but the room proved to be worth a full round of Scrabble with the Browns as I tried in vain to unload my X tile.

When Roger and Ruthie finally left us in peace, Frank and I collapsed on the bed. It took all of two seconds for Frank to make his move.

"This is weird," I whispered. "What if they hear us? It's not like they're deaf."

Frank, dejected, pulled away. "We can wait until they go to sleep," he suggested with a tinge of hope in voice.

"Roger's probably still plotting his next triple-letter move," I said as I rose from the bed to poke around. I opened the closet. Empty. Then I moved on to the bedside table drawers. Nothing of note. I spotted a built-in cabinet flanking the fireplace.

"Go ahead," Frank said. "The suspense is killing me."

I fiddled with the latch and the cabinet door swung open. "Nice," I said as I reached in and pulled out an old photo album. "I think I just hit pay dirt. It's Ruthie and Simon's wedding album." I held the album up and Frank laughed.

"Bring it here," he said patting the bed.

For the first time in the last hour, Frank was actually focused on something other than jumping my bones. I opened the album and turned the pages slowly.

"What an awful decade for wedding dresses," I said as I took in Ruthie's prairie girl dress. "There's enough ribbon here to hog tie a calf."

"Check out Simon's tux," Frank added. "He looks like an Earth, Wind, and Fire reject."

I felt a stab of guilt. "I feel so badly about Katrina's wedding," I admitted. "I'm barely on board with all the work that goes into one of these events," I said as I leafed through the album.

"You're a pretty crappy friend when it comes to that kind of stuff," Frank said.

"I am. It's all the paraphernalia. I'm just not interested in the excess, even for a bare-bones Freegan wedding. Can you imagine if I was planning a regular wedding?"

"So let your mother and Gayle handle the consumer part. They're into it, and they want to help."

"Then what's my contribution?"

Frank ground his jaw for a bit and then held up his finger. "A painting of Roon."

I felt my eyes go wide. "Frank," I gasped. "That's brilliant. I'll offer to babysit, give Katrina a break, and then I'll make some sketches."

"By the way, if you can get that kid to fall asleep, we'd all appreciate it," he said. "I'm not that bad of boyfriend. I know Katrina is important to you." This was true, so I leaned over and kissed him. I would have kissed him again, but there was a knock on our door. I shoved the album under the pillow.

"All good in here?" Roger called out.

Frank got up and opened the door. "It's wonderful, Roger. We really appreciate it."

Roger just nodded, and Frank closed the door. He was about to return to the bed when I rose and reached for his hand. "Pretend it's our first dance."

"At our pretend wedding?"

"Yes," I said as I walked toward him with my arms open. I settled comfortably against Frank's body, and he wrapped his arms around me. It was less of a dance position than a full-body embrace.

"Hum something," I said, and he started to whistle Eric Clapton's "Wonderful Tonight." He moved his hips back and forth and I melted into his rhythm. We turned slowly and I caught a glimpse of the snow falling. *Could this be any more perfect?* I thought as Frank swayed, tightly against me.

"Frank," I whispered.

"Shh."

"There's something wrong with Ruthie and Simon's wedding photos."

"Later," he said, pressing his cheek against mine.

I titled my mouth up to his ear and in a breathy tone I said, "There's no *this* in their photos."

He pulled me closer and whispered something mildly dirty as his kissed my neck.

"They never loved each other," I continued. "Ever."

Frank stopped moving and then released me. I felt suddenly cold, as if I'd been stripped naked and forced to stand outside in the storm. He walked over to the album and turned to the page of Ruthie and Simon's first dance. Their bodies were a mile apart.

"No wonder there were no children," he said.

"What do you think happened?" I cringed as if the demise of the Fletcher marriage was somehow contagious.

"I don't know," Frank said, "but I don't want to think about it now." In an uncharacteristic move, my boyfriend was walking away from casework. He turned down the bed covers and reached for me. I figured that Ruthie and Roger must know how romantic their former bedroom was when they offered it to us. Could Frank and I be blamed for enjoying something the Browns clear partook of for the last twenty years?

I slid under the quilt and considered the chaos I had just

uncovered. As Osbaldo Rivera had advised, the more questions and diversions that surfaced, the better chance we had of confusing the jury. If I believed the photos in the wedding album, then Simon Fletcher had never loved his first wife. He was an ego-maniac in a loveless marriage, waiting for a chance to reinvent himself. I believed Ruthie Brown when she said she didn't hold a grudge, and I believed that there was something off about the new Mrs. Fletcher. Even I had noticed her unusual attachment to her husband. What type of young woman breaks up a twenty-year marriage to pursue an older man? Simon *was* a rising star at that point. Was she a bad person or simply a damaged soul in search of a father figure to protect her?

Every scrap of information, no matter how small, could save Charlie, but the man next to me was the biggest piece of the puzzle. He had to believe that Charlie was innocent.

Frank gazed deeply into my eyes. I had a feeling he knew I was thinking about Charlie.

"Can you do the song again?" I asked.

He whistled quietly and just like that magic filled the room, and I felt as if I were spinning on the dance floor again. Tomorrow I'd have to break my Freegan buying freeze and get a basket of fruit or cookies for the Browns. It was the least I could do, seeing as they had lent us their love shack for the night and possibly saved our relationship.

———

Ruthie and Roger were finished with their breakfast when Frank and I stumbled downstairs at ten in the morning.

"I'm sorry we overslept," Frank said, "but that bed really sucks you in."

140

Roger smiled. "It's a modest house, but we've tried to make it as comfortable as possible."

"I was wondering about that," I said as I sipped my coffee. "Your house is lovely, but I thought, given Simon's wealth, that there'd be more. . . ." I wasn't sure how to finish my sentence without offending the Browns.

Ruthie pushed a plate of pastries toward me, and I happily reached for a blueberry muffin. "Oh, there was no money when we were married. Simon was still an academic trying to build a following of devotees. The money came after the divorce, when he started the developments."

"Developments?" Frank asked. "Plural? I thought Green Acres was newly built."

"There are ten in total," Ruthie said as if we already knew. "The initial ones were only a two or three houses. I wouldn't call those *developments*. But as I understood it, he'd been expanding. The last time we spoke, maybe a year ago, he'd built ten in different cities."

Frank wiped crumbs from his mouth. His day-old beard trapped a handful of strays, and I motioned for him to wipe again, but he ignored me. Ruthie's statement had intrigued him. "There are nine more eco-friendly housing developments like Green Acres?" This was clearly news to both of us.

Roger nodded. "There sure are. Fletcher focuses on high-end suburbs located outside major cities."

"The first one he did was in San Francisco," Ruthie said, "and then he moved on to Sedona, Austin, Charlotte, Aspen, and Savannah. I don't know why it took him so long to tackle the Northeast."

I could see Frank's gears turning, and I was curious to know how the housing developments might fit into this case. At this point I'd take anything to divert his attention from Charlie. I took Frank's lead, and we quickly concluded our breakfast with the Browns. As we said our good-byes, I asked Ruthie one more question.

"Is Jamie a bad person?"

"Some people might think so," she said, her voice ringing with honesty, "but I don't."

Roger nodded and I chose to believe the Browns.

TWENTY

THE ROADS WERE STILL covered with snow by mid-morning, and Frank had to focus to stay in our lane.

"You missed the exit," I said, motioning to a sign for Long Island.

Frank barreled past the sign and instead took an exit headed north. "Turns out, Fletcher built a Green Acres development in Westchester, a town called Ardsley. We're going to check it out while we're here."

"What's the connection?" I asked. "So what if Fletcher started a bunch of these developments?"

Frank raised his eyebrows and started to explain his concern. "We know that his Long Island development has issues. Residents feel Fletcher misrepresented the homes functionality, and we know the neighbors have convened to express their disappointment. If this pattern is consistent in all of his developments, that means he's made enemies along the way. With ten developments and an average of six homes per development, that's sixty new people with a beef."

"I'd buy that," I said. "What else?"

"The building industry is notoriously corrupt. There are grafts, shady deals, town corruption, sleazy real estate agents, sketchy contractors. I have to believe that not all ten of Fletcher's projects got built without a hitch. Someone somewhere doesn't like Fletcher."

"Hopefully enough to kill him," I said, "but it still doesn't explain why someone would move the body."

"If we don't figure that out, then that puts Charlie back in the bedroom with his love interest."

"You need to talk to Jamie Fletcher," I insisted. "Why haven't you spoken to her yet?"

"I have," Frank said. "The night of the murder. If I want to speak with her again, I need a new question."

"How about, *why the sudden redecorating inspiration the night your husband was murdered?*"

"We might be able to get her to admit she moved the painting, but she'll claim she couldn't physically move the body."

"But what about Ricky? He was in the house at some point. He could have helped her."

"I've been wondering if they'd been having an affair. I had Cheski look into it, but he couldn't find anything. Both Ricky and Jamie offered their credit card receipts, and there was no record of a hotel or fancy dinners."

"Fletcher's house is so damn big, they wouldn't even have to leave the house to have an affair. Think of my mother's house. Fletcher's was built in the same era, but it's even larger now that he renovated it. You could hide a second family in his house."

Frank nodded, and I let him think in peace as I stared out the window.

"Why does an environmentalist need an oversized mansion?" he finally asked. "It seems contradictory."

"Big ego, big house."

"I wonder if it's that simple," he said and then he pointed to a row of exceptional homes built on cliff overlooking a winding river. "Some serious money up here."

Westchester, unlike Long Island's flat plains, was a series of steep hills and tight turns. "I feel sick," I complained as Frank turned too tightly around a six-foot-high stone wall. The houses, mostly Tudors, gave the towns a European feel, although I guessed most of the homes had been built in the forties and fifties. The only thing European, it appeared, were the imported vehicles in the driveways.

"Here it is," Frank said as he pulled into a cul-de-sac.

"Oh my god," I said slowly. "This is like something out of a *Twilight Zone* episode."

"It does feel a little weird," he agreed, referring to the layout and design of Simon Fletcher's Westchester development. It was identical to the Long Island version, right down to the style and placement of the mailboxes.

"If George Fraser walks out of that door," I pointed in the direction of George's house, "I'm hauling ass back to the highway."

"Do you have your sketch pad?" Frank asked. I patted my bag and he added, "Let's show the picture of the kid with eyebrows. At the least, it will get us past the front door."

Out of habit, we chose what would have been the Calhouns' house. A woman in her mid-thirties answered and Frank quickly flashed his badge. She invited us in, and Frank explained that the developer of these homes had been murdered and that he was investigating the crime.

"I saw it on television," she said. "My husband wasn't that upset. These houses have a lot of problems."

"Can you give us an example?" Frank asked, and she ran through the same sorts of complaints we had heard from the Long Island residents.

"Basically, we've got a bunch of malfunctioning gadgets that aren't synchronized. We thought this would be a harmonious, socially conscious experience, and it's absolutely not what we envisioned. In fact, when things go wrong—like the heat resetting itself to thirty degrees when we were on vacation—it's pretty stressful around here. Who wants to come home to burst pipes?"

"Did the heat go off due to a power shortage?"

The woman stopped. "No, that's one thing we haven't had, knock on wood. It's more about the individual 'smart' devices and how they work, or don't work, in unison." She paused. "Now that you ask, we haven't had a power outtage exactly, but the electric bills just don't make sense. We were supposed to be feeding the grid and possibly getting credits, but our bills are still pretty high. It makes me wonder if these solar panels are even hooked up."

Frank raised an eyebrow. "Did you ask Fletcher about the bills?"

"We actually had a neighborhood meeting two years ago, here at my house. Fletcher came and gave a presentation with his assistant." She shuddered slightly. "I've heard Fletcher speak before. He's not as sharp as he used to be, though honestly, I still could have sold tickets to the meeting."

"He's got a following," I agreed.

146

The woman nodded. "Well, he's also got quite a few years under his belt. His assistant, Ricky, tried to fill in the gaps, but he's no Simon Fletcher. I think that's when my husband started to lose confidence in our decision to move here."

It was a descent description of Ricky. He was the backup man, not the front man. I guessed it was his job to shadow while Fletcher commanded the center stage. I considered Jamie's personality, since she had apparently been Fletcher's assistant before Ricky. She, also, had no interest being the center of attention. Similar to Ricky, she placed herself a few steps behind Fletcher, hanging on his every syllable like it was gospel. People like Jamie and Ricky don't ask questions, they don't challenge. They're there to support. Maybe that's all Fletcher wanted.

"So what was Ricky's explanation?" I asked.

"He said we underestimated the size of these houses. Before we moved here, we lived in a city apartment, and I suppose we didn't understand how much electricity a large house could consume. He was also quick to remind us that we owned hybrid cars and the recharging is costly."

I wasn't sure I bought Ricky's excuse either, and I wondered if Fletcher had installed the panels properly on the roofs. I'm not an expert on solar energy, but I did know there was a science behind panel placement to ensure maximum sun exposure. Interestingly, what a homeowner wanted and what the electric grid needed were often two different things. Homeowners with southern-facing panels feed the grid during the longest span of sun hours. Conversely, the grid requires more power when the sun starts to fall. If every solar panel in the country faced south, then the grid would be oversupplied during the high daylight hours and underserved as the sun set. Most panels do face south, though, because as consumers we tend to think in volume and this is essentially what happens on a daily basis. Unfortunately sunlight isn't efficiently storable; therefore, the grid as a whole is often working inefficiently.

I put that thought aside and showed the woman the picture of the bushy-eyed teenager, but she had no recognition. More importantly, the development had not been plagued by break-ins. In fact, they hadn't had a single incident of home invasion.

She led us to the door and repeated her original concern. "This was a really bad investment."

"You can probably get your money out when you sell," Frank said. "Your home is very attractive."

"Thank you," she said, "but I think we'll be here until the kids graduate."

We returned to the car and Frank cranked the heat. "I'm starting to wonder if Fletcher was solvent," he said.

"It sounds like there's a big up-front investment," I agreed. "Maybe that's why he was so eager to work with Charlie." I thought about all the money Charlie had accumulated by selling apps while living as a Freegan. All revenue, no expenses. It was a great formula. "Charlie's got a green thumb; maybe Fletcher thought it would rub off on him."

"I think you're right about that."

I rolled down the window and stuck my head out into the frigid cold. "Which way is south?" I asked, and he pointed toward the first house on the left. "If your internal compass is correct then all the panels face south," I noted.

"Isn't that the goal?" he asked.

"For the average consumer, yes," I said, "but Fletcher's not an average consumer. He's a famous environmentalist, and I have to believe he worked with the local utilities company when he placed these panels."

"You're too green for me. I'm confused."

I smiled because I secretly enjoyed the few chances I had to one up my highly intelligent boyfriend. "Alternative energy supplies increase when users demand more of it. Even a two-bit environmentalist like me knows that if you really envision a day without oil, you have to create more market demand than supply, and then the supply will catch up."

"Okay, but it seems like this housing division is adding plenty back to the grid."

"Too much at the wrong time of the day. Simon should have placed a bunch of panels to the west, which catches some light at the latter part of the day, when people really need their lights. Think about it. During the day, your lighting needs are often satisfied by sunshine. A solar panel contributor is more likely to access the grid in the later part of the day, when their panels are not producing. Right now, these panels are maximizing the credits, but not the output of the overall grid."

"Interesting," Frank said, and I knew I had him. "Maybe Fletcher felt pressure to design the homes to deliver the most amount of utilities credits back to the homeowners." He shook his head like he didn't agree with his own statement. "And even then, it seems the Green Acres residents don't feel as if they're getting enough back in solar dollars. Kevin Calhoun mentioned the same thing."

"Based on what I'm seeing, it's as if Fletcher didn't care about the big picture, and the weird thing is that his lecture circuit spiel is all about the big picture." Frank got out of the car and snapped pictures of the panels with his phone. I pointed to the position of the sun in the sky. "I'm guessing it's about noon. I'm supposed to visit the caterers with Katrina today."

He frowned. "I thought we agreed you'd give up the wedding planning."

"It's a food tasting. I'm not passing up free food."

TWENTY-ONE

HARVEST TIME CATERING, FORMERLY known as the Meyer family farm, was wedged between the two major highways servicing the east and west ends of Long Island. The highways run parallel to each other and cover almost all 124 miles of the island. In a few towns, Huntington included, the highways run so close to each other that a driver can practically read the heater settings on the neighboring cars. Over the years, the Meyer farm had been chopped and hacked into smaller parcels that were eventually sold off for development. A handful of the Meyer grandchildren had managed to retain the main section of the farm and, to my sheer delight, had converted grandpa's agriculture concern into an organic farm-to-table catering company.

Our own farm was one of their smaller suppliers, as the Meyers had recently discovered Katrina's jelly-making prowess. The chef now ordered jelly by the vat, converting it to the most delectable tarts I'd ever tasted. Although I wasn't much of a cook, Katrina and I had started our fledgling Kat's Kans jelly venture about two years ago, and local businesses had started to take an interest. As a result of our networking, Katrina had worked out a wonderful deal with Harvest Time for her wedding dinner. Harbor House's farm would supply Harvest Time with whatever we could grow by the time of Katrina's wedding and they would only charge for the cooking, delivery, and set-up. Since we didn't raise animals, the only food expense would be free-range chickens and pigs. Katrina had already paid down the meat purchase in cases of traded jelly.

Charlie and I had given Harvest Time a list of vegetables and roots we thought we'd be able to deliver before the wedding. Given the timing of the event, early May, we agreed to force a handful of vegetables in our hot house. It wasn't a perfect science, and we weren't sure how much of each item we could grow to maturity, but the Harvest Time chef seemed up for the challenge.

Frank pulled in to drop me off at the farm just as the others were arriving.

"Last night was fun," I said.

Frank smiled. "I'm a big fan of Scrabble too."

"So what's our next move?" I held up my hand. "No references to board games, please."

"My next move," he said, "is to re-interview Jamie and Ricky. I think I can justify bringing them in to ask about the other developments."

"What do you need to exonerate Charlie?"`

"A blood-stained weapon and a motive," Frank said, and then his face dropped. "What the hell is Cheski doing here?"

"He's a master bread baker now," I said, as if Cheski's new hobby was yesterday's news. "He offered to supply fresh loaves for the wedding."

Frank shook his head and watched as his fellow officer got

out of a police cruiser with a bag of steaming baguettes. "So he's attending the tasting?"

"Kelly, Gayle, Charlie, and my mom are coming too," I replied, and then I realized we'd left Frank out. "I'm so sorry. Did you want to come?"

"I'm not even sure you still want me to be your date for the wedding."

At that moment, my mother's car turned into the caterers with Charlie at the steering wheel. Charlie let himself out and then held the door for my mother. He glanced at Frank and me, turned his back, and then walked into the converted farm building.

I exhaled slowly out of my mouth and waited for Frank to blow a gasket. It didn't take long.

His ears twitched and I imagined his jaw was about as tight as an un-sprung mouse trap. He started and stopped a few times, finally settling on the following observation: "Charlie and Cheski should not be breaking bread at the same table."

I tossed my head from side to side to show that I was open to interpretations. "He's out on bail," I offered. "It's not like he's on house arrest."

"But Cheski shouldn't be socializing with Charlie. In fact, you, Cheski, and Charlie shouldn't be hanging out together, especially after you've just spent time with me interviewing Fletcher's ex-wife." Frank turned to me and took my hand so I had no other choice but to face him. "For the record, my world works better if Charlie is found innocent. I'd go so far as to say that we might not last if Charlie goes to jail."

That last part hurt, but we both knew it was true. We'd already weathered Teddy's murder and my father's twisted plan to separate Teddy and Frank. How much more could this relationship stand?

"You must recognize that I'm highly motivated to find the real killer."

"I do realize that," I sputtered. "I don't want what we have to end. The dance, last night." I blushed. "It was special."

"Do you also see that your friendship with Charlie and your role in this case might jeopardize the outcome?"

"I never thought about that," I said.

"The last thing Charlie needs is for me to be taken off the case." My face fell. "Can they do that?"

Frank nodded and for the first time I realized that this investigation had taken a toll on him. His rich olive skin seemed pale and his eyelids were full, almost as if he had been crying. It was faint, but I also spied a tuft of gray hair around his ear. How could I not have seen how conflicted he was over progress of the case? He scratched the shadow around his chin and continued.

"Charlie has a lawyer—am I right about that?"

"He does," I said, wondering what Osbaldo Rivera had uncovered in the last few days.

"Hopefully, he's come up with something," Frank said, rooting for Charlie's defense.

"When are you going to try meeting with Jamie?"

"Tomorrow."

"Can I tag along?"

"At this point, you'll need a *reason* to tag along. It's one thing for you to come to Connecticut and meet Fletcher's ex-wife, but Jamie could be involved at much higher level. You can only attend in your role as a sketch artist, and I'm not sure there's anything left to sketch."

"What about the alterations to my painting?"

He frowned. "If you could work up a side-by-side comparison

of the portraits to show the changes, then yes, we could present you as an expert. We could then show Jamie the evidence and see how she reacts."

I kissed Frank hard on the lips. "Charlie's innocent. I promise."

———

The interior of the Meyer farm house would make even the most adherent Amish person grumble in approval. The rooms were pared down with an eye toward functionality. The furniture—a mishmash of Shaker-style and vintage farm pieces—gave the setting a clean and purposeful feel. The deep kitchen sink was filled with fresh-cut vegetables waiting to be scooped into heavy baking crocks and there were bowls of pre-cut and peeled potatoes begging to be roasted.

Katrina was in heaven. "I'm so glad you're here," she said as she hugged me tight.

"Where's Roon?" I asked as my ears searched for the perpetual bleep of his cries.

"One of Gayle's friends agreed to babysit," Katrina said and then turned to Gayle. "So nice of her to give up a school holiday to help me out."

Gayle leaned into to me. "She won't be my friend much longer if Roon cries all day."

I gave Gayle a squeeze and made my way around the room. Charlie seemed surprisingly relaxed, but my mother appeared out-of-place in the rustic setting with no chance to even turn down a cocktail.

"You can do this," I said as I embraced my mother. She was wearing a silk Hermes scarf, lined wool trousers, and tasseled loafers.

"Should I lose the jewelry?" she asked as she fiddled with an armful of gold bangle bracelets.

"Just don't volunteer to milk a cow," I said with a wink. "The clanking might cause performance paralysis."

She pinched my arm, and I moved on to Cheski, who was a pig in heaven as he sliced his homemade bread and slathered it with organic butter. He had brought his own apron with *World's Best Grandpa* embroidered across the front.

"It's a good look for you," I said, tightening the strap around his waist. Cheski pecked me on the cheek, and it occurred to me that Frank may have been right. This group was a bit too chummy to be involved in a murder case. I looked over at Charlie, Cheski, my mother, and then Gayle and her dad, Kelly. Almost everyone here was instrumental in the success of Charlie's case, yet in the festive environment, none of us seemed to appreciate the gravity of the situation and the importance of our roles. Charlie was goofing off with Gayle, who had already gone undercover to figure out what was making angry Adam hate the world. My mother, sipping her soda water, had proved to be an important connection between my altered painting and the forger. Then there was Kelly, who had secured a top-notch lawyer for Charlie and was lending his own legal time free of charge. And if Katrina's wedding hadn't brought us to my mother's house, I would have never seen the stranger running across my mother's lawn.

We were all a part of this, and we were all motivated to help Charlie. We were also all intent on having a really good time today.

The chef was a local fellow who had grown up eating in fast food joints and strip-mall restaurants. On a class trip to France, he experienced a food epiphany, a rebirth of sorts. He returned to Long Island to rediscover what was left of its agricultural society.

He wouldn't have to look far, as most of Long Island was originally covered in potato farms. Bits and pieces had survived the mass post–World War II suburban development, and there were still enough like-minded people on the island to fight for what was left of the farm land. The Meyers' farm was a piece of that fractured puzzle.

As instructed by the chef, we settled at the lengthy farm table as rounds of tasting trays circled amongst the diners.

Cheski handed me a bite-size hors d'oeuvre. In the palm of my hand, it looked like a miniature nest with an egg in it. "Shredded baked Brussels sprout filled with a roasted whole garlic clove," he said as he popped one in his mouth. No argument here. The food was spectacular *and* free. I followed up Cheski's selection with barbequed asparagus wrapped tightly in a bacon strip. Again, another hit. The chef slowly made his way around the table and offered a detailed explanation of each dish. I didn't want to disappoint him and let on that I supplemented my farming with the occasional Dumpster dive, so instead I appeared enthralled as he described his onion caramelization process.

"So who is the worst catering client you've ever cooked for?" I asked as the chef handed me a small bowl of fresh peas laced with hollandaise sauce.

"Hands down, the Fletcher event," he said proudly.

The room fell silent, but the chef didn't notice the drop in acoustics. "Don't get me wrong," he continued, "Fletcher didn't deserve to die, but that was a difficult night for the crew."

I looked at Cheski. This wasn't, of course, a formal interview, but if anyone was in the clear asking the chef about the Fletcher catering event, it was him. I glanced at Charlie, and he signaled Cheski to start the inquisition.

"So an upscale party goes downhill," he said as he wiped his mouth. "Did you burn the soufflé?"

"I would have loved to burn something, but their house lost electricity."

There it was again. The electricity. It was as if a light bulb had gone on in my head—or in this case, off.

Cheski, a master of the soft sell, put his fork down. "Sounds like it was more than a flicker."

"We lost a good half hour of prep time," the chef said. "Fletcher was fuming and his wife was screaming at me—as if I had any control over it."

So Jamie did have a range of emotions and now anger was added to the list.

"Did Fletcher think you caused the outage?" Cheski asked.

The chef started to laugh as he remembered the event. "Me? No. Fletcher's a smart guy. He knew I had nothing to do with it. He did, however, give his assistant a rough time. Sent him outside like he would be able to solve the problem." The chef paused and placed a food tray on the table. "Then one of the guests followed Fletcher's assistant outside and the two of them got into a heated argument." The chef appeared incredulous.

"The assistant and Fletcher?" Cheski asked.

"No, the assistant and the guest."

I couldn't help myself, so I butted into the conversation. "What was the event?"

"Fletcher was hosting a party for his new homeowners."

The entire table stopped chewing at once, and I prayed the chef hadn't noticed that our undivided attention was focused entirely on him. Cheski wiped his mouth calmly and then pretended to find the humor in the situation. "Who won?" he asked, likely hoping to get a description of the Ricky's opponent.

"My bet was on the banker, but Fletcher's assistant was pretty quick on his feet."

"How did it end?" I asked.

"The two men left the party in a huff. Then an older guy offered to return to the development to make sure nothing further happened. I found out the next day that one of the homes had been robbed during the blackout."

An older man? I wasn't surprised that George had offered to command the neighborhood watch. I mulled over the events of the world's worst dinner party while I chewed on an asparagus tip. So the lights go out while the residents of Green Acres are gathered at Fletcher's manse for a neighborhood celebration. Fletcher instructs Ricky to check the rest of the neighborhood, so Ricky leaves Fletcher's but not before he and Kevin get into it. Kevin and Ricky go back to Green Acres, and George follows the two of them. Did Ricky accuse Kevin's stepson Adam of being involved? Did Kevin return to Green Acres to make sure Adam was at home?

On the night of the murder, another blackout occurs. Fletcher probably instructed Ricky to check out the electricity at Green Acres. That would have put him in the area on the night of the murder. Had Kevin and Ricky gotten into it again that night? Maybe Kevin had accused Ricky of faulty services while Ricky accused Adam of taking advantage of the problem. And where was George in all of this? Did George see something that night that upset him?

I started to wonder if Ricky ever had a day off. He seemed to be at Fletcher's beck and call. If Fletcher was disappointed with his assistant's work managing the development, then the two of them may have also fought that night.

"Now that's bad timing," Cheski chuckled to lighten the conversation. "So when did this all happen?"

"The day that will live in infamy?" the chef said. "As it turns out, the party was on December seventh. We've been referring to it as the Pearl Harbor of catering jobs ever since."

A server came to clear plates and the conversation turned to happier topics. As soon as the table resumed its natural patter, I excused myself and headed for the bathroom. I looked over my shoulder to see Charlie hot on my heels.

"Ricky is so in on this," he said.

I nodded and reached into my bag for my sketch pad. I flipped through the pages and found the notes I had made when I visited George's house. There it was. The starred dates on George's calendar matched the dates of the blackouts.

"Look here," I said to Charlie. "George keeps track of the blackouts."

Charlie shrugged. "So? He's a retired guy with nothing else going on. Maybe he wants to bill Fletcher for the times he has to use his generator."

I looked at my notes again and pointed. "But what about this date here?" I pointed to today; George's calendar had a star on it. "If he's simply tracking the blackouts, then he'd have to put a star on his calendar after the event and not before."

Charlie nodded. "It's a good point, but we're not even sure the stars on his calendar are linked to the blackouts. Maybe it's just a coincidence." He ambled over to a bench facing the open fields. I sat down next to him and we looked at the farm's outer buildings. Charlie pointed to the roofs.

"This place is making us look bad," he said. "We've got plenty more room for solar panels. Are you okay with me investing some of my money into an energy overhaul?"

"I don't have money," I said as I thought about the check my friend had so easily written to Osbaldo. "So, yes. Feel free to spend."

One of the servers came by with a small plate for us, which I thought was above and beyond the call of duty, though I certainly wasn't turning down any delicious bites.

Charlie pointed to the buildings through the window as he chewed. "Is the farm running at break even?" he asked.

"We don't require any outside utilities, if that's what you mean," the server, who appeared to be a Meyer relative, said. "And we have plenty of leftover to feed back to the grid. We turn the excess supply into RECs."

"RECs?" I asked.

"Renewable energy credits," Charlie supplied. "They're a traded commodity. We never applied for REC status since we're essentially a single family home. Commercial properties, like this one, generate enough volume to be considered a full-fledged provider as opposed to simply a residential user."

"That's really the catch," the server said. "The farm is certified by New York State. Last month RECs were trading in New York at $680 a unit."

"Holy shit," Charlie said as he stood up and walked to the window. "You've got miles of panels. How much can you make in a month?"

"If the weather is good and the rates are high, we can make about twenty grand. And that's after we've satisfied our own demand." The server munched on a wafer. "The catering is really just a hobby. We could have sold the land to a developer and cashed out, but this gives our family a reason to stay together. It's fully self-sustaining, and it makes money."

"A solar farm," I said.

"Too bad Grandpa Meyer didn't own land in Florida," Charlie said.

"Tell me about it," the server replied. "This gray winter has set us back a few grand. We're working with a bunch of other farms to lobby the state in hopes that the state will readjust their rebates and make us whole with our west-facing panels."

"I'd heard about that," Charlie said. "Haven't a few states started offering more credit for units produced during lower sun elevation?"

"Yup," the server said. "We've voluntarily mounted west-facing panels, so we don't make as much money since they technically produce less, but our day will come."

"Getting paid fairly to serve the greater good," Charlie said. *A point Fletcher had unfortunately missed*, I thought. Turns out the Meyer grandkids were twice the environmentalists Fletcher ever proposed to be.

As the server headed to the kitchen, I turned to Charlie. "Something's not right about Fletcher's solar setup."

"I wonder if his developments are certified energy providers," Charlie added.

"I think I should let Frank know what we've discovered."

"Screw that," Charlie said. "Frank will find a way to make this work against me. I've got to loop Osbaldo in on these developments. He said he needs one other person who was at the house with a legitimate motive, and you can't tell me that Ricky or Jamie aren't somehow connected."

"I'm sure Adam was at Fletcher's too," I offered. Charlie's face

162

turned ugly. "Don't even think about it," I said. "You can't approach Adam. Frank already got rebuffed by the stepfather. You can't just bring a teenager in for questioning without solid evidence."

"There are other ways to infiltrate a teenage boy's life," Charlie threatened. "Your daughter got further than Frank in one afternoon."

I heard Katrina calling for us. "Let's wrap this up and get back to work," I said as I grabbed Charlie's arm.

TWENTY-TWO

By the time we got home, Katrina was so exhausted I offered to put Roon down for a late-afternoon nap. Katrina disappeared into her bedroom while Roon and I had a face-off in the kitchen.

"There's no way you're falling asleep anytime soon," I said to the nine-month-old as I strategized on the best way to capture his features for the wedding portrait. Roon answered me by blowing milky bubbles in my face. I wiped his mouth with, what else? A pink washcloth. He started to breath heavily and his little huffs and puffs of frustration filled the room. I was certain a mega meltdown was about to occur, and I decided an immediate intervention was in order. I wrapped Roon in another layer of pink blankets and grabbed Katrina's diaper bag and the car seat. I strapped his wriggling body in and dragged him out to the Subaru. It took me fifteen minutes to secure his seat while I prayed he wouldn't explode in a nasty fit that only Katrina could handle.

"Work with me, kid," I said as I kissed his chapped cheek. He grabbed my finger and shoved it in his gummy mouth. *Poor baby*, I thought. I could feel a swelling where he was about to break a tooth. I considered my options and settled on a destination that would soothe both of us.

———

My mother was happy to see me.

"Hey, Mom," I said as I handed over Roon. "He's fussy," I added, but it seemed redundant.

My mother stroked his head and examined his red cheeks. "Teething," she confirmed. "I have just the thing."

We settled in the kitchen and my mother pulled a stool over to the refrigerator. On her tippy-toes, she reached for a high cabinet and produced a dusty bottle of rum.

"As I suspected," I said.

My mother pooh-pooed my accusation. "Just for emergencies," she said as she noted the very full bottle. "Once in a while I allow myself a quick sniff." She unscrewed the bottle, took a whiff, and smiled. "I miss those days," she said dreamily. She dipped her finger and then ran a line of brown rum along Roon's gums. I was right behind her with a chaser—a bottle of warm breast milk.

My mother pushed my hand away and then opened the refrigerator. "I'm not judging Katrina, but this kid is what? Nine months old?"

I nodded.

"He needs some solid food," my mother said. "He's crying all the time because the breast milk isn't cutting it anymore."

"What do you suggest?" My mother opened a tupperware and I peered inside. "Mashed potatoes."

"He'll love them," she said as the plastic container rotated in the microwave. "Watch this," she said as she mixed in a splash of breastmilk and spooned a lukewarm dollop into his mouth. It disappeared in seconds.

"Wow, he was hungry."

"Now you can give him the breast milk," my mother said.

Roon sucked down the milk, but not before my mother gave him another rum rub along his gums. We watched as his lids grew heavy.

"Elixir of the gods," I said.

My mother nodded. "An organic home remedy," she laughed. "Even your father approved of this when you were a baby."

"He must have hated when Teddy and I cried."

My mother tossed her head back. "He simply walked out and left me to tend to you two. That's when I hired outside help," she said in reference to the string of nannies the Prentices had employed over the years. My mother cradled a now-snoring Roon in her arms. "He's actually kind of cute when he's sleeping." Without missing a beat, I grabbed my sketch pad as I explained my idea of painting a baby portrait for Katrina's wedding gift. "Love it," my mother said. "We've got to stage this properly."

We wandered from room to room in search of the perfect setting for his wedding portrait.

"I think he's old enough to sit up," my mother said.

"I wouldn't know," I laughed. "Trina never puts him down."

"We could prop him up at your father's desk and put a phone under his chin," my mother suggested with a sly grin.

"With a baby bowtie," I laughed. We scratched the infant MBA pose in favor of a beautifully upholstered chair that had belonged to my grandmother. Still sleeping, we let Roon curl up in a ball on the chair with his face turned towards us. His bottom was tilted up and his hands were positioned under his chin like he was hoarding a secret. Probably the secret to stop his crying.

"Even I have to admit that is one precious baby," I whispered. I set up my pad and started to sketch like crazy, since Roon's sleeping stretches had the half-life of expired milk. I started to draw and found it was easy enough to eliminate his pink clothing. I simply pulled out a colored pencil from my case and added a dash of traditional blue. It was amazing how the socially ingrained association with a particular color changed the nature of picture. I knew it shouldn't matter that much, but suddenly Roon was a boy again.

It took me about an hour to get something solid on paper, which I could then easily transfer to a canvas without the subject. For backup I snapped a few photos of the sleeping baby in case I had missed a detail that Katrina would notice. Just when I thought we were out of the woods, my mother's doorbell rang. Roon stirred and my mother made a mad run for it. I kept drawing and listened as a line of footsteps followed my mother back into the living room.

It was Charlie. And Gayle.

Charlie's hand was placed firmly on Gayle's back as he led her forward.

"Look what I found at Adam's house," he said.

"Look what I found at Adam's house," Gayle repeated.

"Let me guess," I ventured. "You found each other at Adam's house." I wagged my finger at Charlie. "You tried to approach Phoebe? How could you? What did you hope to accomplish?"

Charlie shrugged and walked away from me into the kitchen, but I was hot on his heels, my finger still pointed accusingly. He saw the bottle of rum on the table and poured himself a glass. "I couldn't help it. The chef's story stuck with me. Something's not right at Green Acres and I figured, what the hell? Phoebe Purcell is just shallow enough to let me pick her brain as long as I throw in a few compliments."

"You're impossible," I moaned.

"Impossibly charming. You'd be surprised how much I got out of our pal Phoebe, and as it turns out, Gayle worked her own magic there too."

Gayle slid a piece of paper toward me. "I think these are the names of Adam's Hide and Creep friends." There were four names on the list: Tobey, Mike, Jake, and Matty. I recognized Tobey, but not the others.

"How did you get these names?"

"They're video gamers. I joined one of Adam's multiplayer games and tracked who he played with regularly. I figured it was the same group that plays Hide and Creep. They're basically acting out online what they're doing in real life." Gayle sighed and took off the overcoat she'd found in the basement. She was tall and slim underneath the weight of the coat, and I wondered if Adam suspected why my attractive daughter was paying him any attention. "Everyone's got fake names online, which made it kind of tricky," she said. "I spent a few hours with Adam today and pretended I could set up my girlfriends with his friends. Eventually, the names started to surface."

Video gaming. Not my forte. It wasn't my age that held me back in the tech world but rather my interest level. My senses required stimuli of a physical nature, like wet paint and moist dirt. If I could make it to the end of my life without a single password, I'd be thrilled. "What's your gaming name?" I asked.

"It's stupid. I didn't want them to know it was me so I picked something a boy would choose." She paused. "A gross boy."

"So?" I prompted.

"Crotchkid," she said without hesitation.

Charlie laughed. My mother flinched.

"This is quite a score," I said as I studied the paper. "I'll have Frank check them out, although I'm guessing you're one step ahead."

Gayle smiled. Thank god I hadn't actually raised her. If I thought she was a rule-breaker now, she'd have been a terror had I been her no-holds-barred mother. I turned to Charlie. "And what did your long lost love reveal?"

Charlie leaned across the table and twirled his glass. "Kevin bought Adam a brand-new car. He's probably only old enough to have a driver's permit."

"The nouveau riche," my mother moaned. "A bunch of show-offs." She took Charlie's glass and sniffed it without running it over her lips.

"A car?" I was bewildered. "Why the hell would Kevin buy Adam a car? He can't stand the kid."

"The first year I went to camp, my dads bought me a gigantic My Little Pony play set," Gayle said.

"A reward for going to camp?" I asked.

"No way. I wanted to go to camp," Gayle admitted. "They bought me the pony set so I wouldn't say anything about having two dads to my camp friends. They thought my feelings would get hurt if someone teased me."

"So they bribed you to lie," my mother added.

"Pretty much," Gayle said.

I turned to Charlie. "Do you think that's what Phoebe was trying to tell you?"

He nodded and wiped his mouth. "I'm convinced Adam or one

of his friends saw or did something that night. He either told his parents or they caught him, and now they're afraid if it comes out, he'll get in more trouble."

I stared at the list again and wondered if one of these was the name of the boy I saw on my mother's lawn. With the list in hand, I considered which one of these kids I'd seen. Where exactly had I spotted someone? I thought about the path the kid must have run from Green Acres to our house. I put the list down and opened a side window. A cold breeze filled the room. With the top half of my body hanging in the frigid air, I surveyed the side of the house.

"There really isn't a good way into the house from this side," I said.

Charlie took my lead and walked to the far end of the kitchen. He opened a door that led to a walkway connected to the front drive. "If I were to break in, this door would be optimal. Or"—he walked toward the back of the kitchen and pointed to an over-sized window—"this would work too."

"So we agree that the other side of the house, where I saw someone, doesn't make sense if the goal was to get in and out unnoticed."

Everyone nodded and I suggested a quick field-trip.

My mother agreed to watch a miraculously still snoozing Roon while Charlie, Gayle, and I prepared to inspect the exterior of the house. We put on our coats and headed outside. My first stop was the basement window. I tapped my foot on the frame. The window opened from the inside, but if the kid had a screwdriver or a similar tool, he could have easily popped it open from the outside. I eyeballed the size of the window, wondering if a teenage boy could fit through. Even I remembered it as a tight squeeze as a teenager. If he was more than five foot three, some crucial body parts might be compromised—parts a teenage boy probably valued. Hence Gayle's gaming name, Crotchkid.

"What do you think?" I said to Gayle and Charlie. Ignoring my question, Gayle started to run across the lawn toward Green Acres. She stopped about a hundred yards away, turned, and waved at us. Then she ran back to us.

I looked at Charlie. "She's clever."

She stopped in front of us and took a deep breathe. "The house looks like a locked fortress as I ran here. I could see the main road up ahead, but barely."

We turned and stared toward the street. "I focused on the telephone pole," Gayle said as she pointed to the pole on our driveway.

"I always hated that pole," I said as I eyed the loopy wires that sagged, almost begging for support, on their way over to the corner of the house. "I don't know why there was never an effort made to sink the electrical underground."

Charlie walked slowly to the electrical pole and then climbed up using the metal footholds inserted by the electric company.

"What do you see?" I yelled, but before I finished my question, Charlie had scrambled back down the pole.

"Let's go inside. I need to speak to your mother," he said.

We hurried back into the warm house and resumed our seats at the kitchen table. My mother was applying another layer of rum to Roon's gums. *Child protection services be damned*, I thought as I watched my mother wipe her finger clean.

"Elizabeth." Charlie's opening was exceptionally formal; he rarely addressed my mother by her first name. Apparently, he had seen something on that pole. "You mentioned your lights have been tempermental."

My mother nodded.

"And you called the utility company?" Charlie asked.

"I've never called the utility company," my mother said. "I assumed a neighbor called because the lights usually go back on in about a half hour."

I shrugged. In old days, the Prentice household had people that handled these types of details. I already knew the answer, but I asked anyway. "So you sat in the dark and waited?"

"It's not that bad," she said. "The lights always go back on."

Charlie turned to me. "The night of the murder, when the lights went out, where were you?"

"I was in the basement and then I was here, in the kitchen. I was on the phone with Frank."

Charlie paused and I could feel his momentum. "Think hard. When your lights went on, what happened at Green Acres?"

I had to think about that, so I rose from my chair and walked over to the window. "I'm not exactly sure, but I think our lights went on while Green Acres was still dark. I don't remember the sky lighting up all at once."

Charlie smiled. "That's exactly what happened, and I can confirm it. You mother's house is not on the same wiring schematic as Green Acres." He paused and then continued. "When I was on the utility pole, I could see that this house is not connected to the development. Your mother is connected to the transformer by the main road. Green Acres is probably connected to another transformer located closer to the entrance of their cul-de-sac."

Gayle nodded as she recounted her run toward the house. "If all the houses were connected then the wires from the pole would have to have gone over my head to Green Acres. Grandma's lines run from the pole in the opposite direction to the street."

It wasn't Gayle's observation that stopped us cold, but rather her choice of words.

"Grandma?" my mother gaped.

"I thought I'd try it out," Gayle said sheepishly, "but I'm not feeling it just yet."

"Me neither," I said and then I turned to my mother. "Let's tackle this now. What should Gayle be calling you?"

My mother swirled the rum in the tumbler. "How about Mimi?"

I looked at Gayle, and she smiled in confirmation. "So here's the problem," she continued. "Mimi's wires would have to be traveling over my head if they were connected to Green Acres."

"Exactly. This house and Green Acres are electrically independent," Charlie said. "I think the kid was running to the pole to connect and disconnect the electricity here. He could have been up on that pole waiting to reconnect when you were in the kitchen."

"But why?" my mother asked.

Gayle snapped her fingers. "Because Adam and his friends were getting bored with their game. Adam mentioned that to me today; only ten houses, not much to choose from. They must have wanted to expand the size of their gaming field, so they manually disconnected this house to expand their reach."

"I'll bet if we checked, we'd find that Green Acres had electrical trouble first," Charlie said.

"I wonder how many of these houses they've actually been inside," Gayle said.

"We don't know they hadn't been in all of the houses," Charlie added. "We only know they stole from a few. The way Gayle explained the game, these kids could have gone in and out of the houses without anyone knowing if they didn't take anything. It doesn't sound like stealing is their primary motive. They could have even been in this house without you suspecting."

My mother frowned.

"Maybe," I said. "But they haven't been in George's house since right after they moved in. He's got enough security equipment hooked up to his generator to know who's coming and going."

"And it sounds like Adam is aware of that," Charlie added. I remembered Katrina's sample wedding dresses. George's house was like the one without a belt—an outlier.

My mother got excited. "This makes sense now. I talked to a neighbor across the main road from me and her electric problems started at the same time as mine."

Charlie rocked back in his chair. "And the game board just got bigger."

"So," I summarized, "the electrical issues at Green Acres have nothing to do with my mother's electric, except to the extent that all the houses are part of this teenage-delinquent game."

"I think one of Adam's friends was simply manipulating the lights here manually." Charlie paused again. "Ce, can you describe this kid again?"

"I saw very little," I confessed. "Male, jeans, sweatshirt." I stopped and then remembered a ridiculous detail. "His hands looked big, like he was wearing ski gloves."

Charlie smiled. "Those weren't ski gloves. They were rubberized gloves. Probably the same kind the utility men use when they work on the poles. You can buy them at any home improvement store."

"It would be nice if we could find the gloves," I added.

"I wonder," Charlie continued, "if Fletcher's electricity is attached to Green Acres. If not, then Adam, or one of Adam's friends, must have also disconnected it separately."

"That would put one of them at the scene of the crime," Gayle said.

I winked at Charlie. "And you know teenage boys; one of them must have purchased a condom in the last few months. That would make two males, you and perhaps Adam, at the scene of the crime with a condom in their pocket."

"After a comment like that," Charlie sniffed, "you can bet I won't be wasting my last condom on you."

I dangled the Subaru keys in front of Charlie. "But would you still be up for a ride to Green Acres to see if the electric is connected to Fletcher's?"

TWENTY-THREE

WE LEFT MY MOTHER at home with her open bottle of rum, but I felt fairly confident she'd return it to the shelf above the refrigerator. She'd had such a good time at Dominic LaSalle's Hampton studio that they'd made plans to see other again, and we all knew her sobriety was having a positive effect on her happiness.

The rest of us, with Roon in tow, decided to tackle the neighborhood's electrical system before it got too dark. Charlie pointed to the transformer powering my mother's house as he turned the Subaru from our drive to the main road. "That's what we're looking for. A bulky box mounted high on a utility pole."

He hooked a left and headed around the corner to the Green Acres entrance. On the mile-long route, we watched as the wires multiplied and divided in their quest to deliver power to the various pockets of houses along the way. Electricity, of course, is something homeowners expect, literally at the flip of a switch. Even for me, a die-hard Freegan conditioned and willing to accept less, I demand an immediate result when I turn on the lights. Yet, as I surveyed this massive wiring overhead, I realized it takes nothing more than a few fallen branches—or a bored teenager up to no good—to cause a massive blackout.

Gayle tapped on the car window as we neared the development. "I'll bet that's the box for Green Acres." Sure enough, a clunky metal transformer was perched atop a utility pole at the entrance to the cul-de-sac. "So if this box is damaged, Green Acres gets zapped?" she asked as she rubbed Roon's toes through his feety pajamas.

Charlie slowed as we neared the transformer. He stopped the car, got out, and walked around the pole, inspecting the wires overhead. We opened the window an inch to hear his assessment.

"This one," he said, pointing to wires feeding the Green Acres homes. "If this thing blows, all the houses in the development go out."

"And the utility company can fix a damaged transformer in thirty minutes?" I asked.

"No," Charlie said. "And that detail has been bugging me. If the transformer was damaged, it takes the utility company a good half hour just to show up. I'm wondering if there's some type of short occurring at the house level."

That seemed odd to me. "At every house simultaneously?'

Gayle raised her eyebrow. "No way," she said matter-of-factly. "I haven't even taken physics yet, and I don't believe that all the houses would short at the same time, unless it's coming from the transformer."

"Let's park up ahead, and we'll see if these wires run over to Fletcher's," Charlie suggested. "We've got about five minutes of daylight left." He backed out of the cul-de-sac and drove around the corner. Fletcher's driveway came up quickly, but we drove right past.

"I can't do this," he said. I realized he hadn't been back to Fletcher's since the night of the murder almost a week ago.

I dug deep into my pockets and pulled out a pair of mittens and then I zipped up my coat snug under my chin. "You stay here," I instructed my friend, "with the baby." Charlie moaned. He and Roon were not the best of buddies. "Gayle and I will walk down the driveway and follow the wires."

Roon started to fuss. "Make it fast," Charlie said.

Gayle and I got out of the car and stomped through the slushy snow.

"It's tough to see in this light," Gayle said, "but I think the main wire is on the left side of the house." We walked slowly towards Fletcher's. There were a few exterior lights on and the main hall was lit. Otherwise the big old homestead was dark.

We moved to the left side of the house and Gayle pointed to a knuckle-like device that connected the street wires to the corner of the house. The rubber-covered cord, about a quarter of an inch thick, ran in the opposite direction of Green Acres.

"Fletcher isn't connected to Green Acres either," I said. It made sense. Green Acres was a new development wedged between my mother and Fletcher's. There'd be no reason to rewire the older homes through the Green Acres transformer. I started to explain my theory to Gayle when she grabbed my arm and shoved me behind a bush. With her hand on my shoulder she lowered me into a squatting position and wet snow filled my back pockets. Gayle opened her mouth but almost nothing came out.

"Saw someone," she gasped. "In the house."

Damn, I thought. Was it possible Cheski hadn't secured the house . . . .again? Maybe Frank was right. Cheski should have being doing his job instead of enjoying the organic food fest at Meyer's

178

farm. I squeezed Gayle's shaking hand. "It could be Jamie," I said. "She's probably picking up some clothes."

Gayle shook her head. "Guy," she stammered.

"It's fine," I said calmly. "Maybe it's Fletcher's assistant, Ricky."

She nodded, but I could see she was spooked and so was I. The house was a crime scene. I looked around for a car but couldn't find one. I wondered if it even mattered. We had walked onto Fletcher's property from the main street without being spotted; anyone else could have done the same. And as far as entering Fletcher's home, it appeared more people had been in the house over the last few days than a McDonald's drive-thru.

"I'm afraid to walk down the driveway," Gayle said. "What if he sees us?" She had a point. If that was Ricky and he was involved in Fletcher's murder, he wouldn't be happy to find us spying on the house—although now it seemed that he was the one doing the spying. Of course, the man Gayle saw could have been anyone.

I surveyed the grounds. "If we can make it across Fletcher's side yard, we'll end up back at Green Acres. Charlie can pick us up there."

Gayle nodded, but I could hardly see her face at this point. "Come on," I said, our hands still clasped. We stayed low and scurried across the lawn, staying below the window line. The sun had just dropped, but I could feel the ground underneath freezing up. My ankle bent two or three times in the troughs of snow. I squinted in the direction of Green Acres. It wasn't my favorite place, but it was our only choice if we wanted to escape Fletcher's yard and his uninvited visitor.

I had an urge to run. Really fast and really far. Instead, we hung close to the tree line and moved carefully toward the well-lit Green Acres homes. We were in striking distance of Phoebe's back yard

179

when the entire neighborhood went dark. I couldn't see two feet in front of my face, so I looked back toward Fletcher's in search of light. There's wasn't a lot of it, but Fletcher's lights were still on.

And then the hall light in Fletcher's house went out, but the exterior lights remained on.

"Oh my God," I whispered, and I could feel Gayle's hand tremble again. It wasn't hard to imagine what had upset her. Whoever was in Fletcher's house had seen the Green Acres lights go out. They must have turned off their own light to get a better look outside.

Gayle and I stepped back into the trees. "We can't stay here forever," she whispered. "It's freezing."

A solid thud echoed in front of us, followed by a crack. "Did you hear that?" I asked.

"Loud and clear," Gayle replied. "It sounded like a basketball hitting the rim and then smashing the backboard."

It was a decent catch on Gayle's part. The thud came before the crack, as if a heavy object hit, bounced, and then damaged a window.

We strained our ears for a follow-up crash, bang, or boom, but I was distracted by the now cacophonous sounds of the outdoors. Sounds I'd normally screen out, like rustling leaves, had taken over my senses and my imagination. It was amazing what you could hear when you actually tried. Unfortunately, my fight-or-flight mechanism was driving my blood pressure up and muffling my hearing.

"I feel like I'm deaf," I complained, but Gayle placed a woolen hand over my mouth.

"I just heard a door close," she said. "Behind us."

"He's leaving Fletcher's," I croaked through the frosty mitte,n and sure enough the faint sound of crunching footsteps echoed behind us. I thought about my mother, alone in her house. From our hiding place in the woods, I couldn't see if her lights were on and I prayed that she'd rescued the vintage rifle from the basement. If I was lucky, she'd also have broken down and swigged a shot of rum to bolster her nerves. Then I thought of Charlie, alone in the car with Roon. Did he have any idea what was going on? And what had I been thinking taking Baby Roon away from his mother, directly to the scene of a crime? Yet another reason I'd make a terrible mother.

Gayle physically turned my head toward Fletcher's, and there, under the clouded moonlight, stood a man. He was motionless, staring ahead at Green Acres. For the life of me, I couldn't make out a single detail.

We watched as he disappeared into Fletcher's yard.

"Look," Gayle whispered and pointed toward Phoebe's house. Sure enough, we watched as muted bodies morphed out of nowhere and darted around the Green Acres homes. "It must be Adam and his friends."

"Game on," I said.

"We have to get out of here," Gayle repeated. "Whoever we saw could be out here."

"Then we'll play along," I said. "We'll join in Adam's game."

"Are you nuts?"

"Going back to Fletcher's is nuts, but blending in among Adam's friends is pretty safe. They won't know we're not one of them in the dark. All we need to do is make it to George's front porch and we'll be safe. He's got a generator."

"Is this your idea of motherly advice?"

"Would you prefer to talk about where babies come from?"

Gayle let loose a nervous laugh.

"Stay behind me," I said. "Not too close or it will look like we're together."

With Gayle lagging behind, we took off through the connected yards. The snow slowed us down, but the biggest challenge was to focus on objects that popped into view unannounced. A low bush, an outdoor grill, a decorative garden stone. All these yard items were invisible until it was almost too late to prevent a fall. Along the way, we passed two people running, just like us, but they paid no mind to our movements, as I'd hoped. We were just playing the game.

We entered the cul-de-sac, and I stopped short on the plowed pavement. Hard ground. It felt good, until I spied George's house.

"Shit," I mumbled, "George must still be in the hospital." His house was pitch black. No generator. I turned around, but Gayle was not, as I had assumed, behind me. I ran back in the direction I had come, but given the similarities of the Green Acres homes and the lack of light, I quickly became disoriented. Where the hell was Gayle? Suddenly my idea to join the game seemed downright dangerous. What if the man we had seen at Fletcher's had tailed Gayle? My body heat skyrocketed, and I felt like Roon, overheated in a fleece sack. I tore at my neck and let the cool night air drench my thoughts. Think. Where had Gayle gone?

I couldn't call for her or we'd be spotted, but I couldn't let her roam free in a neighborhood where a man had just been murdered. I'd run directly into what Osbaldo had referred to as chaos, and that was my mistake. My only choice now was to stop the chaos from spiraling out of control.

I removed my glove and banged on the Calhouns' door. Within seconds, the door flew open.

Adam stood on the other side of the entry.

"What the . . . ?" I said. I certainly wasn't anticipating the neighborhood punk to open the door. Shouldn't he be outside on the prowl? And then I remembered his shiny new car. The bribe to keep him in the house. Adam's friends were running wild, but not Adam. Car or no car, this was one bummed-out teenager.

"Heard you got a new car," I said. Adam slammed the door in my face, but not before I caught a glimpse of Phoebe, her face pink with anger as she held a flashlight. I was about to hit the door again when I heard Gayle yelling for me. I ran towards her voice and we met, abruptly, in George Fraser's lawn.

George, wearing nothing but his green, loosely tied hospital gown and padded, no-slip socks, was half draped over Gayle's shoulder. "I can't hold him," she cried. "Help."

I reached for George, but instead of accepting my help, he grasped at his chest.

"No," I screeched. "You have to hold on." My pleas were useless, and George slid off Gayle's slight frame onto the wet ground.

Without hesitation, I tore off my coat, hat, and gloves and began the awkward process of wrapping a nearly naked man. His breathing labored, I leaned in to hear his heart. He coughed softly and then groaned.

"Look up," he said.

A reference to heaven? Was George looking for the light? Gayle had already run off in search of help, and I was left to tend for a dying man.

"Why are you out here? Why did you leave the hospital?"

George strained. "Keep the lights on."

"They'll be on soon."

"No," he groaned. The air from his lungs was so weak, it barely condensed in the night air. I held him over my knees and listened helplessly as a hollow void filled his chest.

"George, please," I begged. His mouth opened wide and for a second I thought he would come around, but I was wrong. George Fraser took his last breath as he lay across my lap. My cheeks burned, but my insides shivered so hard I lost my grip on George, and his body glided gently across his icy front lawn. His head was tilted toward his house and I wondered, if in his last moments, he'd been looking for his wife Dotty.

I followed his gaze and noticed he was staring at his basement window. And then I remembered George's calendar. The starred dates. Had he known there would be a blackout tonight? Had he somehow found his way home from the hospital, wearing nothing more than his hospital clothing? What could he have possible known about the blackout that put him in this deadly position?

I started to cry and out of nowhere someone handed me a tissue. It was Kevin Calhoun. Like me, he appeared frozen solid, except for the tears running down his face. I didn't think George was anything more to Kevin than a neighbor. I instantly suspected, therefore, that his tears were driven by guilt. Kevin Calhoun was afraid his stepson's game may have contributed to his neighbor's death.

"Why is he here?" I asked.

"I don't know," Kevin replied.

I turned to study Kevin's face. "I think he came home to protect Dotty during a blackout."

Kevin shrugged.

"From your stepson," I added.

"Adam's been in the house the whole night," Kevin said defensively. "I can't vouch for these other people's kids."

"He must have been worried about his wife," I repeated as I pushed the point.

"I called him at the hospital just today and told him we'd look after Dotty." He paused. "I guess he didn't trust me."

I wasn't sure I trusted Kevin either. How did he even know where to find me? And why was he outside if Adam was in the house?

TWENTY-FOUR

CHARLIE WAS LONG GONE before the ambulance or police arrived. It wouldn't have looked good for him to found at the scene of a crime twice in a week. He passed Roon off to me like a pro quarterback and then hit the road before Frank arrived. One the neighbors took Roon into their house while I approached the Fraser home and prepared to console Dotty.

———

Dotty Fraser was shaken, but she had sensed that something was wrong days earlier. She seemed to think that the reccurring blackouts were almost too much excitement for George given his obsessive interest in his fully wired hobby of a house.

"I kept telling him these were just blackouts," Dotty whimpered. "Light some candles, make a fire, but it wasn't good enough for George. The blackouts were too stimulating for him."

Out the window I saw Phoebe come outside to meet Kevin, her short, plump body wrapped in a fur coat. She stood next to her husband, but her rigid body posture reminded me of Hilary and Bill Clinton after the Lewinsky affair exploded. We waited without talking while the paramedics tended to George's lifeless body.

It wasn't until Frank was ready to drive Gayle and I home that Roon was returned to me, fussy as ever. The young woman who'd watched him for nearly thirty minutes seemed totally drained by the experience. Baby Roon balled his fists and reached out toward my face to grab my hair. His lips started to turn downward, and I suspected we were in for a long cry. What I'd give for a bowl of warm mashed potatoes.

Frank looked in the rearview mirror of his cruiser. "I'm not going to ask why I smell alcohol on a baby."

Gayle was about to protest, but I placed my hand firmly on her arm. All I wanted was to go home, and Frank was our only source of transportation.

"We're going to bring Adam in again tomorrow," Frank said as he offered me a withering olive branch. "I should have pushed harder earlier."

"You're too nice," Gayle said. "Why is everyone nice to Adam? How could his parents buy him a car?"

Frank moaned, and I could see his hairline move as his jaw sawed away. He muttered something about Kevin Calhoun under his breath.

"Are we still on for tomorrow?" I asked tentatively. I had promised to compare my altered painting with the original and then make notes for Frank's interview with Jamie. He had been planning on presenting the inconsistencies to Jamie without letting her know we knew about the bloodstains. We also had my photos from the original shoot that showed the new location of the rug.

I knew Frank wasn't pleased to find me, Gayle, and Roon at Green Acres tonight, but I wanted to be there when he interviewed Jamie.

Frank didn't respond.

I searched out Gayle's face in the back of the car. I was tired. No more than an hour earlier, George Fraser had died in my embrace, and the thought of lifting even my lightest drawing pencil seemed like a monumental task. But there was still work to be done on Jamie's portrait comparison.

I didn't know if it was stress, but Gayle's features overwhelmed me. Dark shadows danced across her eyes, and her mouth was pursed like she had something important to say. In this particular moment, she looked like Teddy with a passing nod to Frank. When I first met Gayle, all I could see was my mother. She had inherited my mother's regal stance and although her naturally blond hair was still dyed black, Gayle's demeanor and style mimicked the well-bred Elizabeth Prentice. She presented as much older, and sometimes I had to remind myself that she was just sixteen. Her resemblance to Teddy, her father, was faint but real none-the-less. Behind her eyes, however, I saw myself. There was something about the way her brain worked. In that regard, she was all me.

"Uncle Frank," she said softly. I shook my head and stifled a smirk. Piece of work, my daughter, referring to Frank as her uncle. She had played the family card. *Nice move*, I thought. Frank was, of course, her uncle, but neither of them had formally acknowledged the connection. For the past few months, she'd been testing the waters getting to know me and my mother, but her relationship with Frank had been on the back burner.

"CeCe needs this." She paused and then said, "Mom needs this." Talk about poetic license. This kid was a master of manipulation.

I poked her hard in the arm, and then kept my fingers crossed that she'd hit Frank's soft spot.

Frank parked the car at the edge of Harbor House's porch. "Tell your *mom* to be at the station by ten."

TWENTY-FIVE

Katrina met us at the front door, and I exchanged Roon for a piece of paper with a phone number scribbled on it. "Call him back," she said. "I think it's the guy you get your free gas from." She smothered Roon with kisses, which she then generously bestowed on Gayle and myself. "Best nap of my life," Katrina raved. "Thank you so much for taking the baby."

She had no idea what we'd been up to. She also had no idea Roon had tried solid food. Or booze.

Amazing what a solid couple hours of sleep could do to a person's disposition. Katrina had snoozed straight through to the evening and woke up a new woman. "I can't believe it's almost nine," she said with urgency. "Time for bed," she quipped. One nap and my best friend had become a sleep junkie.

Bed, I thought. It was an interesting concept that relied on a fixed variable: time. There were only twenty-four hours in a day, and I needed every last one before meeting with Frank and Jamie tomorrow morning.

"I'll call Kelly and see if you can stay over tonight," I whispered to Gayle as we spotted Charlie passed out on the couch in the library. Gayle yawned in my face, and I wondered if Harbor House had sprung a gas leak. We trudged upstairs to my attic studio, where Gayle curled up on my futon and made like Charlie and Katrina, dead to the world.

I glanced at the number in my hand. I wondered if Chris, my gas station attendant friend, had spotted Adam or one of his friends doing something nefarious. It seemed moot now that George was dead. How much worse could it get? I decided to call Kelly first.

"Is it okay if Gayle stays here tonight?" I asked, fingers crossed. There was no way I was driving her home. I needed every minute.

Kelly wasn't exactly excited. "I sense a custody fight down the road," he joked.

"I'll take her whenever I want," I offered, "and you pay for college. Deal?"

"Do I get to walk her down the aisle?"

"I assume you'll be paying for the wedding too?"

"My wallet is open if we can get the Meyers to cater the event. The food this afternoon was fantastic."

I couldn't believe that a half day earlier I'd munched on roasted garden vegetables and freshly baked bread. "Crazy good," I said as I shoved George's death to the back of my mind. I didn't have the energy to tell Kelly what had happened at Green Acres. He'd be furious when he found out Gayle had witnessed a man's death. To make matters worse, I had also lied to Katrina about my excursion with Roon. Forget the alcohol-soaked gums and mashed potatoes; I had bounced Roon from my mother, to Charlie, and then to an unknown Green Acres family. I'm not sure how many more lies I could fabricate before the day was over.

"How was the rest of your day?" Kelly asked.

"It was great," I lied again. "I think Gayle and I are really getting to know each other." Cowering in the woods at night while an unidentified man lurks menacingly behind you tends to draw people together.

"Well then, I've got some more good news for you," Kelly said. "Osbaldo is coming from the city to see Frank tomorrow. He must have found something in Charlie's favor."

"What's he got?"

"I don't know," Kelly said. "He wouldn't tell me, but I think it's good." I wasn't sold just yet. It seemed every time we turned over another rock, Charlie's reputation got crushed. As if it wasn't enough that he'd been found hovering over Fletcher's dead body, he had been accused of having an affair with Fletcher's wife. His condom purchase had only added to his guilt, while the transfer clause in his contract with Fletcher gave him the financial motive to off his business partner. The fact that Fletcher's body had most likely been moved from the bedroom led Frank to think that Charlie had indeed had an affair with Jamie.

Whatever Osbaldo had discovered, I certainly hoped it was more than just good.

I'd felt from the beginning that Osbaldo had plenty to work with. There was something off about Jamie, and Osbaldo was savvy enough to unearth her skeletons. My evening with Fletcher's ex-wife Ruthie had confirmed my earlier suspicion that Jamie was, at the least, socially challenged. And then there was Ricky, the assistant du jour. He'd been loyal to Fletcher, almost frighteningly so. If anyone besides Katrina needed a nap, it was Ricky. He seemed to be available around the clock, appearing on the scene only to point the finger at Charlie.

As my mind worked through the possibilities, I almost forgot Kelly was still on the line. "I'll call you tomorrow if I find out anything new." I disconnected and then dialed the number Katrina gave me.

"Chris?" I asked tentatively.

"Hey, CeCe," he said. "I don't think in all the years I've known you that we've spoken on the phone."

"I think you're right," I said. "I guess that means you've got more for me than a tip on free gas."

Chris cleared his throat. "You know that Adam kid you were asking me about? He got a new car, a Chevy Camaro. That damn thing goes for about twenty-five grand." He was clearly perturbed that a do-nothing like Adam had scored a new car.

I already knew about Adam's car so I hoped Chris had more to offer. "Pretty nice car for a knucklehead like Adam," I commiserated.

"Well, it's not so nice now. Phoebe drove it in for gas today, and it had a huge dent in the back."

"Really?" I said, and I was genuinely surprised. Maybe that's why Adam was so miserable when he answered the door. His car, less than a week old, already had a dent in it. "Did Phoebe say anything?"

"For someone who spent four years of high school in the back seat of a car, she made a pretty snide comment about male drivers."

"I don't know what she expected, giving a new car to a kid like Adam," I added.

Chris laughed. "Go figure. I just wanted you to know."

I was glad Chris called, but I wasn't sure a dent in Adam's car was meaningful. Had Adam come home from school today and argued with Phoebe about his Hide and Creep game? Maybe he'd driven off and hit something. It seemed a likely scenario, but not one that held clues to George's or Fletcher's death. It simply painted a picture of a disgruntled teen who dented his car, and that wasn't news to any of us.

I said my goodbyes to Chris and returned to the task at hand, analyzing Jamie's portrait. I threw a blanket over Gayle and slid off her shoes. So far, this gesture had been the extent of my mothering. *Not bad*, I thought.

Baby Roon's drawings covered my work table and easel. I scooped them up to make room for my new project of dissecting Jamie Fletcher. I spared a few minutes to admire my initial drawings of Katrina's little bundle. I felt, despite Roon's chronic crying, that I had captured his impish grin. A smirk he doled out so sparingly, you'd think God had given him a limited supply. Truly, if you blinked, you'd miss Roon's grin. But I knew Katrina would be happy that I'd immortalized his perishable puss on canvas. And I know she'd love the fact that I'd recolorized her son in traditional shades of blue. Her Freegan cheapness may have prevented her from buying new boy clothing, but my finished portrait would easily hide the truth of Roon's feminine attire.

Once I cleared my work space, I settled in for a night of investigative art work. First, I gathered and organized all my sketches and photos of Jamie. I had forgotten that in addition to the photos I had taken of Jamie in the great room, we had also tried multiple rooms of the house to test the lighting. There were pictures of Jamie in the dining room, kitchen, center hall, and finally, the great room, where the light seemed to be the best. In every photo, Jamie's face remained stoic. She wasn't a smiler, but I had to give her credit—she was consistent. I remember reading an article about a movie star who purposely kept her face in a relaxed, neutral pose so paparazzi couldn't snap an unflattering photo. There was nothing worse than a starlet caught grinning too hard, laughing open-mouthed, or worse, frowning. It was like this with Jamie. It was as if she tried hard not to act naturally, for fear she'd look actually look like herself.

That thought stopped me. If Jamie were trying not to look like herself, then who was she trying to look like? Maybe she didn't want to appear to be the gloating second wife or the deliriously happy trophy wife. I tapped my finger on her face. Who the hell was Jamie Fletcher? Former intern marries boss and breaks up twenty-year marriage. Maybe she had a reason to change her appearance. Maybe she didn't like who she was before. I looked closely at the pictures. In a few of the outtakes, Simon could be seen in the background. I remembered him taking control of the shoot at the time. He fussed with his wife's hair and adjusted her clothing as if he were an experienced photo stylist. Like Jamie, Fletcher wanted this portrait to be something I ultimately had struggled to deliver. To this day, I still don't know what the Fletchers expected the portrait to accomplish. In my experience, portrait clients had a desire to look younger or richer or more important. I painted Jamie exactly as she was: an expressionless woman. It was a face I'm sure she'd examined in the mirror hundreds of times. In fact, I was now convinced she had practiced her look long enough to make it stick.

And that's what I had captured on canvas—the look that Jamie had mastered. Our only advantage was that we knew a coverup had occurred. It was important that Frank had enough evidence to back Jamie into a corner and get her to admit she knew the painting had blood on it.

I had two photos. One of my original painting and one by

Kwan Ko. Both photos had been enlarged to 8.5 by 11 inches. Of course, the original canvas was much larger, but I only had access to photos. To accurately compare the two, I used old-fashioned sheets of transparency paper. I added a cross-hatch of lines, maybe an eighth of an inch apart, like graph paper. I'm sure a computer whiz could have scanned the photos and superimposed graphing lines to the same end, but I was hands-on. I lettered the axes and numbered the lines so I could refer to each section by coordinates. Then I made a list of all the sections in the paintings that were different. It really wasn't hard, and I was pleased with my progress. By using clear graph paper over the photos, I could identify subtle differences in color, style, and brush stroke, down to an eighth of an inch.

Two hours later, I looked at my list of fifteen points. The evidence was substantial, and Jamie would have a hard time denying she knew it was blood that had damaged her portrait. In my opinion, she either knew her painting had been moved and altered within forty-eight hours of her husband's death or she knew who was behind it.

By the end of the exercise, Jamie's stoic face had worn me down, but I still had a bit of drive left in me. I tiptoed down the attic stairs into Charlie's bedroom. His room was empty, and I assumed he was still passed out on the couch. I sat down at his computer, typed in Simon Fletcher's name and clicked *Images*. I didn't think Jamie was a significant enough personality to warrant her own Google search, but I thought I might get a glimpse of her on Simon's arm. Sure enough, dozens of photos from charity and speaking events appeared. In every photo, no matter how many years apart the photos were taken, Jamie looked the same, unlike Simon, whose changes were more obvious. I printed out some choice photos and took them back up to the attic, where Gayle was snoozing comfortably.

I lined the photos up in chronological order. Amazing. Jamie's smile, or lack of it, was the same in every shot. Her consistency was so maddening I had an urge to cluck her chin just to get her to crack. Upon closer inspection, however, I could see Jamie's features had softened and rounded over the years. The line of her jaw seemed a bit gentler and her neck was not as rigid as in earlier pictures. I suspected a breast enlargement along the way, but that wasn't any of my business. Jamie was also very tall, while Simon seemed to be shrinking as the years passed. In the most recent picture of the couple, he seemed to be on her arm as opposed to Jamie on his. My Google search also revealed another familiar face. There were a handful of Fletcher and Ricky together, and I noticed the same phenomenon. Placed in dated order, Ricky's persona took on more authority in later years. Gone was the adoring gaze of the new intern in earlier photos. By the last shot, Ricky looked like a peer of Fletcher's and not a subordinate.

I checked the time, 2:00 a.m. Based on the police department's flat rate for this project and the amount of time I'd already invested, I'd earned about three cents an hour.

I curled up next to Gayle and snuck a peek at my daughter's lovely profile. Staring at Gayle was an indulgence on my part, but this time a bit of jealousy surfaced. I thought about how lucky Katrina was to have a baby, even a cranky one. What I'd give to have held Gayle as an infant. I'd missed a magical moment, yet I was so thankful I'd at least discovered that Gayle existed. I lay my head back and wondered what my relationship with Gayle would have been like had she been a boy, like Roon. We probably wouldn't be sharing a bed now, that's for sure. I certainly couldn't envision

Phoebe logging eight hours a night with Adam as her bedmate. I yawned and realized these topics were too complicated to consider at this hour. I let myself drift into a well-deserved slumber.

———

I woke up, not surprisingly, to Roon's cries. Katrina was sitting on my futon with Roon propped up like a puppy dog on all fours. I watched as he rocked back and forth.

"What's he doing?"

"He's trying to crawl," Katrina said as she stroked his back. "I probably have to stop carrying him around all the time or he'll never learn." My mother was right about some things.

I patted Roon on his head and breathed a sigh of relief. Luckily I had moved my sketches of him or the great wedding reveal would have been ruined.

"Aren't you supposed to be at the station helping Frank?" Katrina asked as she passed me a slice of toasted bread with our famous Kats Kan's peach jelly spread thickly on top.

"Is the bread from Umberto's?" I asked as I savored the toast and jelly. The bread, I had noted, was thick and puffy. On rare occasions, Katrina was able to snag extra rolls of pizza dough from our favorite pizza shop, and I suspected she'd turned her last free batch into my morning toast.

"Umberto's closed, and they gave me a bunch of stuff from their freezer."

"Closed?" I asked through a mouthful of jelly-covered pizza dough. "That's impossible."

"Closed for two weeks and then moved a few stores down. Better rent."

"That was a close one," I said. "What time is it?"

"After nine, I think."

I jumped out of bed and sped around the room in search of clean clothes. I settled on the same jeans I'd worn yesterday. The frayed bottoms were still damp from last night's snow, and I slid them on gingerly, hoping the back pockets had dried. "Is Charlie still here?"

"He left a while ago. So did Gayle," Katrina said, and then added, "I know this a bad time to ask, but will you have time to look at YouTube clips of local wedding bands?"

I laughed. "I'll only watch the cheesy ones. The kind of bands that make guests do the Macarena or the bunny hop." I jumped forward twice and then backward once. Roon smiled. I did it again and this time he giggled and rocked harder. "Was that all it took?" I said as I hopped over to my easel to the sound of Roon's gurgles. At this rate, I might be able to get him to crawl. I picked one of Jamie's photos and handed it to Katrina.

"This is Fletcher's wife. First impressions?"

"Phony," Katrina said, as she handed back the shot, "but insecure. Like those feminine hygiene commercials where the girl is afraid she's had an accident in a public setting."

"You got all that from one photo?" I asked.

"I may not be all that sophisticated, but I'm genuine, and this woman is not genuine."

I thought about Charlie's conversation with Jamie before he left the house for the first time. According to Charlie, she'd asked him about Fletcher like she was concerned her husband had become distracted. Did she think there was another woman or were her questions simply driven by her underlying insecurity? Or, as Charlie had thought, had she put out signals?

"Fletcher's first wife said she wasn't a bad person," I said.

"I don't think insecure people are necessarily bad people," Katrina said. "Though they might do bad things when their insecurity surfaces."

I put the photo of Jamie back in my pile and turned to Katrina. "I think you're right about that," I said, and that worried me. I wanted Jamie to be mean. Mean and guilty. I hopped forward and then backward until I'd jumped all the way over to Roon. He laughed ferociously. I kissed him on the head and then headed off to the police station to set a trap for Jamie Fletcher.

TWENTY-SIX

A STUBBORN TRAFFIC LIGHT stood between me and Charlie's freedom. I waited for what seemed an eternity when I realized my Subaru was the only car at the four-way intersection. I seriously considered running the light. To test the waters, I rolled the car forward a few feet. A third of the way into the intersection, I caught a glimpse of Umberto's Pizza on my right. As Katrina had mentioned, our favorite pizza shop had indeed relocated. The sign on the front window gave the new address and a poster announced, "*New Look, Same Pizza.*" I repeated the words to myself, and I then laid my forehead on the steering wheel and banged it a few times. *New Look, Same Pizza.*

How could I have missed it? It seemed so obvious now.

New look, same Jamie.

I wondered if Jamie Fletcher had created a new look for the benefit of her new husband. The clothes, the hair, and the smile, all delivered with the consistency of Umberto's famous pizza. Now I realized the purpose of my portrait. I was supposed to make Jamie look real, as if she'd always been who I'd painted. But I couldn't do it. It wasn't real, because it wasn't the real Jamie.

My photos. I drove through the stubborn red light and into the pizza shop's former parking lot. I fished the photos of Jamie and Fletcher from my bag and displayed them on my dashboard. Then I considered Ruthie's comments about the new Mrs. Fletcher. *She was the right choice for Simon. It had nothing to do with me. We're polar opposites. We're just built differently.*

I scooped up the photos, turned the car around, and ran another red light. Worst-case scenario, a cop would pull me over, toss me in the back seat, and deliver me to the station faster than I could steer the Subaru. My head felt like a wad of pizza dough spinning in the air as I pieced together my thoughts. I now realized that Jamie had worked very hard to maintain her look. Every photo, including my portrait, supported her efforts. If I was right about Jamie's new look, then it meant she wanted her old look to remain hidden. People hide things they don't want others to know. Some even kill for it.

I wanted to roll down my windows and scream the news at the top of my lungs. So I did. "*Jamie has a secret,*" I yelled as I pushed my foot to the floorboard. "*Jamie has a secret.*"

I wanted to be the first to tell Frank. I wanted to be the first to set Charlie free. I wanted to help both of the men in my life without losing either one.

Cheski held the door to the police station open. He must have seen me running from the parking lot, a smug look plastered across my face. I jumped across the threshold and high-fived Cheski. He frowned and pointed down the hall.

Osbaldo Rivera, Charlie's lawyer, was standing next to Jamie Fletcher, their heads pinned together, deep in conversation.

Osbaldo and Jamie? That was an odd couple and certainly not what I expected to see this morning.

"What's with those two?" I asked.

"He's representing her," Cheski said.

"But," I stammered. "That's impossible. He's Charlie's lawyer. He doesn't know the whole story yet." I stomped over to the conspiratorial pair and reached for my photos. Before I could flash Jamie's dirty laundry around the police station, Osbaldo held out his palm.

"Hold your thoughts," he said. "I know what I'm doing."

I looked at Osbaldo's normally chipper face. This case had clearly cut into his personal grooming routine. He needed a shave and his teeth hadn't been bleached in the last week. Then he reached out for Jamie's manicured hand and I nearly spit. It didn't seem real. Osbaldo was treating Jamie like a victim and I had evidence to the contrary.

"Charlie gave you a fat wad of cash," I hissed. "How can you represent her?"

"Have you forgotten my most basic principle?" he asked.

I leaned back on my heels. "Now is the time for the truth," I countered, "not chaos."

Frank poked his head out of his office when he heard my voice. "I think we're ready," he said calmly. "We can use the conference room down the hall." Did he have any idea what was going on?

We took our seats, although it pained me to sit. My legs bounced frantically under the table. It sounded like a troupe of Vaudeville tap dancers was about to introduce Frank.

"Mr. Rivera informed me you have something important to tell me relative to your husband's death," Frank said to Jamie. "I don't know the nature of the information, so I'm going to read you your rights with your lawyer present."

Osbaldo nodded.

I'd never actually heard someone receive their constitutional rights, and I guessed Frank had memorized the statement years ago. But today, the pressure was on, and there was no room for error where Charlie was concerned. Frank read from a card no bigger than the Ace of Spades. It seemed so official.

"I moved my husband's body," she said when Frank finished.

Wow, I thought. Did she miss the part about 'anything you say, can and will be used against you'?

"Start from the beginning," Osbaldo advised as he patted her hand, again. Mister Touchy-Feely was getting on my nerves. "Slowly, we're not in a rush," he added.

No rush? I was in rush and Charlie was certainly in rush.

Frank gave Jamie a glass of water. If I were in her position, having just admitted to moving the victim's body, I'd have thrown the water in the detective's face and run for the door. Jamie, however, was as controlled as her pictures. She took a slow sip of water and continued.

"Jamie is my nickname," she said. "When I was younger, my friends and family called me James."

I thought Frank's head was about to explode. His jaw ground back and forth, and I said a silent prayer on behalf of his overtaxed molars. Jamie turned to me. "You knew," she announced. My face went red. It's not as if I'd been spying on Jamie, but that's how I felt. Ten minutes ago I had prepared my victory speech and thought about purchasing tickets to Disney for the gang. Now I felt like a whistle-blower short on breath.

"I didn't know at first," I said. "I mean, I know now. I think

I figured it out last night, but I wasn't sure until this morning. I really had no idea when I painted you." I bumbled my way through what sounded like an awkward, back-handed compliment. *You're such an amazing cross-dresser, it took me years to realize you were actually a man in woman's clothing!* But that was the truth, and it would have remained so had I not spent an inordinate amount of time analyzing Jamie's face. I thought about all the things that had gone through my head last night, and I realized a flicker of recognition had tapped my subconscious sometime after midnight. Maybe that's why I had been overly impressed with my ability to switch Roon's gender with the stroke of a colored pencil. And then there was my semidream state musings about Gayle. I'd wondered what she'd be like had she been born a boy.

Of course now I understood the softening in Jamie's features overtime. I guessed hormones and plastic surgery had been introduced at some point. I thought about Jamie's sessions, hours sitting in front of me while I studied her face. She must have been terribly self-conscious.

"I got the sense you didn't like my portrait," Jamie said.

I nodded. "Sorry about that. It never felt right."

Jamie laughed. "I've never been very good at this"—she motioned to her attire—"but it's what Simon wanted, and I'm a pleaser."

You might also be a murderer, I thought.

"Are you gay?" Frank interrupted and then quickly apologized. "I'm sorry. I'm confused, and I don't want to violate . . ." He stopped, clearly not sure what was appropriate in this case. He looked desperately at Osbaldo, as if the lawyer had the final say on all things gay.

"Jamie is gay," Osbaldo confirmed, "and Simon was gay. From

what Jamie has told me, it was important for Simon to keep up appearances. He wasn't entirely comfortable going public with his sexuality. It's not unusual for a man of his generation."

"I could have gone either way with the clothing," Jamie admitted, "but Simon wanted a showpiece wife, and I agreed," she sighed. "I loved him."

The room was quiet. If only I had been able to speak with Frank before we entered the conference room, he might have been able to devise a better strategy to counteract this unusual turn of events. This was a murder investigation, not an episode of *Dr. Phil*.

To break the tension Osbaldo threw in his own status. "I'm gay," he said.

"My daughter's adopted father is gay," I added, but our approach didn't help. Jamie looked distraught, and I felt I was to blame. However, I realized that if we indulged in much more of this politically correct verbiage the statute of limitations would run out on this case. I tilted my head toward Frank to remind him the ball was still in his court. He got my drift.

"Mrs. Fletcher, did you murder Simon Fletcher?" Frank asked.

"No," Jamie answered. "I did not murder my husband."

"Where were you when he was murdered?"

"I had barely stepped in the shower when the lights went out. I slipped in the tub, and I think I may have been knocked out for a few minutes." Jamie lifted the hair above her brow to reveal a yellowish bruise. "When I came to, I found Simon on the floor of our bedroom."

"You covered the bruise when I first spoke to you," Frank said.

Jamie shuddered. "I did because I thought you might think I'd had a physical fight with Simon."

"Did you?"

"No, I didn't fight with Simon."

"Did you see anyone in the house?" Frank asked.

"I didn't, but I heard the front door shut. My first thought was an intruder. It seemed to be a pattern with the blackouts."

"There's a strong possibility it was an intruder," Osbaldo said, as he peddled his chaos theory. That would explain the open door when Charlie arrived. "Mrs. Fletcher has indicated that her husband kept a bat under their bed."

Jamie nodded in agreement.

"Why didn't you tell us about the bat?" Frank asked.

"The less you knew about me and Simon, the better," she said. "He lived in fear that we'd be exposed. That's why he kept the bat under the bed, in case someone broke in during the night and saw us in bed. I moved him from the bedroom so you'd be inclined to look for other suspects."

Frank pushed his chair away from the table and took a quick stroll around the room. "So you think someone broke in and Simon went for his bat. The intruder grabbed the bat from Simon, killed him, and then left through the front door with the weapon."

"It's not impossible," Osbaldo offered. "Especially in the dark. The blackouts provided the perfect cover. I'm wondering if someone purposely caused the blackout to create a distraction for the murder."

"Interesting," Frank said under his breath.

I motioned to Frank and he nodded. "There was a blackout back in December," I said, addressing Jamie. "Your husband hosted a party for the Green Acres residents on the night of the blackout. Why did you get mad at Simon when the electricity failed?"

Jamie lowered her eyes. "You've done your homework," she said.

I shrugged.

"I don't like socializing," Jamie continued. "I'm constantly afraid someone will look too closely. Ricky is Simon's right-hand man, but Simon sent him off to solve the electrical problem and that left me to play hostess." I could literally see Jamie's tall frame shrink in discomfort. "Too many eyes on me, even by candlelight."

Frank came back into the conversation. "Do you know what caused the blackouts?"

"We had no idea, and it made Simon crazy. Ricky called the utility company multiple times. He was very diligent, and he insisted it wasn't an issue with Green Acres."

"Ricky and Kevin Calhoun got in an argument that night," I said, ignoring Frank's sharp look. "Why?"

"The residents were not happy," Jamie said dryly. "Their houses are expensive and frankly, they don't work."

Frank opened his iPad and pounded away at the screen. He continued to circle the room. "Charlie said you came up behind him and screamed, but now it appears you knew your husband was already dead. It was too dark to see his body."

"True," Jamie admitted. "I realized later that my scream was ill-timed. The house was dark and I couldn't really see anything definite when I walked in on Charlie. I should have waited until the electricity was restored, but I had no idea when that would happen."

"Please repeat your movements after you found your husband in the bedroom."

"I sat with Simon for a few minutes in our bedroom, and then I realized the murder might be pinned on me. Unless there was a break-in, I was the only one in the house. I was the only suspect."

Jamie's dilemma, unlike her portrait, was real. Now I understood why Osbaldo had treated her like a victim—a victim of social convention.

She continued. "I know there's nothing wrong with our lifestyle, but others might have made me out to be guilty simply because of our choices. I thought if Simon were in a different room, any room but the bedroom, other suspects might be considered."

Her fear was plausible. Simon and Jamie had chosen an alternative path, and I believed she felt threatened by their secret. Her planning, however, was as impressive as her fear. I wondered, given the Fletcher's arrangement, if she was one of those people who always had a plan B.

"So you put Charlie in the great room," I said. I was sympathetic, but my main concern was Charlie. I struggled to control my anger.

"First I rolled the rug in the great room and pushed it to the side. Then I dragged Simon on the rug into the great room and moved the great room rug to the bedroom. Then I texted Charlie." She started to cry as she recounted her effort and then stopped to catch her breath. "It was mean of me to set up Charlie, but I couldn't think of anything else." She laughed uncomfortably. "He's a bit of an opportunist so I knew he'd come back, and fast. Thankfully, I had such an enormous burst of adrenalin it felt like Simon's body floated across the floor. I also called Ricky, but he already knew the lights were out and he was on his way."

I wondered if Ricky was already there.

My shoulders released and my vibrating legs came to a halt. For the first time in a week, I was able to sit back in a chair and relax. I tried to convince myself that years from now, I'd get a kick out of retelling how Charlie had inadvertently propositioned Jamie. Jamie had just provided Charlie with an embarrassing, but valid, alibi. My job was done.

Or so I thought. I then remembered that this case involved something very personal to me.

"I understand why you moved your husband," I said, "but you just admitted it was too dark to see his body when Charlie arrived. How could you possibly have seen blood on *my* painting?"

Jamie's eyebrows cinched tightly over the bridge of her nose. "Why would *my* portrait have blood on it?" she asked.

"You tell me," I shot back.

Suddenly, we were fighting over a painting that neither of us particularly liked. Jamie's response startled me.

Frank lifted his hand and then turned to me. I understood it was time to keep my mouth shut. Jamie's story and the evidence didn't match. Maybe Jamie wasn't all that innocent. For all I knew, she might actually *be* a woman, and her whole story bunk.

Frank returned to his chair. His head bounced up and down as if he were playing through the possible scenarios. "Mrs. Fletcher," he said, "Where is your portrait currently hanging?"

"On an easel in the master bedroom." Jamie seemed genuinely confused.

"I'm referring to the portrait painted by Ms. Prentice."

"That's the only portrait I own," she responded, "and it's in my bedroom."

"We spoke at your house on the day of your husband's death. Please account for your movements from that point forward."

Osbaldo groaned. "For an entire week? That's insane. My client hasn't been on house arrest."

Frank amended his question. "Where did you spend the night of the murder and the next two days?"

Osbaldo gave Jamie the go-ahead, and she answered. "One of your officers told me I'd have to leave the house. I stayed with my sister in northern New Jersey, and she can attest to my presence. I was under the assumption that I couldn't enter the house."

"So you haven't been in the house," Frank repeated.

"No," Jamie said. "One of your female officers packed a bag for me."

Frank passed his finger over his iPad and studied his notes. "After you moved the body and texted Charlie, what did you do?"

"I was afraid to drag evidence back into the bedroom, and I certainly couldn't sit in the great room, so I went into the kitchen and waited until I heard a car."

"The kitchen is in the back of the house."

"Yes."

Frank fixated on Jamie as if he'd just realized she'd changed her gender.

"Thank you for your time," he said. "You're free to go, Mrs. Fletcher." Then he turned to Osbaldo. "Please inform your client, Charlie Knudsen, that he is no longer a suspect."

Before I could protest, Frank said, "In my office."

Jamie stood up uneasily. We were both surprised at Frank's abrupt decision to end the interview. Osbaldo, too, was caught off guard, despite both his clients' favorable outcomes. "Chaos works," he said to me.

The one person who remained focused was Frank, and he left the conference room before the rest of us had accepted his decision.

TWENTY-SEVEN

I MET FRANK IN his office with Cheski.

"What's up, boss?" Cheski asked.

Frank pointed over his officer's shoulder. "Shut the door."

"How could you let Jamie go?" I protested. "She's lying about something."

"She's not lying," Frank said. "She moved her husband's body, but she didn't move the portrait."

"She moved it," I countered. "She said the portrait was in the master, just the way I remembered it. Then it ended up in the great room. She was in the only one in the house. Therefore, she moved it." *Case shut*, I thought. "Plus she set up Charlie. How honest can she be?"

"But she didn't move the painting," Frank said. "If she couldn't see her husband's body in the dark, a point you just made, she couldn't have known her portrait had blood on it."

"Then who the hell moved the painting?" Cheski asked.

Frank sighed. "Someone who knew there was blood on it

212

because they had touched it." I let that explanation sink in. He continued, "Kwan Ko didn't just cover up blood splatter. He covered up a bloody fingerprint."

"Oh my God," I gasped. "You're right."

Frank raised his eyebrows as if I had just complimented Einstein for being really smart.

"I guess I'm driving to the city," Cheski said.

"You are," Frank said, "but I'll bet by now Kwan Ko is in Korea enjoying a steaming bowl of kimchi. He knew damn well why he was hired to touch up the portrait, and he was probably relieved we hadn't figured it out when we pulled him in the first time." He sat down behind his desk and leaned forward. "CeCe, the day you spotted the painting swap, you also smelled acetone in the bathroom."

"I did."

"How long do you think it took Kwan to touch up your painting?"

I had to think about that question. The canvas was four feet by three, but the actual area Kwan worked on was relatively small. I guessed that only the bottom right-hand corner had been altered. The job required about two hours of touch up and probably another hour perfecting my signature. To be safe, I padded my estimate. "Maybe five hours."

"Let's assume the murderer was still in the house when they heard Jamie come out of the shower. Maybe they were still in the bedroom. They watched Jamie move her husband's body while he or she decided what to do with the bloody portrait. They couldn't destroy it. That would be too obvious."

"Way too obvious," I agreed.

"If I remember correctly, the easel in the bedroom was no more than four feet off the ground."

"That's right," I said. "The painting sat just below eye level."

"So when the lights went back on, the blood on the portrait would have been evident."

"I suppose so."

"But that mantel in the great room," Frank said. "It's high and a good ten feet from where we found the body."

"I had to stand on a table to examine it," I confirmed, "and even then it was a stretch."

"It would have been nearly impossible to spot the blood at that height."

Hidden in plain sight, I thought. *How cliché.*

"Above the mantel is also a logical spot for a portrait. Had the murderer hung it elsewhere in the house, it might have raised a red flag," Cheski said.

"We'll have to assume that Jamie was too disoriented to even notice the swap. It probably occurred when she retreated to the kitchen. And according to her, she didn't return to the bedroom that night."

Frank drummed his fingers on his iPad, and then he moved to his white board and mocked-up a calendar. He pointed to the day after the murder. "The next day, the murderer calls your painter friend on the east end and gets Kwan's name. Meanwhile, the splattered portrait is hanging over the mantel, safe from the untrained eye."

Cheski shifted his bulky frame back and forth. "I'm sure whoever moved that painting was under intense pressure. Eventually someone would have noticed the blood."

"And that's why I think time was of the essence," Frank said. "Kwan lied about receiving the painting in the city. I think he met the murderer and did the work at the house."

Cheski moaned. Fletcher's house hadn't been secured. It was his fault Kwan had entered the house.

I avoided Cheski's guilty expression and addressed Frank. "So Kwan lied about the painting being delivered to his lobby?"

"An outright lie," Frank said. "I'm guessing the touchup was done the night after the murder. We'd already completed our sweep of the house, but I'm sure Kwan and the murderer were able to find a way back in."

"A blind man could find a way back in," I said.

Frank hunched over his desk. "Ce, how hard is it to remove a layer of paint?"

I shook my head. I was confused.

My boyfriend sighed, clearly digging for patience. "Can you remove Kwan's paint? I want to see if we can find the fingerprint underneath."

I thought about the errant fingerprint. "If you left a fingerprint, wouldn't you simply wipe it off?"

"I thought about that," Frank admitted. "But then why hire Kwan? Maybe the murderer wiped the print, and it smeared. That would leave a DNA trail. What I'm guessing is that whoever touched the painting figured that slapping a layer of paint over it would be the safest solution, even if the print was smeared. I'd like to see what's under that fresh paint."

"I've got to be honest," I said. "I'm not hopeful that's possible."

"Just try," Frank said. "If it doesn't work, I can still make a suspect believe we found a print and then force them into a confession."

"But with Jamie and Charlie in the clear, who are our suspects?" Cheski asked. It was an excellent question.

I remembered my conversation with Chris, my gas station buddy. I explained the dent in Adam's car.

215

Frank rubbed the tension spots below both of his ears while he rotated his jaw. "Adam and his pals are officially suspects, as is Ricky," he said. "Ricky is the only other person who has admitted to being in the house, and we have to assume Adam or one of his friends was in this house at some point too."

"I'll bet that's why Ricky accused Charlie and Jamie of having an affair," I said. "What do you know about Ricky?"

Frank nodded to Cheski. "Squeaky clean," Cheski said. "White, single, male, twenty-eight years old. Fletcher pays him sixty-five thousand a year, and he owns a modest condo in town. We followed him for a few days, but he's barely left his house. He normally works out of Fletcher's home office in the basement. I'm guessing the only thing he's doing now is canceling Fletcher's speaking engagements."

"Who's running the Green Acres empire?" I asked.

"Is there anything to run?" Cheski said. "Fletcher is a developer. He builds the homes and sells them. Once they're sold, he's out."

"Almost," Frank said. "I followed up with the other developments and apparently, two maintenance men poke around every month or so, and they report back to Ricky. The owners are contractually obliged to participate in Fletcher's research on sustainable living. I guess Ricky gathers data on the homes' efficiency for Fletcher's lectures."

"There's data being collected? How come Phoebe or George or Kevin never mentioned that?" I asked.

Frank nodded. "Because their development was only recently completed. Ricky, it turns out, has been handling most of the on-site reviews until a maintenance team is hired."

"I guess that's why Simon sent Ricky to Green Acres during the catered dinner party when the lights went out," I said.

"Exactly, and that's why Ricky claims he came back to Fletcher's on the night of the murder. It's part of his job."

"It does make sense," I said. "Did you find out what the maintenance men do at the other developments?"

"From what I could gather," Frank said, "the only thing they do is read the meters. If a homeowner is around, they'll write up complaints, but according to the homeowners, the complaints end up in the garbage."

"They read the meters," I said slowly. I sat down and rested my chin in my hands. "There's something wrong with Fletcher's panels, but I don't know enough about this solar stuff to figure it out." I then explained what Charlie and I had discovered about the wiring. "So my mother's house and Fletcher's house are not connected to the same power source as Green Acres. Charlie thinks someone was manually disconnecting the houses."

"I figured it was something like that," Frank said. "We spoke to the utility company, and they insisted the Green Acres blackouts had nothing to do with their service." He stopped and went through a pile of notes on his desk, then pulled out a slip and dialed the phone.

"This is Detective Frank DeRosa," he introduced himself. "We spoke a few days ago about the power outages at Green Acres." He listened while his utility contact droned on. "Yes, I understand that there's nothing wrong with the transformers. I forgot to ask you who your contact is at Green Acres."

Frank listened for a few moments, then put the phone down and frowned. "According to the utility company, they don't have a contact at Green Acres."

"What?" Cheski said. "I thought Ricky's job was to work with the utility company."

"The first they heard about the blackouts was from us, the night of the murder."

"So the neighbors never called the utility company?" I asked.

"The neighbors called Fletcher, and Fletcher sent Ricky."

"Ricky's been lying," I said.

Frank stood up and started to make one of his famous circles around the room. "I wonder if he thought he could fix the problem himself."

Cheski walked over to the white board and wrote Ricky's name in block letters. "Maybe he was afraid to lose his job."

Frank continued to pace. "People lose jobs all the time. He'd been working for Fletcher for six years. It should have been time to move on anyway." He stopped and then started. "Now I'm wondering what was keeping him there. He probably could have made more money elsewhere and not been an underling for the rest of his career."

"What started as a simple work-related lie, *I'll check with the utility company*, is about to catch up with our friend Ricky," I said.

"What concerns me is that Ricky continues to perpetuate the lie even after his boss was murdered," Frank noted. "When I interviewed him, he insisted he was on top of the problem."

"And then he led you to believe that Charlie and Jamie were having an affair," I said.

"He doesn't want us to look at the electrical," Frank said.

"And Kevin and Phoebe don't want you to look at Adam's involvement in the blackouts," I added.

Frank's jaw slid back and forth like he was cracking walnuts shells. "The Calhouns and Ricky are connected, and George knew it. I think it scared him. In fact, I think he was afraid enough to come home from the hospital to protect his wife." Frank stopped circling. "What's Charlie up to these days?"

"Now that the police are off his back, I'm guessing his schedule has miraculously opened up."

Frank suppressed at laugh at his own expense. "Any chance I can get him to look at the Green Acres solar setup?"

Cheski raised his eyebrow as the conversation turned to Charlie. He'd had enough of our awkward triangle. "I'm out of here," he said. "I'll let you know if I find Kwan."

I waited for Cheski to leave before responding to Frank. "You owe Charlie a face-to-face."

Frank grumbled, and I felt like I was negotiating a playground fist-fight between two ten–year-olds. "It would mean a lot to me," I said. "And could you please stop pacing and sit down so we can talk about this?"

He took his seat and I continued. "Cheski has Kwan covered. I'll work on removing the paint from the portrait, and you've got to interview Adam and his delinquent friends. You know you need Charlie's help, but you're going to have apologize to him."

"Fine," Frank acquiesced. "I'll swing by Harbor House."

TWENTY-EIGHT

THE POLICE DELIVERED JAMIE's portrait to Harbor House the next day, and I propped it up on my easel. Frank had come by to speak with Charlie, but unfortunately the formerly accused murderer had decided to celebrate his newfound freedom by drinking his way through every bar in Huntington. It was 10:00 a.m., and Charlie still wasn't home. Could I blame him? If I didn't have to strip Jamie's portrait down to a bloody fingerprint, I'd be right there with him. If there was any time to dance on top of a bar, last night would have been it.

In a moment of wedding weakness, I had actually used Charlie's absence as an excuse to avoid watching wedding band videos with Katrina. I convinced Katrina it would be more fun as a group. Which was luckily true, and she'd agreed to hold off.

So there I stood, staring at Jamie's painting and wondering where to start. Cheski's drive into the city had proved futile. Kwan Ko, the infamous Korean forger, had disappeared shortly after meeting with Frank the first time. Cheski, however, was able to retrieve a sample of Kwan's oil paints. I was pleased to discover that Mr. Ko had, as I suspected, used a knock-off brand. I wouldn't go so far as to label Kwan's paints watercolors, but his selection did appear to be more soluble than a better brand of oils. The question now was how to lift the paint without lifting the fingerprint. And that's assuming I knew where the print was located.

I heard the attic door open and a man grumble. The attic stairs were not for the faint of heart, as Dominic LaSalle had just discovered. I met my mother and Dominic at the top of the flight and invited them into my studio. My mother's face glowed, and it wasn't from the strenuous hike up the stairs. Yet more evidence that she had the hots for Dominic. I liked the idea of my mother having a beau. As for Dominic, he seemed equally pleased to accompany my mother. He held the door for her and then gently placed his hand on her shoulder as they entered my attic studio.

"I'm sorry about the stairs," I apologized. "I guess I could have moved everything to the main floor."

Dominic rested his free hand on my art table and took a few deep breaths. "I'm fine," he wheezed. "It takes a lot to get me out of my own studio"—he winked at my mother—"but this project intrigued me. Let's see what you've got."

The three of us stood in front of Jamie's portrait for a good five minutes before anyone spoke. Frank had challenged me to find and reveal a murderer's bloody fingerprint under layers of oil paint. My strategy was to assemble a century's worth of artistic experience to solve this puzzle. I figured between the three of us we'd find a way to peel back Kwan's work without damaging the layer of incriminating blood.

Dominic tilted his head to the side and my mother took a few steps backwards and then forwards.

"He's good," Dominic said. "If Elizabeth hadn't told me that the blood splatter was on the right side, I'm not sure I would have known."

"He is good," I conceded.

Dominic squinted his eyes and leaned into the portrait. "Elizabeth tells me this little darlin' here is actually a man."

"At some point she was," I said. "Although it's irrelevant to the case at this point."

"Makes me wonder who I've been painting over the years," Dominic said. "But you're right; it's not important. Let's see what else you've got."

I displayed my before and after photos and then laid the transparent graph paper over the photos. "Here's where I think Kwan touched up my work," I said, pointing to the suspect quadrants.

Dominic and my mother went through my notes carefully as they referred to the painting. "You've done a lot of work," my mother said.

"A labor of love." I feigned exhaustion.

"Speaking of love, where is my favorite almost-convict?" my mother asked.

"Probably in a nameless girl's bed wondering if he should chew his arm off to make his escape."

Dominic chuckled. "I knew I was glad I made this trip. When do I get meet your local lothario?"

"He actually lives here," I said. "I'm sure he'll stumble in soon enough. You can trade war stories." Dominic laughed. I liked him, and I think he liked me too.

We returned to the painting, and Dominic asked me to walk through Frank's theory.

I explained the blackouts and the preponderance of teenage boys roaming the neighborhood during them. I then related Jamie's version of the night Fletcher was murdered, and surprisingly, it rang true.

"So the wife was in the shower when the lights went out?" Dominic asked.

I nodded and my mother responded, "I could see that being scary. You're naked, wet, and it's dark. I'd probably slip and fall, too, under those conditions."

Dominic agreed, and I continued.

"Frank thinks it's possible that someone entered the house at that time. There had been burglaries in the past, and the master bedroom is a good target for jewelry." I explained the bat under the bed and how Frank thought Fletcher lunged for the intruder.

"He may have been protecting his wife," Dominic said.

It was an excellent point. Fletcher might have gone for his bat to prevent an intruder from entering the bathroom and harming Jamie.

"The painting was on an easel near the bed," I said. "Assuming Fletcher went for the bat, it would make sense that something physical happened in the area around the bed."

Dominic took a swing as though he had a bat in his hand. As he pretended to release the bat, he took a step back and faked a stumble. "If I reached backward and leaned on an easel, it would tip over."

"It may have," I said. "Maybe that's when the print was left on the canvas."

My mother grabbed an older painting of mine. It was a landscape, and not my best work. "This one isn't very good," she confirmed. "Let's drop some blood on it." With one quick motion, she grabbed a spackling knife from my supply tray and pricked her finger. She let a droplet fall and pressed her thumb down into the canvas. A perfect oval with circular lines appeared. "Now we wait until it dries," she said. "Then we'll paint over it with the low-quality paint."

I sighed. "We'll be here all day. Let me find a hair dryer." I was a drip and dry kind of girl, but I thought Katrina had a dryer to use in extremely cold weather.

I left my mother and Dominic upstairs. We agreed that one bloody print wouldn't be enough for testing purposes, so my mother and Dominic got down to business and pricked their fingers. It was literally a bloody mess.

TWENTY-NINE

KATRINA'S BRIDAL SEATING CHART, a collage of circles and chicken scratch, was displayed on the kitchen table. "Do you think your mother would like to bring her artist friend as a date?"

"She'd love to bring Dominic to the wedding," I said. I asked about a hair dryer and Katrina pointed to the storage closet. I leaned over her shoulder and studied the proposed seating. "So, me, Charlie, and Frank are at the same table?"

"Would that be uncomfortable?"

I flipped a pencil over and handed it to Katrina, eraser side up.

"Am I erasing Frank or Charlie?" she asked.

At that moment, Charlie walked into the kitchen. He tossed his denim jacket over a chair and then went to the sink for a glass of water. He was strangely sober, despite a night of heavy drinking. "Hey," he said as he took a seat. He glanced at the seating arrangement and pointed to our table. "We're all sitting together?" he asked me.

"Is that a problem?" I said, testing the waters.

"Can I bring a date?"

Katrina place the tip of her pencil on her chart. "Does the girl you slept with last night have a name?"

"For your information, Trina, I spent last night with Phoebe."

I shook my head and held back tears of frustration. I had worked so hard to get Charlie off the hook, and now he had gone and slept with the enemy. The married enemy, no less.

"You just had to go and put that damn condom to use, didn't you?" I accused. "Do you have any idea what I've done for you? Katrina was just about to erase Frank's name from the seating chart because of you."

"I didn't sleep with Phoebe last night. I hung with her." He paused. "And Frank."

My eyes popped wide. "Together?" I asked.

"Separately," Charlie said. "Frank found me in a bar last night, and we had a beer. Your name may have come up." I flinched, but I let Charlie continue. "We're good," my pal said as he pointed to the seating chart again. "But we won't be sitting together."

"What about Green Acres?"

"Frank asked if I could review the Green Acres solar setup, and I said I'd think about it."

"It's not a definite?

"I'm conflicted," Charlie said as he rubbed the back of his neck. "I'm psyched to be off the hook, but do I really need to drag someone else into Fletcher's murder?"

"I'm afraid to ask what Phoebe offered to get you to back off from the case."

"It's not what you think," he said. "Frank tried to bring Adam in last night, but he lawyered up. Some of Adam's friends came in voluntarily. Tobey provided the most information. He confirmed

226

that Adam was definitely running around outside the night of the murder, and he was likely in Fletcher's house. Phoebe lied about Adam being in his room."

Again, this was old information. *Frank must be frustrated*, I thought. "How did you hook up with Phoebe anyway?"

Charlie shrugged. "Word was out that I was partying. She came by to tell me how upset she is about Adam. She's worried Frank is going to arrest him."

"Of course she's upset. How would you feel with a son like that?" Katrina asked.

"How would I feel?" Charlie asked. "I *was* that kid. In fact, I got in more trouble than Adam's pea-sized brain can even imagine. I was sarcastic, obnoxious, irreverent, and disrespectful."

"No, you weren't," my mother said. She had just descended the stairs with a rag wrapped around her thumb. "Charlie Knudsen, you weren't any of those things. You also weren't a softie, and I think your sympathies are misplaced. Adam did something wrong. Even if he didn't kill Simon Fletcher, he found a way to break into our houses and turn it into a game."

"So I'm a better person because I never got caught?"

My mother walked over and placed her good hand on Charlie's shoulder. "You were a brilliant kid with a wicked sense of humor. That's all. Please don't compare yourself to a common delinquent."

"Remember when you had crates of live lady bugs delivered to the biology teacher's classroom?" I said.

Charlie started to laugh. "They were ten for a penny. It's still the best fifty dollars I've ever spent."

"Why do you feel badly for Phoebe and Adam?" I asked as I followed up on my mother's thoughts.

"I don't know," Charlie said. "Phoebe is scared. I know she's not all that real, but she's a mother, and she's loves Adam. I think I should stay on the sidelines."

"I'm thinking of it differently," I said. "If you don't help Frank, he's going to continue to pursue Adam. If you want to help Phoebe and Adam and you believe her, then you need to move the investigation in another direction." I waited for Charlie to respond, but he remained pensive. I planted another seed. "Maybe an investigation of Green Acre's solar panels will highlight other suspects."

"Ricky?" Charlie asked.

Now it was my turn to shrug. "It's possible."

My mother walked over to the sink and ran her punctured finger under water. "I have a suggestion. Go see your mother and apologize to her for all the crap you did over the years. You'll feel much better."

Charlie raised his head and stared at my mother. "Do you think that's what's bothering me? I feel bad for Phoebe because of what I put my mother through?"

My mother smiled. "At the least, she'll be happy you stopped by."

"It's worth a try," Charlie said as he rose from the table and headed toward the door. "I'll stop by Green Acres on my way back."

My mother started opening cabinets and then looked under our sink. "So what do you ladies use to clean this house?"

"Supplies are Trina's department," I said.

My mother came over to the table and took Charlie's seat. "Dominic and I want to test a natural substance on the paint. Turpentine and acetone are too harsh."

Katrina smiled and put her pencil down. "Then you've come to the right house."

———

Our numbers had grown as we gathered around the portrait. Katrina brought a fully stocked, toxin-free bucket of supplies to the attic. Her grime-fighting stash included old rags, vinegar, water, and baking soda. "Au naturel," she said as she dabbed the corner of an old towel into her eco-friendly cleaning concoction.

"Are we dying eggs or solving a crime?" Dominic asked as he pinched his nose.

My mother, Dominic, and Katrina went to work cleaning the samples while I finished blow drying the last stack of test canvases. "This seems hopeless," I said over the drone of the dryer. I held my hand steady while I calculated the amount of hours Phoebe had wasted styling her hair. I'd never had the patience for perfectly coiffed hair. The dryer emitted a burning smell, and I gave it a rest when I heard the phone ring. I ran down the stairs and caught it on the fifth ring.

It was Chris from the gas station. "Hey Ce," he said.

"We're certainly making up for lost time, aren't we?" I joked.

"A few more calls, and I'll have memorized your number."

"Have you seen Adam again?"

"No, but another car came in today with a dent in the rear bumper. I didn't think twice about it, until I realized it was another resident from Green Acres. There was a bit of paint on the fender—same color as Adam's new car."

"Do you know whose car it was?"

"You know the old guy from Green Acres? He's a real motor head. Knows more about cars than me."

Oh no, I thought. I didn't have the heart to tell Chris that George Fraser was dead. "Who was driving his car?" I asked.

"I think it was his wife."

"Did she say anything about the dent?"

"She seemed a bit out of it."

George had only been dead for a day, so the fender bender must have occurred very recently. Adam hadn't had his car all that long. One possibility was that the accident happened while George was in the hospital. If that was the case, then maybe Dotty had been driving the car. With George in the hospital, she may have been flustered and backed into her neighbor, Adam. It seemed like a logical explanation.

I wondered about George's connection to Adam. George knew Adam was breaking into the neighbor's homes. After Fletcher's death, he may have approached Adam and warned him to stay away from his home. Maybe Adam refused to comply, and it ended with two bumpers connecting. That was another possibility. If George had argued with Adam, it may have been enough stress to trigger his heart attack. Then there was George's unexplainable return to Green Acres. Was he trying to protect Dotty from Adam? Was he afraid Adam would break in while he was in the hospital?

Unfortunately, I couldn't let it rest. I could have called Cheski and Frank and let them follow up on this possible thread, but I could also call Dotty directly myself. So I did.

THIRTY

THE PHONE RANG so long that the repetition actually had a soothing effect on my nerves. Good thing too, as I knew I shouldn't be calling the Fraser home without Frank's consent. Dotty picked up just as my heartbeat synced with the rings.

"Hey Dotty," I said. "I wondered if you needed any help at the funeral."

"Oh," she replied. "That's sweet of you." She stopped speaking, as though she needed to search for the second part of her sentence. I waited until I was sure she'd finished her thought.

"I could help drive your guests," I suggested, and then paused. "I saw that your car had a dent in it. Is everything okay?"

Dotty's voice was raw, and I had to assume she'd spent the last day crying. "George's car," she said, and again she couldn't seem to finish her sentence. At that point, I suspected that she was on something stronger than a glass of wine.

"Did George dent the bumper?"

I heard a chair squeak along the kitchen floor. I listened as

Dotty sighed and sat down. "I suppose there's no one to lie to now," she admitted. "I got in a little fender bender when George was at the hospital."

"I'm sorry," I offered. "Tell me what happened."

"George badgered me about bringing his computer to the hospital, but I took your advice and told him he needed his rest. I was upset about our confrontation. We never fought, but George can be stubborn. Anyway, I was frazzled and backed out of the hospital parking lot too quickly."

I took a page from Frank's book and started to circle my kitchen, but the phone cord was too short. "Who'd you hit?" I asked as I returned to my original spot.

"I hit a parked car in the hospital parking lot," Dotty whispered. "And then I drove away." She started to giggle, and I felt certain her personality had been pharmaceutically mellowed. "It all seems so silly now that George is dead."

"Do you know who you hit?"

"No idea," Dotty said, and she started to laugh again. I heard some voices in the background, and I hoped she had a solid support system. "My sister is here," Dotty said. "Will I see you tomorrow?"

"Sure thing," I replied as I processed Dotty's new information. The car she hit belonged to Adam. That meant either Adam or someone with access to Adam's car had been at the hospital, but that didn't make sense. The Calhouns weren't that close to George. In fact, George had made it clear he didn't like Adam or his parents. "One more thing," I said. "Is everything okay at your house? Do you feel safe?"

Dotty started to whisper again, and I imagined her cupping her hand over the phone. "I don't feel safe. George came home for a reason, and I don't know why."

Neither did I, but I had some ideas. "Dotty, I'm sorry to keep bothering you, but would it be okay for me to look through George's desk in the basement? I'm wondering why he came home too, and I'd feel safer if we looked into it."

"It would be nice to see a friendly face," Dotty responded. "I can't stand my sister." She giggled again.

———

I walked slowly up the stairs to the attic. I poked my head into Roon's bedroom on the second floor. He had pulled himself up and was calmly peering over the edge of his crib. "You got some moves there," I whispered, and then I picked him up and balanced him on my hip. "Let's find your mom."

Instead of crying, this time he smiled. Those potatoes, I thought. Our little secret. I jogged up the final flight of stairs and then placed Roon on the floor. He immediately assumed his four-legged pose. "How goes it?" I asked.

"Not good," my mother said. "Not good at all." My mother's shirt was untucked and she'd discarded her shoes. The attic reeked of vinegar.

"If I donate any more blood to this project," Dominic said, "I'll need a transfusion."

I leaned over the samples. Even Katrina's non-toxic solutions and pastes had removed our bloody prints. On the upside, it made me feel pretty good about the cleanliness of our house. Dominic came over and held up a small canvas for me to look at. Clean as a whistle. "Quite the quandary," he said, "but we'll keep at it."

He smiled and I had to admit, he was a charming man. Dominic winked at my mother. She lowered her eyes, and I realized this thing between the two of them was real. Dominic had the cool confidence of a younger man, but it was tempered by his years of life experience. Kind of like an older Charlie. With his scraggly ponytail and his beach-weathered skin, I could see how my mother found him attractive, and it wasn't an aging hippy vibe either. The beach bum look on older men creeped me out, but Dominic had style. His button-down shirt was expensive, as were his belt and shoes. I was impressed. *Good for you, Mom*, I thought.

I also realized their newfound attraction would buy me a few hours. These two were looking for a reason to be together, and my fingerprint project had them engrossed.

"Are you guys okay if I step out for a few?" They nodded in unison. I could have asked them to skin a cow and they would have said yes.

Katrina trailed behind me with Roon reattached to her side. "I need a cigarette after hanging out with them," she laughed. "They're like two horny teenagers."

It was true and apparently, I wasn't the only one who had noticed the attraction between my mother and Dominic. I stopped short on the main floor and turned back to Katrina. "When I get back, we'll watch the band videos. Cross my heart."

I hoped I could keep my promise.

———

I had no difficulty finding Charlie. He and Frank were sitting in a police car, parked in front of Dotty's house. I knocked on the window.

"Open the door," I mouthed, my breath condensing on the window. Frank released the lock, and I climbed in the back. Since I'd met Frank, I'd spent way too much time in a police car. It tended to raise eyebrows. The curtain on Dotty's living room window slid open and then closed. The unlikeable sister wasn't pleased by our presence.

"What's up?"

"I didn't kill Fletcher," Charlie said, "but I came close to ripping Ricky's face off today."

I stared at the back of Frank's head. "What happened?"

"Charlie gave us a reason to bring Ricky in," he said. "I couldn't have set it up any better myself."

Charlie's neck was red as he continued to seethe from his apparent altercation with Fletcher's assistant. He shifted his shoulders and spoke to me through the police grate. "I'm checking out the meters and little Ricky comes marching across Fletcher's lawn. He accused me of trespassing, seducing Jamie and—oh yeah—murdering his boss."

"Two out of three ain't bad," I said. Then I turned my attention to Frank. "Is that why you're here?"

"Charlie called us. It was the right move; by the time we got here, Ricky's behavior had escalated. It was enough to cuff him. Neither he nor Fletcher own the Green Acres properties, and he had no right to threaten Charlie."

"Charlie must have done something specific to piss him off," I said.

"That's where it gets interesting," Frank said. Then he turned to Charlie and grinned.

Charlie held his cell phone up for me to see. The glass face was shattered, but I could make out the word *beta*. "It's the app Fletcher and I were working on."

"Ah. What's it do?"

"Something Ricky didn't want it to do," Frank said. "Hence the smashed phone."

Charlie nodded and his expression became animated. For a guy who had mastered the art of blasé, he couldn't hide his enthusiasm for his pet projects. "Solar panel companies offer software with a few nice tracking tools," he started. "Most homeowners slap up panels and then forget about them. They'll check their monthly bill, see the savings, and move on. However, if a homeowner is so inclined, the standard panel software allows you to analyze your system in real time. You might notice that one of your panels is underproducing, so you decide to cut back a few trees. The software can also alert you to a damaged panel."

"Okay, I get it," I said.

"The software also provides the homeowner with energy comparison reports by day, month, and year. This way you can see how much you're actually saving within specified time frames," Charlie said. "Remember how I showed you our meter after we got the panels?"

My knowledge on this topic was thin, but I did remember feeling a certain level of satisfaction seeing an arrow move in the opposite direction. "The meter shows energy being subtracted."

"Basically," Charlie explained, "the meter is doing two things at once. It's calculating the kilowatts consumed and the kilowatts produced. The left arrow shows your panels at work and the right arrow indicates the electricity being used. At the end of the month, your bill compares the cumulative production versus consumption and then credits your account appropriately."

"You may get a check back," I said.

"That's correct."

"So what does your app do?"

Charlie tapped at his splintered phone and a small chart appeared. It was difficult to see through the cracked glass, but I could make out the outline of a house. It looked like an open doll house.

"My app is for the discerning environmentalist. It allows the user to enter all of their household items that use electricity. Everything from your washing machine to your curling iron. The app ties into your meter and gives you a granular breakdown of kilowatt hour consumption by device. This way you can see which gadgets or appliances are counterbalancing your production."

Frank nodded. "Interesting," he said, although it obviously wasn't the first time it had been explained to him.

"It also links to your utility company. Depending on where you live, utility companies charge varying amounts at different times of the day. That's why the eco-nuts will do their laundry in the middle of the night. My app helps you adjust your energy-using activities based on utility pricing."

I had a hard time imagining Phoebe waiting until after midnight to blow dry her hair. "It's an environmentalist's dream," I complimented Charlie. "Was Ricky upset because you and Fletcher left him out of this groundbreaking new app?"

"I think he was upset he couldn't stop the app from getting past the beta phase," Frank said. He motioned to Charlie, who worked his way up to the punch line.

"I'd tested the app at our house, and I'd tested it at Fletcher's," Charlie said, "but it never worked properly at Green Acres and that set us back a few months. Today, I decided that maybe my app wasn't the problem."

"And?"

"A few months back, I thought my app was faulty because this neighborhood's houses' net output didn't make sense. The Green Acres houses appear to be overproducing kilowatt hours, but the appliances and gadgets, when studied individually, weren't draining the excess. Their individual usage didn't match the total usage on the Green Acres meters. I kept going back to my code, but today I thought, maybe it's the meters. Maybe the Green Acres meters are off."

"So all of the meters are broken?"

"More like a leak," Frank explained.

Charlie raised his eyebrow. "In the industry, it's called siphoning. If my app is correct, someone is siphoning off the excess capacity produced by Green Acres."

An intangible theft. I was intrigued. It's not like stealing jewelry or a television or even cold hard cash. You can't touch power. You can only see the result of it, and Charlie's application provided residents with the detail behind the power. Without his application in full roll-out, the siphoning was undetectable.

"That's why the residents aren't getting utility credits," I said.

Frank's smile stretched across his day-old beard. He loved a good brain-teaser and hearing the solution explained twice in the last hour was doubly satisfying.

"So why would Fletcher endorse your app?" I asked.

"He didn't know what was happening," Frank said. "Remember you mentioned the angle of the panels in Westchester. Those panels, like these, are positioned to produce the most energy, but not in a way that benefits the grid as a whole. Someone, I'm guessing Ricky, created this setup for volume."

"So he could convert the excess into Renewable Energy Credits and sell them on the commodities market," Charlie added. "Ricky benefits, not the grid; and certainly not the homeowners."

I sat back and thought about the solar-stealing scheme. "Times ten developments."

"And that's where it really gets interesting," Frank said. "If Ricky is doing this at every development, then we're talking big money."

"That's why he still works for Fletcher," I said.

Frank held up a utility bill addressed to Green Acres, Inc. "Cheski remembered the day Ricky came by Fletcher's to pick up the mail. Apparently he wasn't too keen on leaving empty-handed."

"He was interested in the bills," I confirmed. I wondered if Ricky was in the Fletcher home looking for those bills the night Gayle and I were snooping around Fletcher's yard.

Frank unfolded a sheet of paper and held it up.

I whistled when I saw the credit. "A family of four could get by on this."

"It's enough to power a stadium for a month," Charlie said.

I just shook my head at the waste of that scenario. "I can't believe Fletcher didn't know."

"I had a discussion with his general practitioner earlier today," Frank said. "His doctor said there were signs of early dementia."

Charlie agreed. "In retrospect, we could have completed this app much faster, but every time I met with Fletcher I had to explain it from the beginning. I thought he was just being thorough."

"I think Jamie suspected Fletcher was losing it," I said to Charlie. "That's why she asked you if Fletcher had appeared distracted. She wanted confirmation."

"So she wasn't hitting me?" Charlie asked, crestfallen.

"Amazing," I said and frowned, "but true." I felt badly for Jamie, but if you marry a man twice your age, time eventually catches up.

Frank was still studying the bills. "I believe Ricky was waiting Fletcher out. He probably thought his duties would expand as Fletcher's deterioration accelerated. But here's my issue: Fletcher's murder draws a lot of eyes to Green Acres. Ricky needed Fletcher's role in the business to wind down naturally so he could step in without drawing attention to the transfer of leadership. Fletcher's untimely death works against Ricky."

"Maybe Charlie's app forced his hand," I said. "He needed to get rid of Fletcher before his siphoning scheme was discovered."

"Cheski's got Ricky at the station," Frank said. "He'll stall until we can come up with something concrete."

Frank's phone rang. He listened without speaking and then hung up. "We've got a problem," he said gravely. "That was Gayle. Adam's friend Tobey texted her about Adam. Apparently, Adam has gone gaming commando on his friends. He's blowing the crap out of his own online team members."

I looked over at the Calhouns' house. Somewhere in their overpriced eco-friendly home, an unhappy teenager had melted down. "He's afraid," I said. "He knows his friends told you he wasn't in his own house the night of the murder. He knows you're getting closer."

"I think it's time to check out George's basement," Frank said.

THIRTY-ONE

DOTTY SEEMED RELIEVED TO see me and although the timing was awkward with a house full of relatives, she gave us free reign of the basement. Frank took the time to speak privately with Dotty and positioned the visit as a safety precaution, which seemed to satisfy her skeptical sister. Dotty gave us a list of potential passwords for George's computer, and we ducked downstairs with plates of food.

George's basement looked exactly as I'd left it. I made a beeline for his paper calendar and proceeded to explain the starred dates to Charlie and Frank.

"So you think he tracked the blackouts?" Frank asked.

"But not after the fact," I explained. "*Before* the fact." I opened my bag and pulled out my notepad. "See this date?" I pointed to the day George died. "It was on his calendar before he passed away, but the event occurred the night he left the hospital. Somehow he knew when the blackouts were going to occur."

Frank tilted his head and looked down at George's desk calendar and then turned to Charlie. "If you had to set up a system

241

to siphon electricity from all of these houses, wouldn't it be easier if the homes were connected? Literally, wired together?"

"Of course," Charlie said. "I'm sure Ricky had these houses wired to a central site like a master meter. Wherever that meter is located, it's generating the bills you showed us. His siphoning setup must accumulate credits through one meter with one bill. Otherwise he wouldn't be able to control all the credits."

Frank walked the perimeter of the room and returned to George's desk. He pointed to the computer. "Every six months or so, I read about a national retailer whose credit card system gets hacked. Consumers all over the country worry that their bank information is compromised," Frank took a breath and looked at Charlie. "How does that work? From the hacker's perspective."

Charlie shrugged. "It's pretty easy. The hacker isn't going after each outlet in the chain. They're simply tapping into the store's centralized system."

Frank nodded. "So if we think these houses are connected, couldn't the houses be hacked the same way? Through a central system?"

"It couldn't be," Charlie laughed as he spun around in the desk chair. He patted George's computer like a puppy and pulled open some drawers. "Expensive tools, a state-of-the art security system, and a high-end computer. I think we've underestimated our friendly neighborhood watchman," he said and then began to pound away at the keyboard. "If the houses are connected—and I'm sure they are—then George could have hacked the central system with one easy program." Charlie reached for George's calendar with the starred dates. "He could have preprogrammed these blackouts."

"But why?" I asked. "Even if he was capable of hacking the

electrical system, why would *George* cause an uproar in his own neighborhood?"

Charlie looked at me like I was nuts. "Because that's what hackers do. And based on the setup of this basement, George was no Sunday DIYer. He probably got a kick of inconveniencing his neighbors for a half hour every few weeks while he cranked up his generator."

I wasn't convinced. "He started his generator manually. Why wouldn't he simply program it to start when the blackouts occurred? It's not like he didn't know when it would happen."

Frank jumped in. "Because he needed to appear as if he was as caught off-guard as the neighbors. If his behavior was prescient, the neighbors would have picked up on it."

"Or Dotty," I said. "She's no dummy. She would have noticed if George wasn't tinkering with the generator." I paused. "But I'm still questioning his motivation."

"Big-time hackers shut down entire government systems just for the thrill of it," Charlie reminded me. "George got his rocks off in his own backyard, and he had a front-row seat to his own events. It probably seemed like benign fun in the beginning."

"Until something went wrong," Frank noted.

"Very wrong," I said as I moved my finger across the calendar. People were dead and George's hack may have been the catalyst. "I wonder what George saw from that front row."

"Apparently enough to cause a heart attack," Frank said.

Now I understood why George wanted Dotty to bring his computer to the hospital. He wanted to un-program the mess he'd made. "And here's our problem," I said. "If George did hack the system, then we're due for another blackout sometime today."

Frank tapped the date with a pen. "Adam was on to George,"

he said. "He must have been in this basement at some point and seen George's calendar. Then he planned his own game by piggybacking on George's hacking. He opened it up to his friends, and now his friends have ratted him out."

"So he's blowing them up virtually," I moaned.

"Look," Charlie said. "I'm not saying I'm the poster child for teenage delinquents, but based on personal experience, I think you've dismissed Adam's friends too quickly. Who's to say they're not guilty?"

"It's a good question," Frank said, "but their actions subsequent to George's death have been appropriate. They've all shown up at the station, no lawyers, and they've admitted to being participants in Adam's game. And now we find out that Tobey has contacted Gayle to warn her about Adam's online gaming activity. The only one who hasn't cooperated is Adam. He's definitely the kingpin."

"Phoebe was worried about that," Charlie confirmed. "She knows her son is the ringleader."

"I think Kevin tried to get his stepson to stop roaming the neighborhood a few months ago," Frank said. "Adam's behavior was probably taxing his marriage."

Phoebe and her men. There was never a shortage of guys lusting after Phoebe. I shook my head. "So you guys really think Phoebe is cute?" Both of the men in my life nodded affirmatively. "Cute enough for her husband to intervene in Adam's issues?" I asked. "Kevin is just the stepdad. He could have ignored it."

"I think he tried to do the right thing by Phoebe," Charlie said. "He stepped up to the plate and tried to discipline Adam."

Frank continued in his support of Kevin Calhoun. "Like the other residents, the Calhouns blamed the blackouts on Fletcher and Ricky, but for them the blackouts were magnified by Adam's bad behavior. I think Kevin knew Adam had spiraled and then their worst fear came true. A serious crime occurred with Adam mixed up in it."

"So let's assume Adam saw something," I offered. "He's scared. His parents are scared. They buy him a car as a bribe to stay put and keep his mouth shut."

"If he didn't kill Fletcher, why wouldn't he just tell Frank what he saw?" Charlie asked.

"That's where I'm stuck," Frank said, and then he turned to Charlie. "Can you de-hack a hacked system?"

Charlie ran down the list of potential passwords from Dotty. He tested a couple of combinations until 'name of first pet' with 'birth date' worked. "First we'll have to confirm that George is the hacker," he said as his fingers flew over the keys. "I'm not totally ruling out Ricky or Adam or one of Adam's friends."

It took all of ten minutes before Charlie lifted his hands off the keyboard. "I stand corrected. Our hacker is definitely Mr. George Fraser." He pointed to the screen, and it filled with lines of what appeared to be Greek. Charlie leaned into the screen. "It's a straight-forward sequence of code," he said as he ran the cursor about halfway down the page. "Should I disable it?"

Frank twirled a pen in his hands. "What if we just played with it? You know, like maybe turned it off and on when no one expects it."

"That would really mess with Adam's head," I said.

Frank smiled and crossed his arms over his chest. "Let me throw something out there. What do think happens here, at Green Acres, when the lights go out?"

I took a stab at Frank's question. "Assuming Adam knew George's schedule, he and his crew descend upon the neighborhood. They enter houses, maybe steal a few items, and leave before their time is up."

Frank scratched his day-old beard. "What about Ricky?"

"Based on what we know," I said, "Fletcher sent Ricky to Green Acres to investigate the blackouts."

"But now that Fletcher is gone," Frank challenged. "Is there any need for Ricky to follow up on the blackouts?"

Charlie hit a few keys and answered. "Forget Fletcher. It was in Ricky's best interest to come to Green Acres during the blackouts. He would have shown up even without Fletcher's instructions because the blackouts threatened his siphoning scheme. The last thing he wants is someone examining the meters."

"George's little hack must have been driving Ricky nuts," I said. "Every time the lights flickered, Ricky's scam could be exposed."

"And then Fletcher came down on him," Charlie said.

"What about Phoebe and Kevin?" Frank wondered. "What do you think they did during the blackouts?"

"They tried to keep Adam in the house to avoid more trouble," I said, and then I stopped. Something didn't make sense. "The night George died, Adam *was* in his house. I know because I ran up to the Calhouns' door and Adam answered."

"But he could have been outside before you arrived," Frank said.

I shook my head. I wasn't so sure.

"And that bothers you?" Charlie asked.

I pinched my fingers together to demonstrate. "A bit," I said as I tried to re-create the events of the night in my head. I remembered Kevin handing me a tissue as I cried over George's body. Now his presence seemed too convenient. If Adam was inside, why was Kevin outside during the blackout? Then I remembered seeing Phoebe when I knocked on the door. Her face was rosy and she

246

had blown on her hands. I thought it was anger, but maybe she was cold. Had she been outside with Kevin while Adam was in the house? I explained my recollections to Frank and Charlie.

Frank searched around George's desk. Then he leaned over Charlie's shoulder and pushed a button on the side of the computer. A CD ejected. It had the same label as the one I had given Frank. "This is George's copy of the security footage from the night Fletcher was murdered. It shows Phoebe calling for Adam on the night of the murder. Let's watch it again."

Charlie started the video and my stomach turned uneasily. Simon Fletcher was alive before the blackout, but by the end of this footage, he'd be dead. I thought about Jamie, taking a shower, unaware that her husband was about to be murdered. Within the next fifteen minutes, she'd drag her husband's body through her house in an effort to cover up a secret driven by love. It broke my heart.

We watched as Phoebe came down her driveway. With her hands around her mouth, she called out into the night and then returned to her house. We let the video continue for fifteen more minutes. Periodically, either Adam or one his friends darted across the screen.

"No different than the first time," Frank said. Charlie was about to stop the video when a figured appeared by the side of the house. "Well, I guess that confirms it," Frank said. It was Adam returning home. We waited another minute and watched as Phoebe opened the front door to let Adam inside. But then, like the first scene, she walked down the driveway again, and repeated her calls. "This part was cut from the version I received," Frank said slowly. "Let it roll."

"She just let Adam in the front door," Charlie said, brow furrowed. "Who the hell is she calling for now?"

We watched a cold and frustrated Phoebe Calhoun as she called out into the night. It was dark and the footage was grainy, but light from George's generator cast just enough glow to detect Phoebe's body language. She wasn't happy. After about a minute, she turned on her heels and marched up to her front door and slammed it.

"Maybe her dog snuck out?" I asked.

Frank shook his head. The CD ended and he ejected the disc. "There's only one other possibility. She's calling for Kevin," he said. "He must have gone after Adam."

"This is getting ugly," I said. "Adam is home, Kevin is still outside, and by now Fletcher is dead."

Charlie took the CD from Frank and pushed it back into the slot. He pointed to the top corner of the screen. "Look at the time. I'd just returned to Fletcher's house and found his body and Kevin is still not home."

"So now we've got two people, Kevin and Adam, who weren't where they said they were," Frank said. "We also know, by Ricky's own admission, that he had returned to the property." Frank stopped and rubbed his jaw. He smiled and I could see he was agitated, but in a good way. Like he was two twists away from solving Rubik's cube.

"What is it, Frank?" I asked. "You've thought of something."

"I have," he admitted and then turned to Charlie. "You've only been to this development a few times. What's one of the first things you noticed?"

"That I'd rather die than live in an overpriced cookie-cutter neighborhood with a bunch of misinformed blowhards."

Frank laughed. "After that."

Charlie ejected the CD. "I have to say that George's house

caught my eye. He's got cameras mounted in an inordinate number of places. It's a little odd."

"I notice that too," I added.

"If we noticed," Charlie said, "I'm sure the neighbors were aware that George was keeping watch." He twirled the CD on his finger.

"Keep going," Frank said.

Charlie spun the CD around his finger faster. "If all of these people were up to no good on the night Fletcher was murdered, they may have been worried that George's cameras captured their activities on that fatal night."

"Exactly what I was thinking," Frank said. "I wonder if any of the suspects approached George about it. Maybe even threatened him and his wife." Frank made an efficient circle around the room, almost as if he was narrowing in on the answer. "Ricky suspects George is manipulating the electrical, but he's not sure how. Ricky tries to circumvent his boss's anger by arriving on the scene of the blackout before he's been summoned. His perfectly timed arrival also prevents Fletcher from calling the electric company himself, which Ricky can't allow. If Fletcher spoke directly to the utility company, someone would eventually figure out Ricky's siphoning scheme."

"Go on," I encouraged.

Frank nodded and then continued. "It's possible Ricky argued with George first and then marched over to Fletcher's. In the meantime, Adam and his friends are on the loose. Kevin comes outside to look for Adam. Maybe he stops by George's first and then follows Adam and finds him at Fletcher's."

"Three men and one bat," I said.

"And one security tape," Charlie said.

"They're all worried that they're on this tape—Ricky, Kevin, and Adam," Frank said.

I suddenly remembering the dents in both Dotty and Adam's car. "One of the Calhouns was at the hospital while George was recuperating," I said as I explained the connection. "I think one of them threatened George."

Frank nodded. "I'm not surprised," he said. "It appears everyone had something to lose and George was the keeper of their fate. If George was able to hack the system, then he had probably figured out that Ricky was siphoning energy. He was also well aware of Adam's game, and he must have realized how angry it had made Kevin."

"How do you think George figured out Rick was siphoning the solar power?" I asked.

Charlie tapped on the keyboard and pulled up a schematic of George's roof panels. "We have the same software at Harbor House. It's pretty easy to get a feel for your panel productivity." Charlie pointed at one of the panels. "This panel is underperforming the others. If I were George, I'd be up on a ladder to make sure nothing was obscuring the panel."

"Okay, but I don't see how George made the leap from this drawing to his bill."

"George was smart enough to do by hand what my app is programmed to perform," Charlie sighed. "He calculated his usage for his major appliances and computed the total of his bill and then subtracted the panel production."

"So he knew Ricky and Adam were up to no good and yet he continued to manipulate them," I said as I frowned. "I don't think I like George much anymore."

"I think George enjoyed being a master manipulator," Frank

confirmed. "Remember how quickly he found us when we were walking the neighborhood?"

It was true. George had materialized out of thin air.

"I don't think he could control what he'd created."

"So what now?" I asked.

"Well," Frank replied. "We've got three suspects, no murder weapon, and almost no circumstantial evidence."

We sat quietly for a few minutes. I listened to Dotty and her family moving around upstairs. Poor Dotty. Did she know what George had done? I looked up to find Frank staring at me.

"What?" I said.

"I need that fingerprint," he said.

I shook my head. "I don't know if we can make it work," I protested. At this point, I guessed my mother and Dominic had given up and were rolling around on my futon leaving a different type of evidence. "It's not that easy."

"You have to keep trying," Frank insisted.

"What do you want to me to do about the program?" Charlie asked. "Should I shut it down?"

"Shut it down," Frank confirmed. "Our priority is safety and this neighborhood is not safe with no electricity." He motioned to leave, but he left the CD out in plain view.

"You're leaving it here?" I asked.

"I'm hoping someone steals it," he said. "And maybe leaves a fingerprint in the process. A print I can match to the one you're going to find."

"That's a bit of a stretch. We leave and the suspect strolls in," I said.

"Not now," Frank said. "During George's funeral, when the house is empty."

"You seem pretty confident about this," I said.

"I do. That's because Charlie's going to rewrite George's program to shut off the electricity at eleven a.m. tomorrow. Dotty and her family will be out and their security system will be down without George here to start the generator. If I were a thief or a murderer, I'd take full advantage of the situation. It may be their last chance."

Frank picked up his phone and dialed. "Release Ricky," he said to Cheski. "I'll explain later."

"What if more than one person shows up?" Charlie asked.

"That's why CeCe is going to get me a fingerprint by morning. That bloody print has to belong to someone."

THIRTY-TWO

KATRINA MET ME AT the front door with a bowl of popcorn. "It's time," she said as she two-stepped across the room. My mother and Dominic had already settled on the couch, ready to vote on Katrina's wedding band.

"No luck on the print?" I asked.

They both shook their heads. I didn't have the heart to tell them our work wasn't over. Katrina brought over a bowl of pennies and made equal piles. "We'll use the pennies to vote on our favorite bands."

"One penny per vote?" I asked.

"Oh no," Katrina said. "If you really like a band, you can blow the whole stack."

The doorbell rang and Gayle and Kelly arrived to join the festivities. "I have a soft spot for seventies disco," Kelly admitted as he grabbed for his pile of pennies.

"I'm a big band man, myself," Dominic offered. "Though I'll settle for a good Sinatra impersonator if the mood strikes me."

Katrina was so excited I couldn't help but get swept up in the wedding-band fervor. "I'm partial to sappy movie themes," I said as I hummed the tune from *The Bodyguard*.

Gayle took her pennies last. She seemed preoccupied as she created an orderly line of coins.

"Gayle?" Kelly asked. "Is this too corny for you?"

"I'm fine," she blushed. "I'm not really a dancer. I don't think I'll be much help picking wedding bands."

Dominic titled his head. "At my age, I don't have time to beat around the bush. I'm guessing what you're saying is that you've never been asked to dance by a boy."

Gayle's face grew redder still.

"I've danced with plenty of boys," Kelly said with a smile. "You'll get the hang of it."

Gayle's face relaxed, and she hugged her dad. I enjoyed seeing Kelly and Gayle interact. Kelly was open and understanding with his daughter, and they seemed so natural together. I wondered why Kelly's life as a gay man had turned out so differently than Jamie's. Why had Jamie chosen to hide while Kelly lived an open and fulfilling life? I understood that Fletcher's generation coupled with his public persona made it more difficult for him to live openly, but I wasn't sure I understood why Jamie was so content to accommodate Simon. At the police station, she clearly stated that she could have gone either way on gender, but she then chose to please Simon. According to Simon's first wife, Simon had plucked Jamie straight from a master's program, so I assumed she had half a brain. This couldn't have been purely about money. It's not like the secretary marrying the boss. Had Jamie been that starstruck by the famous Simon Fletcher?

I looked at my mother, and I remembered how she had always

allowed my father, the famous doctor, to take the lead. It was all so typical, but as typical as Jamie and Simon's relationship seemed, it still held close to traditional male/female roles. I considered the videos we were about to watch and my stomach turned in discomfort. If you want a primer on traditional gender roles, all you had to do was watch a bride being "given away" by her father. Throw in two cows and some chickens and you've got yourself one hefty dowry. I guess my future husband would have to be happy with a bag of garbage.

As Katrina set up the videos, I wasn't sure I could watch the brides dance with their fathers. Who wrote "Daddy's Little Girl," anyway? If she's that little, why the hell are you giving her away?

Katrina fired up the first video of a band with more hair than Phoebe could produce in a lifetime. "This hurts my eyes," I mocked and the room burst into laughter. We continued to watch as band after band put forth their best effort to impress future brides. These promotional videos were the best of the best, but it played more like a reel of wedding bloopers. The funniest parts were the awkward footage of couples dancing their first dance. About halfway through, we switched to using our pennies to bet on the future of the marriages based on the couple's dancing coordination.

"He's stepped on her foot twice," my mother chuckled. "I give it a year."

For all the bad match-ups, I was sincerely impressed with, and somewhat jealous of, the couples who appeared deliriously in love, their embraces so tight they barely moved on the dance floor. Katrina stopped the video and started to tear up.

"What is it?" I asked.

"They just seem," she blathered, "so in love."

"But so are you," my mother consoled. "Isn't that why we're here?"

"It is, and I am in love," Katrina said. "I love Jonathan with all of my heart, but I'm watching these videos, and I wonder how much of a sacrifice marriage will be."

Interesting, I thought, borrowing a word from Frank. I wondered about Jamie's sacrifices for Fletcher. I wondered if Dotty had politely ignored George's basement shenanigans, and I wondered about Kevin's commitment to Phoebe. Katrina was right—this marriage thing seemed like a lot of work. My face soured, but then I thought about Charlie. We weren't in love, but our friendship alone was enough to get me to stand by his side, almost threatening my relationship with Frank. Yet what had I done for Frank? He was the man I loved, but I hadn't done what he needed. I hadn't found the bloody fingerprint.

I counted up the pennies on the coffee table and made an important announcement. "Remember the hair band in the first clip?"

"Oh no," Katrina said. "Not them."

I laughed. "The clear winner."

I looked at my watch. It was past eleven. I had about two more hours in me before I passed out. I turned to my mother and Dominic. "One last try for the team?"

———

We gathered in my attic studio and stared at the sample canvases.

"You know what I love about the art process?" my mother asked, and without waiting she answered. "It's malleable. You paint over what doesn't work." She paused as she studied the photograph of Kwan's forged work. "All Kwan had to do was cover and blend."

"Cover and blend," Dominic repeated. "Cover and blend." He walked over to a sample canvas and held it out, his arms fully extended. He held the frame to its side and then flat like a serving tray. He rested the corner on a table and studied the canvas as he ran his hand over it. "The paint is thicker where we covered up our prints."

My mother and I approached the canvas and moved our hands over it. "The bigger the mistake, the more paint you add," he said as my mother and I felt the slightly raised surface. Dominic pointed to Kwan's forged painting. We laid it carefully on the ground and kneeled around it like a Ouija board. Then we methodically moved our palms over the picture as if we expected Jamie's face to levitate.

"Ohmm," my mother snickered.

"Here," I said as I rubbed a thick spot, "and here." My mother and Dominic confirmed my findings with their own fingertips and we isolated two points of raised paint. "I think we've narrowed down the location, but we still can't remove the paint without ruining the print," I sighed.

Dominic lifted the edge of the frame. "Push lightly on the first spot," he said as he inched his head under the frame. "Okay, now tilt the frame on its side so it's perpendicular to the floor." My mother and I stood up while Dominic stayed on his knees to examine the back of the painting. He winced and I realized the position was uncomfortable for him. I heaved the painting back to my easel. "You can see the back from this position too," I offered.

"I've got an idea," Dominic said as my mother helped him up. "Flip it so the back of the canvas is facing us," he instructed. He then moved quickly to my work table despite his aching knees. He seemed excited as he yanked a desk lamp from the socket. He removed the dusty lamp shade and dragged it over to Jamie's portrait. He stretched the cord to the wall, plugged it in, and stood behind the portrait, lamp in hand.

"These LED lightbulbs are for shit," he grumbled. "I need a good old-fashioned incandescent bulb. The highest wattage you've got."

I frowned. This was not the house for outdated bulbs. We had replaced all of our fixtures years ago in favor of the energy savings. I scooted over to the stairs and called down for Katrina.

"In my closet," she yelled back. "I'm sorry," she apologized as I descended the stairs. "I can't stand dark closets, and the old lightbulbs just work better." Poor Katrina. Her carbon footprint was in the negatives, and yet she still felt guilty for using a single inefficient lightbulb.

I shook my head and ran back upstairs with one eco-unfriendly bulb. I passed it carefully to Dominic. If it broke, we didn't have a replacement. He swapped the bulbs and then stretched the lamp behind the easel.

"Stand in front of the canvas," he instructed. We positioned ourselves as instructed and stared at the back of the canvas. Slowly, very slowly, Dominic slid the lamp, like a metal detector, across the portrait. At one point, Jamie's eyes inadvertently lit up and it freaked me out. Otherwise, the light showed minor imperfections in paint distribution.

"We need more contrast," I said as I turned off the room's overhead light. The layer of darkness accentuated Dominic's work. "Keep going," I said. "Focus on the thick spots. To the right." He moved the lamp. "My right," I correct him, and he laughed.

On the third sweep, we saw it. "Oh my God," I gasped. "I think that's a fingerprint." I could feel the heat of the bulb through the canvas. Any closer and we'd have a small house fire on our hands, but ultimately Dominic's idea was working. A splotchy round image hovered over my signature. I bet Kwan spent most of his time on this very spot because he needed to make sure my signature appeared authentic, despite the extra paint. *That's a lot of cover and blend*, I thought.

I eyed the print and then looked at the pads of my fingers. "A thumb?" I said, but I really had no idea. Frank, of course, would find a print expert.

"Whichever digit it is," my mother added, "it has an owner. It has to belong to someone."

Dominic switched places with me to get a look at his handiwork. "Genius," he said. "I've still got it."

"What now?" my mother asked.

"I guess I'll call Frank and supply him with the evidence."

Dominic reached for my mother's pin-cushioned hand and kissed her fingertips. "Dinner?" It was midnight, but they didn't care.

My mother stretched her free hand out to me and we put our palms together. Our hands were nearly identical. I took one last look at Dominic and my throat closed. Fingerprints are unique to a person, but fingerprint patterns can be inherited. Those are the kind of facts you learn when grow up in the home of a famous geneticist. Just your basic dinner conversation at the Prentice household. My mother and I probably shared similar patterns. If not, then maybe my print patterns matched my father—my biological father, a man I'd never met.

I closed my hand around my mother's and said, "Can I talk to you before you leave? Then I turned to Dominic. "I'll have her downstairs in a jiffy."

Once we were alone, I walked my mother over to a tiny alcove in the corner of the attic.

"Maybe," she said before I could even ask.

"How long have you know?"

"Well," she said, "you're twenty-nine, so I guess I've suspected for about as long."

I leaned against the wall. "Does he know?"

"I don't think he has any idea," she said. "And I'd like to keep it that way. I'm not even sure myself."

"Not to be nosy, but how many men could you have slept with in the year before I was born?"

My mother shrugged. "Have a little sympathy and try to remember I'm currently coming off a thirty-year dry spell."

Thirty years did seem like a long time. "I thought you said my biological father was a German artist."

"That's possible too." My mother squeezed my shoulder. "Don't be mad."

I wasn't mad. My life had unfolded so completely in the past two years that re-creating it was like cutting new puzzle pieces for the same puzzle. It would all come together in the end, but the picture would different, maybe even better. I looked at the stack of canvases with our sample fingerprints. I sighed. Dominic had left behind his own trail of evidence. If I really wanted an answer, I could spend hours comparing our fingerprints, mine and Dominic's, for common patterns, but my neuroses would have to wait. Frank was my priority.

I followed my mother downstairs and then thanked Dominic profusely for his diligence. As soon as the porch door swung shut, I called Frank. He picked up on the first ring.

"Tell me you found the print."

"We found a print," I said. "I think I also may have identified my biological father."

Frank laughed so hard he coughed uncontrollably. He cleared his throat and asked, "Can I tell Cheski?"

"It's not confirmed," I said. "Just a hunch. I'll get back to you when I'm sure."

"Next question," Frank said. "Have you got a black dress?"

I groaned. "I guess that means I'm going to George's funeral." I didn't own a black dress. I didn't even wear black to my brother's funeral, but I chose not to remind him of that fact. "What's my job?"

"I'll need to know who's there. If any of the suspects show up, you'll have to keep your eye on them."

"I'd actually enjoy that," I said, and I meant it. It's much easier to go to a funeral with a purpose other than crying.

"One more thing," Frank added. "Cheski found Kwan. Our forger returned to his apartment after he thought the heat had cooled."

I imagined Cheski pinning Kwan against the wall of his city apartment and threatening him with an empty tube of paint.

"Turns out, Kwan did do the touch-up work on site, at Fletcher's house. According to Kwan, he was met by a man. We showed him pictures of Ricky, Adam, and Kevin—no match."

"That's weird," I said. "I wonder who'll show up tomorrow in George's basement."

"If I'm right," Frank said, "the murderer."

THIRTY-THREE

By mid-morning, I was clothed in a drippy black dress that was too tight in the waist and too long to the ground. My noticeably thinner and taller daughter had brought three dresses for me to try on.

"I can't breathe," I said as I sucked in my stomach.

Gayle grabbed a scissors and snipped the button. "We'll pin it," she said.

I exhaled gratefully and then asked, "What about the length?"

"I usually wear this one with combat boots, but you need an inch or two," she said as she rooted through my closet. "All you've got is sneakers," she laughed as she held out a white tennis shoe with a blue stripe.

"Let's see what Katrina's got in her closet," I said as I unscrewed the bulb in my desk lamp. We hustled over to Katrina's bedroom, where she was curled up with Roon.

"Have you got black heels?" I whispered. I held out the coveted bulb as collateral. She pointed to the closet, where I found a pair of black platform heels only one size too big.

When all was said and done, I bulged at the waist and slid forward in my shoes. My blond hair hung limply to my shoulders and I looked sad without trying. Perfect for George's funeral. I'd be out of luck, however, if I had to make a quick getaway; the dress's hem caught the edge of my new shoes. It would be a miracle if I didn't trip and break my leg before the day was out.

Gayle walked me to the front door to meet Charlie in my ill-fitted funeral attire. "Happy Halloween to you too," he said.

"So what's your assignment today?" I said, ignoring his criticism.

"One of George's neighbors agreed to vacate their house. After I drop you off at the funeral, I'll handle the computer work from the neighbor's house."

"Where will Frank be during the funeral?"

"He'll sit in George's basement and wait."

"In the dark?" I was appalled by Frank's plan.

"Pitch black," Charlie said as he eyed my get-up. "You'd fit right in."

Gayle laughed and then gave me a hug. "Watch out for Adam," she said. "He's got a bit of postal in him."

"Good to know," I said as I pulled Gayle's vintage overcoat around my shoulders. "Let's get this over with."

Charlie and I drove the short distance to St. James church, where my brother was buried.

"This did not end well for us last time," I reminded Charlie as he pulled into the parking lot. Two years ago, Charlie and I were hijacked from this exact spot and then catapulted down a hill into the Long Island Sound.

"That's why I'll be leaving," he said. He pointed to the church doors. "The line is forming."

I winced. "This sucks."

"I think George would agree," Charlie said and then looked at his watch. "Let's hurry it up. I have to get over to Green Acres." He turned and kissed me. A real kiss. The kind I couldn't tell Frank about. "Don't do anything stupid, Ce."

I unhooked the hem of my dress from my shoe. "Too late for that," I said.

———

The church filled up quickly, but I took my time surveying the crowd. I had a purpose this morning, and that was to take a visual inventory of the attendees. Faces were easy for me to remember, and I did a quick sweep of the reception area. Although I'd never met Dotty and George's children, the resemblance was strong. Apparently, the Frasers had two boys, now men in their forties, and a daughter who looked a few years older. They seemed tearful and reserved, as one would expect. Dotty's sister, on the other hand, had taken it upon herself to manage the event like she was backstage at a rock concert. She pointed directly at me and motioned to the door leading to the church's chapel.

I blanked and ran toward the ladies' room. I wasn't ready to sit down, but Dotty's sister had put the pressure on. On my way to the bathroom, I spotted a few of the Green Acres neighbors and then I hit pay dirt. Phoebe Calhoun, hair freshly sprayed, walked out of the bathroom. I stepped behind a statue of the Virgin Mary and lowered my head in genuflection. Phoebe walked past me to take her seat.

Another face caught my eye, and this time I was genuinely

surprised. Ricky was here, and he was making the rounds among the Green Acres neighbors. *That little slime ball,* I thought. He was working George's funeral like a public relations event. I assumed his purpose was to ensure the neighbors that Green Acres was still a safe and desirable place to raise a family. Now that Frank had released Ricky, he probably figured he'd get right back on the horse undermining his dead boss. As far as Ricky was concerned, he was Fletcher's obvious successor. I reached for my phone and texted Frank.

That leaves Kevin, Adam, and his friends unaccounted for, he texted back.

I walked into the church and spotted a seat in the last pew, closest to the door. Dotty's odious sister came up behind me. "I think Dotty would prefer if you sat toward the front."

I leaned in and whispered, "I'm a crier. It would be best for everyone if I sat in the back." I dabbed at my eyes and eventually Dotty's sister gave up and moved on to pester the next unsuspecting funeral guest. I took my seat and noticed Ricky had claimed a spot right up front, as if he expected the priest to give Green Acres a special blessing. Like there was a designated environmental saint— St. Francis of the Ozone. Clearly, Ricky was here to be seen, a sign that the company was still in good hands.

A few rows behind Ricky and off to the side sat Phoebe. Her motive for attending? She wanted guests to believe her family was unconnected to the break-ins and deaths in her neighborhood. Unfortunately for her, I knew better, and I knew someone in her family had visited George in the hospital the day before he died.

The ceremony started promptly at eleven. Charlie, despite his many flaws, was a fanatic when it came to computer programming. I had no doubt that at the moment the priest started his eulogy,

Green Acres had gone dark. My thoughts raced to Frank, crouched in a corner of George's basement. I wasn't happy, but I assumed Cheski was close by and that the two men had a plan of action. Charlie, of course, would also be looped in from his location in the neighbor's home. I tried to take deep breaths and think pleasant thoughts, but the dress's narrow waistline caused me to emit small gasps. The woman next to me patted my arm. Again, I was inadvertently playing the part of mournful parishioner.

I listened while the priest said some surprisingly wonderful things about George. Apparently, George Fraser had volunteered countless hours to computerize the church's files. *Oh boy,* I thought. *That's a bad combination. George and over hundred years of church files? So much for the congregation's privacy.*

I nearly let out a snort of laughter, so I leaned over to yank on my dress hem. Then I saw the back of Ricky's neck snap up. He rose slowly and politely asked his fellow congregants to make room for him as he slid out of his pew and down the side aisle.

He must have somehow known that Green Acres had gone dark. I started to text Frank when I saw Phoebe flip her hair dramatically over her shoulder. An exit, apparently, was as important to her as an entrance. Without any regard for the solemnity of the event, Phoebe heaved her fur coat over her shoulders and made for the doorway.

At this point, George's friends and family started to glance around awkwardly. It was unusual to bail on a funeral, and Phoebe and Ricky's behavior had not gone unnoticed. I texted Frank and then breathed slowly. The woman next to me must have thought I was truly distraught by George's death. "Take a little break, honey," she said. As soon as the crowd refocused on the eulogy, I took my pew-mate's advice and snuck out.

The frigid air and bright sun caught me off-guard. I buttoned Gayle's overcoat and reached into her pocket for my keys. Shoot. I didn't have a car. Charlie had dropped me off. I hobbled in my oversized shoes down to the main road, my dress hiked up to prevent a fall, and then I took off down the street. As I had hoped, my friend Chris was working the pumps at the station.

"You look like you just came from a funeral," he said, as he stared at my outfit. "Or a witches' coven."

"Funeral," I panted. "I need a ride."

Chris was more than happy to drop me at my mother's. He looked at my get-up as he drove. "Who died?" he asked.

"Adam's neighbor."

"The old guy?" Chris cringed. "You sure you're okay?"

I wasn't sure I could answer that question honestly, but I gave Chris the thumbs up. "I'm good," I said as I closed the door of his truck and walked to my mother's front door.

I didn't bother to ring the doorbell even though I assumed Dominic had spent the night. As I suspected, my mother was in the kitchen wearing an alluring cashmere bathrobe. Dominic was wearing my father's pajamas. I'd already seen too much.

"What the hell are you wearing?" my mother asked.

"It's just clothing," I screamed. I had suddenly had it with the comments about my ad-hoc funeral wear. I ran up to my old room and tore through my closet. Luckily, not a lot changes when you're a Freegan, and that would include my style choices. The ten-year-old jeans were a bit tight, but the sweatshirt fit perfectly. *Wildcats* it said across the chest, my high school mascot. In place of Katrina's shoes, I borrowed a costly pair of leather boots from my mother's closet. The boots were for show, not snow, but they fit. I grabbed Gayle's coat again and left through the back door of my childhood home.

"Don't let anyone in," I instructed my mother, still camped in the kitchen with Dominic.

The yard was still thick with snow, and I said a silent prayer for the fate of my mother's designer boots. I jogged slowly up to the back of Charlie's hide-out and texted him.

Have you seen Phoebe or Ricky?

Phoebe is in her house. No sign of Ricky.

How about Adam or Kevin?

I starred at the screen. It was blank. I started to panic. There was something Charlie didn't want to tell me.

Stop stalling.

Kevin entered George's house five minutes ago. No word from Frank.

Where's Cheski?

In the bushes, on the side of George's house. If for some reason I can't get the lights back on, he'll manually turn George's generator on.

I poked my head around a stone wall to get a better view of Phoebe's house. A side door opened and Phoebe stepped outside with her son. Both were bundled up in winter coats. If they were headed to George's, one house over, their layers seemed unnecessary. Conversely, I couldn't imagine them building a snowman together. What was so important that Phoebe had left George's funeral?

I watched her point to their roof. Adam came around to the garage, opened the side door, and dragged out a ladder. Did Phoebe think her delinquent son could fix the problem causing the blackout? Adam leaned the ladder against the side of the house and started to climb. Phoebe planted her sturdy legs in the snow and held the ladder for her son.

Are you getting this? I texted Charlie.

Bizarre, he texted back.

My phone rang. It was Cheski. "I can see you," he said. "Step back."

I buried myself in an evergreen. "Can you see Adam and Phoebe?"

"He's almost on the roof," Cheski said. "What the hell is he doing on the roof?"

"Maybe it's an assisted suicide," I chuckled.

"I can still see you," Cheski said. "Get down," he instructed and then signed off.

I crouched down and the back pockets of my pants met the snow, similar to the night I was out prowling with Gayle. I looked up at the Calhouns' roof. Cheski was right; what the hell did Adam plan on doing once he mounted the roof? Did Phoebe suspect there was something wrong with her solar panels?

I shifted positions to avoid a case of frostbite on my rear end. As scared as I was the night I was out with Gayle, this situation seemed somewhat more unnerving. At night you expect people to do bad things, but it was daylight and Phoebe and Adam's actions didn't feel right. I looked up at the roof and then I remembered the sound Gayle and I had heard on our late-night romp. We'd been behind the Calhouns' house when it happened. A thud and then a crack. Adam was nearing the last rung on the ladder. I watched as he struggled to find his footing.

I dispensed with texting since my fingers were nearly frozen and called Charlie.

"Charlie," I whispered. "You know the schematic you showed us of George's panels? Are you able to access the Calhouns' panels?"

"Yeah, you want me to see if there's something on one of those panels?"

I explained what Gayle and I had heard the night George died. "Something hit the roof and then we heard a crack. Could something hard have damaged a panel?"

I heard Charlie's fingers banging on a keyboard. "Panel number ten," he said. "It's down."

"Where is it?"

"On the other side of the house. He's got a ways to go."

We watched from our separate locations as Adam inched his way across his icy roof. Phoebe stood at the bottom of the ladder, her hands now in a praying position.

"In two key strokes, I could turn the electricity back on and scare the shit out of that kid."

"Don't," I said. "Let's see what he's got and then you can pitch him off the roof or fry him like an egg."

Charlie laughed. "You're sick, but I am worried. Even though the power to the houses is down, that doesn't mean the panels aren't hot and working. Those panels conduct regardless of the electric connection. That's why my app can still read the panels. Adam better watch his step."

From the peak of the house, Adam leaned over and reached down for a solar panel. He pulled his hand quickly away and then rifled in his pocket for a glove. He came up empty-handed and tried, instead, to pull his sleeve over his hand. Once he had some protection, he slid forward using the panel as an anchor. About halfway down the width of the roof, he spread his legs as far apart as possible, like an ice skater with no motor control. Using his free hand, he swung his arm along the roof, and it looked like his hand connected with an object. He walked back toward his mother with something resting along his side. Given his angle and the tilt of the roof, I couldn't make out what he'd retrieved, but his steps quickened, and I could see he wanted to get back to solid ground. I didn't particularly like Adam, but I secretly willed him to slow down. If he fell off the roof onto a pile of ice, it wouldn't be pretty.

Adam picked up his pace and sure enough, he wobbled, straightened, and then lost his balance. It was nearly noon and the roof was a mixture of melting ice sheets and hot solar panels. A solid sheet of ice released and shattered on the ground below. Adam's foot slid out from under him and his hand opened. He went down hard, but not before I saw a Louisville Slugger slip from his fist.

I don't know how many baseball bats were floating around the neighborhood, but I felt strongly that this hunk of polished lumber was the murder weapon.

I heard Phoebe yelp. I waited, unsure what to do, but after a moment, Adam righted himself pushing his skinny video game arms to the limit, and limped toward the ladder. He was hurt ... and empty-handed.

"Holy shit, the murder weapon is on the roof," I cried into the phone, but I wasn't connected to either Charlie or Cheski. I stood up and watched as Adam descended the ladder. Within seconds, Cheski flew across the cul-de-sac, gun in hand. He slammed Adam to the ground and buried the boy's face in snow. He jerked Adam's arms around his back and cuffed him to a copper downspout. Phoebe, in her fur coat, crumpled to the ground like road kill. Cheski pointed his gun at Phoebe and then back at Adam. He repeated the motion, swaying back and forth between the two suspects, and I realized he needed backup.

I was all he had.

THIRTY-FOUR

CHESKI FROWNED AT ME. "Don't you usually bring an infant and your teenage daughter to these showdowns?"

"You're lucky I'm here."

Cheski took a Taser out of his pocket and handed it to me. "Ta da," he said. "You're deputized. You escort Phoebe into the house. I'll take Adam."

Phoebe walked willingly into house. Once inside, I removed my coat and held firm to the Taser. My high school sweatshirt stood out as a reminder of my history with Phoebe.

"You never liked me," she said.

"Nope," I replied.

I led Phoebe into the kitchen and asked her to stay put. Cheski placed me in the hallway to watch Phoebe and then he sat Adam down in the living room.

"Did you put the bat on the roof?" he asked Adam.

Adam's face crumbled, but he refused to answer.

Phoebe yelled from the kitchen, "I threw the bat on the roof."

Cheski nodded at me and I motioned to Phoebe. "He needs ice on that ankle," she said as she grabbed a pack from the freezer. I followed her into the living room and Cheski allowed her to sit next to her son and tend to his ankle. "Adam didn't kill anyone," she said.

"You lied about the bushy-eyed boy outside your window," I shot back.

Phoebe tossed her hair. I took that as a yes.

"Where did you get the bat?" Cheski asked.

"None of your business," Phoebe answered.

"I'm a cop," Cheski said in disbelief. "It's my business to ask about a murder weapon."

Phoebe clammed up, and I thought Cheski was about to choke her. Instead he turned to Adam. "If your fingerprints are on this bat, you're going to jail for murder."

"You saw me touch the bat."

Good point, I thought.

"Did your mother ask you to retrieve the bat?" Cheski asked.

"Ask her," Adam said defiantly.

"Ask him," Phoebe shot back.

This was quickly spiraling into a "Who's on First" sketch.

Cheski stood up and put his hands on his slimmed-down but still thick hips. "Mrs. Calhoun, where's your husband?"

Phoebe looked nervously at Adam. He shook his head. Apparently, they didn't know Kevin was in George's basement.

"Here's a heads-up," Cheski said. "Your husband is with Detective DeRosa, and you won't have a chance to speak with him to concoct a story before this blows up." He smiled. "That means you've got a dilemma. You're either protecting your husband or you're protecting your son. You'll need to make a decision in . . ." Cheski started to count off his fingers.

"Stop," Phoebe yelled. "Adam was out on the night Fletcher was murdered, but he didn't kill anyone."

"So that leaves your husband," Cheski said, satisfied with his line of inquiry.

Phoebe sobbed as strands of over-bleached hair stuck to her powdered cheeks. "We don't have to talk to you," she said. "We don't have to say anything."

"I'm not interviewing you as a suspect," Cheski challenged. "I'm interviewing you as a witness. If you've got nothing to hide, then just tell me what you know."

"I don't know who killed Fletcher," she insisted. "I found the bat in my garage under a tarp. I waited for a blackout, then I threw it on the roof when I thought no one would see me."

Just like Jamie's portrait, I thought. *No one ever thinks to look up.* And then I remembered George's final words – *Look up.* He knew.

"That's your story?" Cheski said.

Phoebe wiped her eyes and reached for Adam's hand. He inched away. Cheski caught Adam's body language and decided to focus on the boy. He pulled a puffy hassock toward the couch, sat down, and got right up into Adam's face.

"You called your mother at the funeral to tell her there was another blackout. You two figured it would be an opportunity to get the bat and hide it somewhere safer than your roof."

"I figured most people were at the funeral and the panels would be off," Adam admitted and then added, "I didn't realize they would still be hot."

"Your prints are on that bat," Cheski said, and then he cocked an eyebrow. "You seem to think I saw you pick up the bat, but I don't remember it that way at all." He paused and then raised his palms. "It's your word against mine."

Adam started to shake. The movement started in his legs and then travelled up his torso. He had a three-inch metal cross hanging from his earlobe. It vibrated. That's when I knew we had him.

Cheski reached for the earring and Adam recoiled.

"I was in Fletcher's house," he said. "My friends and I were sneaking into houses around the neighborhood."

"Tell us something we don't know," I muttered.

"Go on," Cheski said.

"I came in a back door and snuck into the master bedroom." Adam paused and put his hand up to his quivering chin. "I think my stepdad might have followed me."

"Why?"

"He doesn't like my behavior."

"So your stepdad was in Fletcher's house?"

"Yeah. That's what I said."

"What happened in the master bedroom?"

"The shower was on," he said. "It freaked me out. I wasn't there to see naked people."

"That's what the Internet is for," Cheski chuckled, trying to soften Adam up.

Adam actually smiled. "I was about to leave when I heard someone coming down the hall toward the bedroom. I was trapped so I crawled under the bed."

"And then?"

"I heard my stepdad yelling at Mr. Fletcher. He blamed the blackouts on him and said it was causing us problems. Someone reached under the bed while I was lying there and took the bat."

"Would you be able to identify the person?"

Adam shook his head and shrunk into the couch. His ankle actually looked swollen, and I could tell he just wanted this to be over. "There was a quilt under the bed. I covered my head after that."

"Could you hear anything?"

"Just a bunch of muffled sounds. Maybe some people yelling. I heard someone cry like they were in pain. I waited until it stopped, and then I left."

"How much time passed while you were under the bed?"

Adam looked surprised. "It felt like forever, but it all happened so fast. Maybe the whole thing happened in like ten minutes."

"I think you have more to tell me," Cheski said.

Adam sat farther back into a velour cushion and reluctantly continued. "The bat from under the bed was on the floor of the bedroom when I left."

"Did you see Mr. Fletcher?"

Adam shook his head no. I wondered if Jamie had moved him by this point. Adam bit his bottom lip and stuttered. "I figured something bad had happened, because all of a sudden there was no noise, like too quiet. It was pretty dark, but I could see the room was messed up. Someone had knocked a painting over."

Jamie's portrait.

"Why did you take the bat?" Cheski asked.

"Like I said, I thought someone might have gotten hurt, but I didn't know anyone had been murdered. I didn't know where my stepdad was and I wanted to protect him."

Phoebe hung her head as tears rolled down her face. It was probably the only nice thing her son had ever done, but then Adam momentarily lost control of his face. Not a cry; his mouth twisted into a sneer.

I looked at Cheski to see if he noticed. Adam hadn't tried to protect Kevin—I'd bet anything he took the bat as blackmail. That's why Kevin got Adam a car. Phoebe must have found the bat and then tried to hide it. But now that George *and* Fletcher were dead, the stakes had increased. The mother and son needed to get the bat off the roof before some eventually thought to look up.

Cheski's phone rang. He listened carefully and then put the phone back in his pocket. He addressed Adam directly. "Your stepfather is across the street. According to him, he did follow you into the Fletcher home, but he couldn't find you. I tend to believe him since you admitted you were under the bed. Your stepfather left the house and waited outside the Fletcher's home. He saw you leave with a bat. I'm sorry to tell you, but he thinks you killed Simon Fletcher. He's been trying to protect you all this time. In fact, he was at your neighbor's house today in an attempt to destroy security footage of you and your friends wandering the neighborhood on the night of the murder."

Phoebe lifted her head. I just raised my eyebrows at her. *Yup, your husband loves you enough to cover up for your son. Go figure.*

Adam's smirk melted and a dark spot pooled at his crotch. Cheski turned his nose up and then addressed Phoebe. "You hid a murder weapon. That has consequences." Cheski took Adam by the arm and sat him a distance from his mother. "Don't talk to each other," he ordered. Then he took me into the kitchen while he kept mother and son in sight.

"Adam didn't see Kevin kill Fletcher," I said in a low voice.

"And Kevin didn't see Adam swing the bat," Cheski replied. "It's a problem."

"Is it possible Ricky was already in the house? Could he have hit Fletcher?"

Cheski nodded, deep in thought. We both jumped when my phone rang. Charlie was on the other end with an update. "Ricky

277

just entered George's house through the front door. I don't like that type of bravado. At least Kevin went through a basement window."

"Oh shit," I said. "If Frank still has Kevin and Cheski is here, then he's out numbered." I rubbed my hands together in frustration. "Charlie, maybe it's time to turn the lights back on."

Cheski weighed the pros and cons of my recommendation.

"Wait, I think we've got even more company," Charlie said. "Go to the window in the kitchen. The one over the sink."

Cheski and I rushed to the window. A man was standing about two hundred yards from Phoebe's kitchen. He appeared to be staring at the ladder leaning against the house.

"Who the hell is that?" Cheski said, grabbing my phone.

"Too far for me to see," Charlie replied.

Cheski's phone rang. It was Frank. I grabbed his phone as he held mine.

"I've got everything under control over here," Frank said. "Ricky was aware of George's hacking, and he came to steal George's computer. Kevin showed up for the security tape. A patrol car is on the way to take them in for questioning. It's a good thing we've got the fingerprint. Both of these bozos insist they're innocent."

Cheski took his phone back from me. "We've got a problem," he informed Frank. "There's an unidentified male walking toward the Calhouns' house from the direction of the Fletcher mansion."

I listened to Cheski and Frank strategize as they scrambled to come up with a plan. "Call off the patrol car. If this guy is spooked, he'll run," Cheski said. I leaned into the phone and listened to Frank's concerns. He wasn't comfortable with Cheski holding down the fort while a strange man approached the house. Phoebe and Adam sat quietly, but they had no idea what was going on. If the man attempted to enter the house, we could lose control of the situation. But if Frank left George's house with two suspects in tow, he might be spotted by the unidentified man.

Frank had Cheski relay a message to Charlie. "Can you babysit two suspected murderers while managing the hack?" Charlie was game and the three men agreed that Charlie would enter through George's back door. Frank would secure Kevin and Ricky with cuffs while Charlie held watch. Then Frank would come over to the Calhouns to support Cheski. When instructed by Frank, Charlie would turn the lights back on. The exchange ended in a jumble of sign-offs and two ended calls.

I looked at my watch. "It's almost noon. The funeral will be ending soon."

"Great," Cheski said. "The last thing we need is a funeral procession rolling through the neighborhood."

We focused on the man outside. He had closed about half the distance. If Frank moved quickly, he could make it to the Calhoun house without being spotted.

"Keep your eye on him," Cheski said. He returned to the living room and moved Adam and his mother to the powder room. He cuffed the two of them to each other and then to a pipe under the sink. I heard Phoebe whine and then I heard the front door open and Frank reprimand Phoebe for complaining. By the time Frank and Cheski made it to the kitchen, my back was against the wall and tears rolled down my face.

"He's got a gun," I whimpered. I slid down the wall.

"Get up," Frank said. I couldn't move, but he grabbed my arm and shoved a pair of binoculars into my hands. "This is what you do best," he said sternly but not unkindly. "Check out the face. Maybe you saw him at the funeral."

"I can't," I said. "I'm afraid."

Frank curled my fingers around the binoculars and lifted them on my nose. "Are they focused?" he asked.

I turned the dial on the bridge and the view cleared. A man's face loomed large in the lens, and I backed up a step. The police-grade binoculars were almost too strong.

"What do you see?" Frank said.

"He's slim. Short hair. Almost shaved." I adjusted the binoculars a bit and stared ahead. I knew I was supposed study the man's face, but the gun distracted me. I couldn't help but turn my attention to the man's hand. At any second he could raise the gun and fire. It was like a western. Do you look into your opponent's eyes or try to spot the slightest movement of their hand? My eye traveled back to the gun. Something wasn't right. A flash of red filled my lenses. I dropped the binoculars and let them smack the tiled floor.

"Oh my god," I said as I moved my feet like I was dancing on hot coals. "Shit, Frank, it's Jamie."

Frank's face went blank.

"Her hand," I said. "There's nail polish. I remember the color from the day you questioned her at the station."

"What about the face," Frank said. "Are you sure?"

I hadn't studied anyone's face the way I had examined Jamie's over the past two weeks. Whether it was my own painting, old photos, or Jamie in person, there simply wasn't another face I had dissected in such excruciating detail. The curve of her chin, the shape of her eyes, the length of her neck. I had no doubt that the person heading toward Phoebe's kitchen was Jamie Fletcher. The cropped hair threw me for a second, but then I realized that Jamie had most likely worn a wig during our previous encounters. I always wondered how her hair stayed exactly the same through multiple portrait sittings.

Cheski grabbed the binoculars off the floor. "She's right," he said. "Mrs. Fletcher is about to unload a barrel in our direction."

"Why does she have a gun?" I cried. "Why is she here?"

Frank rubbed his face. "Maybe she thinks Adam killed her husband."

"So throw Adam out back and let's see what happens," I suggested.

"Wait," Cheski said. "She keeps looking at the ladder."

We watched as Jamie headed toward the ladder. In front of her was a small berm with a stone bench. She climbed the hill and stood on top of the bench. Then she rose up on her toes and craned her neck.

"She's interested in the roof," I said, and then stopped to think. The only thing on the roof was the bat Adam had failed to retrieve. "I think she's looking for the bat."

"I think you're right," Frank said. "Didn't you say there was a man in the Fletcher home the night George was killed?"

"There was," I confirmed. "Gayle saw him."

"It could have been Jamie."

"But why? Why dress as a man and return to the scene of the crime?" Jamie was still staring at the roof. I grabbed Frank's arm and dragged him to the bathroom. I opened the door an inch to find Phoebe and Adam twisted awkwardly around the toilet. The tiny powder room smelled like fear and urine. I reached for the fan switch, and then remembered we still had no electricity.

"Adam," I said. "Are you sure you didn't see who took the bat from under the bed?"

He shook his head. "My eyes were closed."

"Do you remember any details after you climbed out from under the bed?"

"The room was messed up."

"You told us that already," I said, exasperated. "There must be something else."

Adam frowned slightly and appeared to actually think. It must have occurred to him that any information, no matter how inconsequential, might lead us away from him as a suspect. "The floor was hard on my knees. I crawled over to the bat. It was on the floor by the painting. I picked up the bat and left," he said.

Frank walked away from the bathroom and down the front hall. When he reached the front door, he pivoted and turned back.

"Thanks," he said to Adam as he passed the bathroom.

THIRTY-FIVE

"SHE HASN'T MOVED," CHESKI said when Frank and I returned to the Calhouns' kitchen.

Frank turned to me and spoke quickly. "According to Jamie, she was in the shower. She hit her head, passed out, and then found her husband dead. Based on her account, the house was empty and she dragged her husband on the rug into the living room."

I nodded to confirm. "That's what she said."

"If we believe Adam, he heard Fletcher and his stepdad argue. Someone reached for the bat from under the bed. He covered his head and waited it out. When the coast was clear, he crawled out."

"The floor was hard on his knees," I added.

Frank pointed his finger directly at me. "Because Jamie had already dragged her husband into the living room on the bedroom rug."

I gasped. It had finally started to make sense.

"She returned to the bedroom to swap the paintings. At that

point, Adam had already picked up the bat and slid out the door while she was in the great room," Frank said.

"I'm with you," I said.

"So, Kevin spots Adam leaving the house and follows him home."

"But why is Jamie on the hunt for the bat?" I asked. "Is she trying to prove who killed her husband?"

Cheski laughed. "That's the last thing she'd want to do."

I was lost again. "Why?"

"Because *she* killed her husband," Frank said. "She came out of the shower and heard her husband and Kevin arguing. She grabbed the bat."

I reached for the binoculars and stared at Jamie. Was it possible she had killed her beloved Simon Fletcher? The man she adored? The man she had altered her entire life to please?

"Why does she think the bat is here?" I asked.

"She knew Kevin had followed his son into her house. She knew Adam and his friends were breaking into homes. She knew someone had been in her home that night, and that it was most likely Adam," Frank said. "I don't think she's been at her sister's place the last few days; I think she's been spying on Adam and Kevin from her own home. I think she spotted Adam on the roof today."

Cheski continued, "As the victim's wife, she was also privy to inside information."

"And we told her about the painting," I said. "She knows we know it's been touched up."

Frank sighed.

"She must have met Kwan as a man," I said. "It's her print on the painting."

"And hopefully on the bat," Cheski said.

Outside Jamie stopped and stared at the ladder.

"She really wants that bat," I said.

Frank nodded. He hadn't taken his eye off Jamie. "That bruise she showed us by her eyebrow. I don't think she got it falling in the shower."

I picked up the binoculars and refocused on Jamie. "Why'd she do it?"

"It was dark," Frank said. "She came out of the shower and heard her husband arguing with Kevin. She grabbed the bat for protection."

"And hit the wrong man?" I said. Ridiculous theory. Even in the dark, I could make out the man I was sleeping with, and Simon and Kevin were decades apart.

Frank frowned. "I think she'll argue she hit the wrong man."

"Or the right man," I said. "Maybe the blackout worked to her advantage. Maybe Charlie was right. Maybe Jamie thought she was about to be replaced like Simon's first wife."

"If her print matches the bat *and* the painting, it doesn't matter," Frank said. "With hard evidence like a murder weapon and prints, all the DA has to do is spin a believable story. We just have to stay alive long enough to bring that story to a jury."

I watched as Jamie raised her gun slightly. Her hand shook, and I could tell that wielding a gun was not in her repertoire. "She's an amateur," I moaned. "I can't die in Phoebe's kitchen because Jaime Fletcher's got a loose trigger finger."

"No one is dying," Frank said. "If she wants the bat, she'll have to put the gun down at some point. She's only got two hands."

"Shouldn't we get to the bat before she does?" I asked.

Cheski sidled up to the kitchen window. "Absolutely not,"

he said. "The bat is our bait, and I can't think of anywhere more compromising to corner a suspect than an icy roof."

Frank nodded. "She'll be a sitting duck."

Jamie put her gun down and kneeled down in the snow. She was studying the house.

Frank dialed Charlie. "All good over there? Great. I'm going to text you in about five minutes. When you get my signal, I want every light in this neighborhood to go on." He hung up the phone and looked at his watch. "When do you think the funeral will be over?"

"It's been more than an hour already," I croaked. My voice was hoarse from crying. "Only the immediate family will go to the graveyard. Dotty said her sister will come back early to greet the guests. Expect cars in about ten minutes."

"Perfect," Frank said.

"You want people here?"

"The more witnesses," he said, "the better."

"She's got a gun," I disagreed. "What if she shoots an innocent person?"

"Then she blows her own alibi," Frank said. "If she claims she accidentally hit the wrong man in self-defense, then she has no reason to shoot someone today."

"You're taking a big risk with people's lives." We watched as Jamie came within fifty yards of the ladder.

Frank lowered his head and paced. "What would make Jamie so mad that she'd brutally kill her husband with a bat?"

"An affair is sufficient motive," Cheski said.

"But we don't know there was another woman," I countered.

"If Jamie believed there was another woman," Frank corrected me, "then that's all that counts."

"What else?" I pressed. "Why else would she purposely kill her husband?"

"Maybe she got tired of playing his game," Frank said. "Think about how happy Ruthie Brown was after she and Fletcher divorced. Maybe Jamie wanted to live freely and Fletcher refused. Ten years ago, gay marriage was taboo. Now, it's not."

"She could have met someone else," I said and my thoughts race to Charlie. Was it possible Jamie *had* actually hit on Charlie?

"She's going for the ladder," Cheski said. "When she's on the roof, we'll need to move outside." He looked at me. "You stay here, away from the windows."

Frank and Cheski snuck out the front door. I had no other choice but to watch helplessly as Jamie's feet passed the window on the way up the ladder. Within seconds, the roof creaked and I could hear a slight thud as Jamie made her way across the roof.

I peered through the window and watched as Frank fiddled with his phone. Out of the corner of my eye, a line of cars with their headlights on turned into the Green Acres entrance. The funeral procession had arrived. Several minutes later the last car parked.

Just then Charlie worked his magic and the entire neighborhood popped like a firecracker. Despite the early hour, the snow-laden clouds created a dark and dreary cover. Although not as impactful as a nighttime sky, it was immediately noticeable when ten houses lit up. The lights were officially back on and Jamie Fletcher was supposedly perched on the roof like a frozen gargoyle.

Cheski stepped forward into my line of sight and removed the ladder leading to the Calhouns' roof. I didn't see that coming. I guess Frank wasn't kidding when he said sitting duck. Despite

Cheski's protests, I opened the kitchen window so I could hear what transpired between Frank and Jamie.

"Mrs. Fletcher," Frank raised his voice toward the roof. "We'd like you to come down. We'll bring the ladder to you."

Frank appeared to be listening, although I couldn't hear Jamie's response. Instead, another chunk of ice came loose. This one, the size of a pool table, slid off the roof like the ominous start of an avalanche.

"Put the safety on the gun and toss it into the yard," Frank yelled. He waited for Jamie to make her move, but nothing happened. I'd had enough. I grabbed my coat and left by the side door.

Frank sighed when he saw me trudging through the snow. "It's not safe outside."

I pointed to the funeral guests making their way into George's house. "How come you're not worried about them?"

"I'm worried about everyone."

"Is that CeCe?" Jamie called down. Her voice was thin and I could tell she knew her options were limited. She hadn't had much of a plan from the get-go.

"It's me," I responded.

An icicle, as sharp and as long as a javelin, detached from a gutter and pierced the snow about three feet from Frank. Jamie screamed. Frank barely flinched.

"Please come down," I begged.

"Were you telling the truth? You really didn't know when you painted me?" Jamie asked.

It seemed like an odd time for this question, but I imagined Jamie, gun in hand, was reassessing her life.

I went with the truth. "I really didn't know," I said I as inched my way toward the house. "And I'm pretty good with faces."

"That's why Simon hired you," she answered. "He said if you couldn't tell, no one could. But then—" Jamie faltered and more ice flew off the house.

"We can talk about this when you come down," I offered. I pointed to the ladder and Cheski rested it carefully back against the house. I climbed up a few rungs. Ice tracks had formed on the rungs from Jamie and Adam's wet shoes.

"Don't upset her," Frank cautioned.

As I climbed the ladder, I could see a gaggle of funeral guests milling in the cul-de-sac. Clearly, our rooftop meeting had not gone unnoticed. I wondered if Dotty's family realized that Charlie was guarding two suspects in the family's basement. Suddenly, the Green Acres development was a theater in the round. There was action in every direction.

My head popped over the edge of the roof and Jamie turned to look at me. The gun was at her side and the bat had rolled into a snow-filled gutter. Sections of the roof were covered in solid ice. The panels that were exposed were hot to the touch. Jamie was sitting on a section of ice, her feet planted firmly on a panel.

"He started to forget," she said morosely.

"Charlie mentioned that Simon had started to slow down," I said.

"No," Jamie said. She was frustrated. "He started to forget about me."

"I think that's fairly common," I sympathized.

She shook her head in disagreement. "He knew my name. He knew we were partners. He started to forget." She paused, and I held up my hand.

"I get it," I said. Simon, in his deteriorating state, must have forgotten that Jamie had been born a male.

"It confused him," she said. "He'd go off like I'd been tricking him." She shook her head. "I gave my entire life to him. I alienated my family. I lost friends. Why?" she asked.

I wondered again about Jamie's motives. Maybe she'd actually hit Simon out of self-defense. "Did he know who you were that night? In the dark?"

Jamie started to cry. "I don't know. There was someone else in the house. I heard them arguing, but when I ran to intervene, Simon seemed rattled and the person was gone. Simon turned and saw me holding the bat. I'm not sure he recognized me."

I reached in my coat pocket and pulled out a wad of tissues. I attempted to throw the ball to her, but it floated aimlessly until it caught on an outcropping of ice. Jamie wiped her nose on her sleeve. She was still holding the gun.

"I'd just come out of the shower. My wig was off and I was naked," she sobbed. "It was so dark. He came at me. How could I blame him?" She looked directly at me and smiled. "I don't always look like me."

Or at least what Simon remembered her to be.

"He ran toward me."

"Did he think you were an intruder?" I asked.

Jamie nodded and reached for her forehead. The bruise. Simon must have hit her. She peered down at the bat and wiggled forward.

There was no way she could get it. "It's over Jamie. Let's go down."

And then a thunderous crack rattled the house. I glanced up, but the sound hadn't come from the sky. The roof was the issue. With the power up and the solar panels on, the largest section of ice had melted sufficiently to cause a major slide.

"Get off," I screamed. I reached out for Jamie, but we were yards away from each other.

Jamie flipped to her stomach and stretched forward in hopes of grasping the top of a secured panel, but the ice chunk moved south an inch. Jamie was like a stranded baby seal on an iceberg floating from shore.

Her feet tore at the roof, but with each peddle of her legs, the ice plate broke looser. A section disengaged and tumbled to the ground. I heard Cheski curse. Mercifully, the fissure left Jamie in place and exposed a part of the asphalt tile.

"Quick, put your foot down."

Jamie placed her foot on the solid surface and rested her cheek on the block of ice. She sighed. I lowered my head on the top rung of the ladder. I needed a break. We both needed a break. "That was close," I said. I looked up to catch Jamie staring directly at me, her eyes stretched wide.

"It's moving," she whispered. And just like that, an enormous floe of frosted ice released from the panels and sailed out into sky, taking Jamie Fletcher with it.

I screamed out of shock. I also screamed to muffle the horror I was about to hear. Jamie and her ice saucer hit the ground with incredible force. In my frantic state, I had tilted my head back and bobbled the ladder. I threw my arms forward and clung to the copper gutter.

"Frank," I cried. I was too afraid to look down, but I felt a hand at my foot.

"One step at a time," Frank said.

THIRTY-SIX

JAMIE AND SIMON FLETCHER were buried together, a week to the day after George. The church was filled with environmental luminaries and at least one senator. Simon Fletcher was an important man. However, without Ricky managing the standing-room only event, the funeral was a bit disorganized. Unfortunately for the former assistant, he had his own legal problems.

I sat with Frank, Charlie, and Cheski. Simon's first wife, Ruthie, and her husband, Roger, were in front of us. After that, the seating was haphazard at best.

An attractive woman in her early seventies sat in the fourth pew near the end of the row. It didn't take me long to realize that it was most likely Jamie's mother, although someone had forgotten to leave room in the front for immediate family. I waited until the end of the ceremony, after the church had thinned out, and then I approached her. She was standing quietly behind the same Virgin Mary statue that had provided me refuge just before George's service began.

"It's a good spot," I said as I held out my hand.

Jamie's mother shook my hand and smiled. "We'd been estranged for some years," she said.

"It happens."

"It wasn't me," she said. "Simon didn't want Jamie to associate with her family."

I nodded. "He was a secretive man," I agreed, and then paused. "Will you be taking the portrait of Jamie?"

Her eyes filled with tears. "It's the only thing I'm keeping."

I smiled.

"Souls don't change," she said as she came out from behind the statue. "My Jamie was always the same person on the inside. I hope she knows I how I felt."

"She knew," I said.

THE END

CPSIA information can be obtained
at www.ICGtesting.com
Printed in the USA
LVHW041527280619
622667LV00002B/401